ARCHIE & FRIENDS ALL-STARS

Betty and Veronica

Beach Party

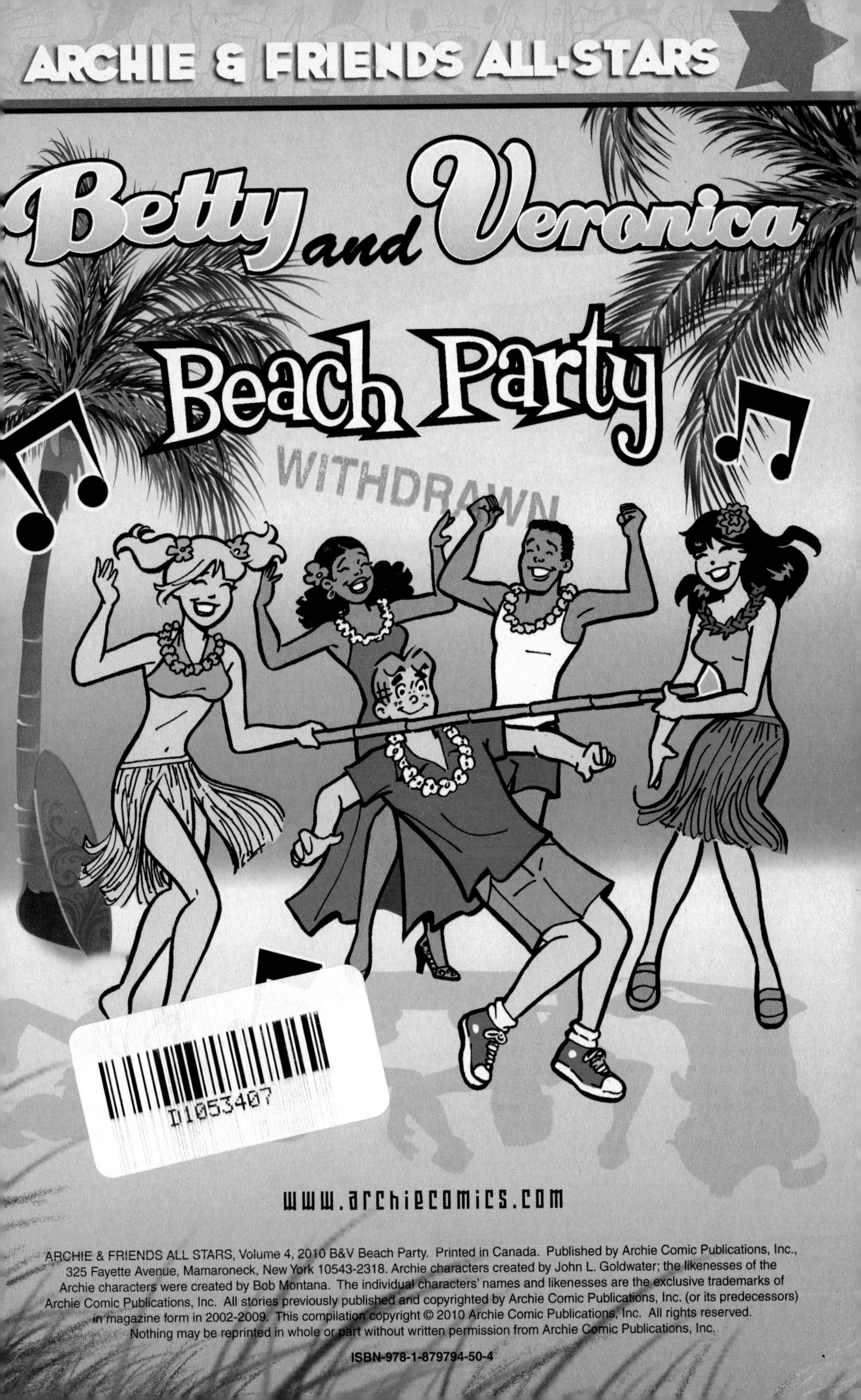

www.archiecomics.com

ARCHIE & FRIENDS ALL STARS, Volume 4, 2010 B&V Beach Party. Printed in Canada. Published by Archie Comic Publications, Inc., 325 Fayette Avenue, Mamaroneck, New York 10543-2318. Archie characters created by John L. Goldwater; the likenesses of the Archie characters were created by Bob Montana. The individual characters' names and likenesses are the exclusive trademarks of Archie Comic Publications, Inc. All stories previously published and copyrighted by Archie Comic Publications, Inc. (or its predecessors) in magazine form in 2002-2009.

ISBN-978-1-879794-50-4

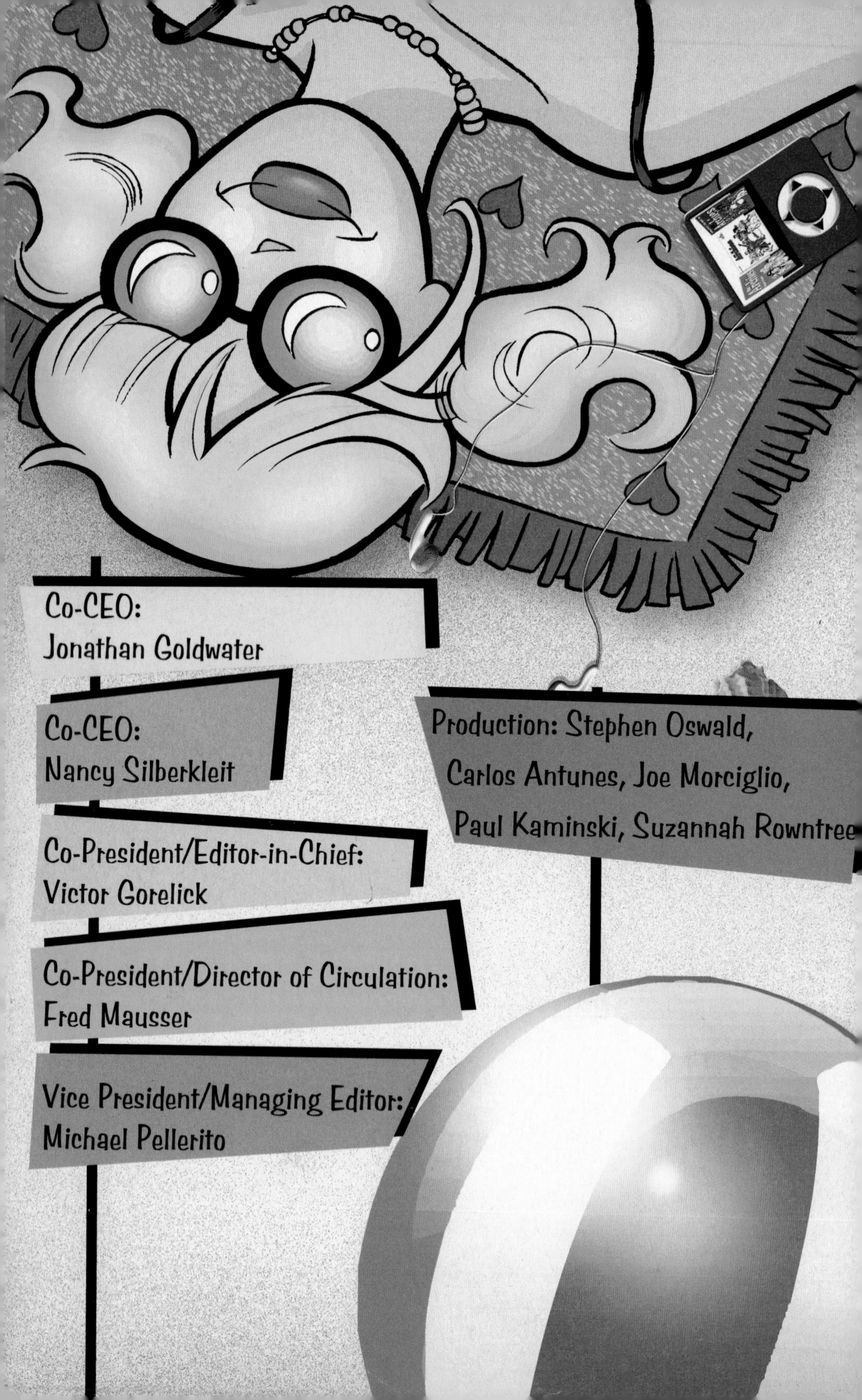
Co-CEO:
Jonathan Goldwater
Co-CEO:
Nancy Silberkleit
Co-President/Editor-in-Chief:
Victor Gorelick
Co-President/Director of Circulation:
Fred Mausser
Vice President/Managing Editor:
Michael Pellerito
Production: Stephen Oswald,
Carlos Antunes, Joe Morciglio,
Paul Kaminski, Suzannah Rowntree

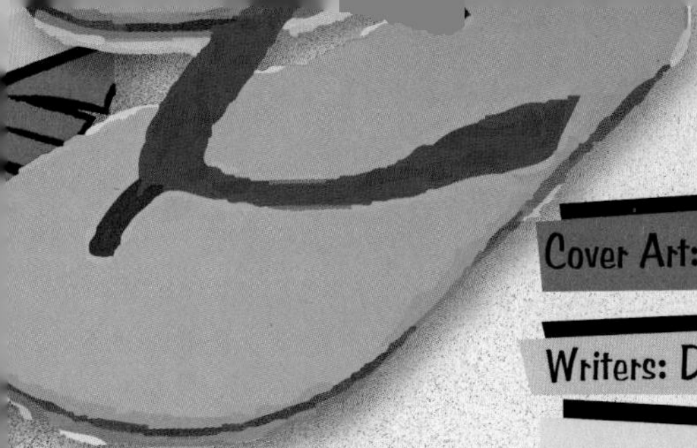

Cover Art: Dan Parent

Writers: Dan Parent, George Gladir, Angelo DeCesare

Pencils: Dan Parent, Jeff Shultz

Inks: Rich Koslowski, Al Milgrom, Henry Scarpelli

Letterers: Jack Morelli, Bill Yoshida

Colorists: Barry Grossman, Dan Parent

www.archiecomics.com

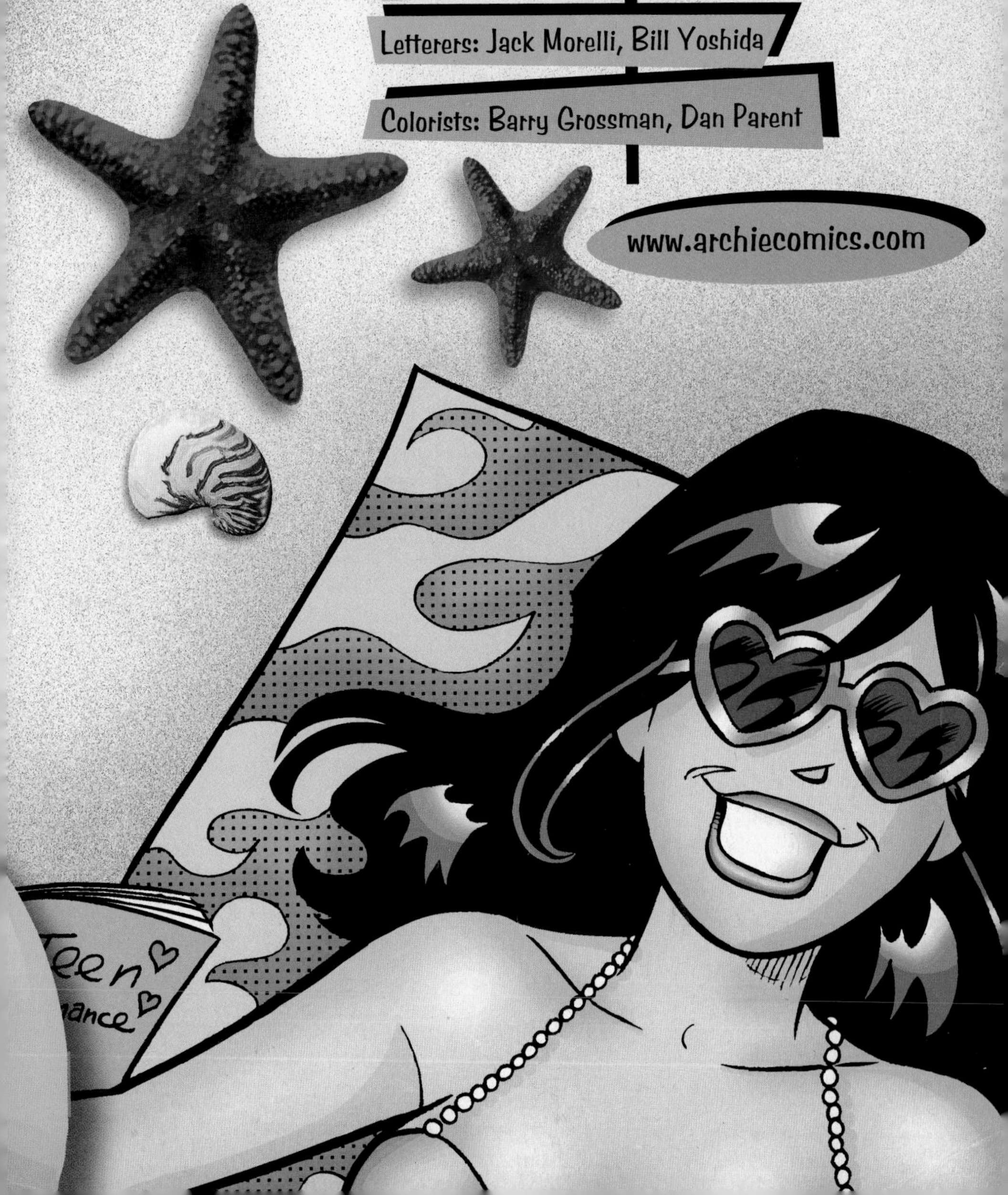

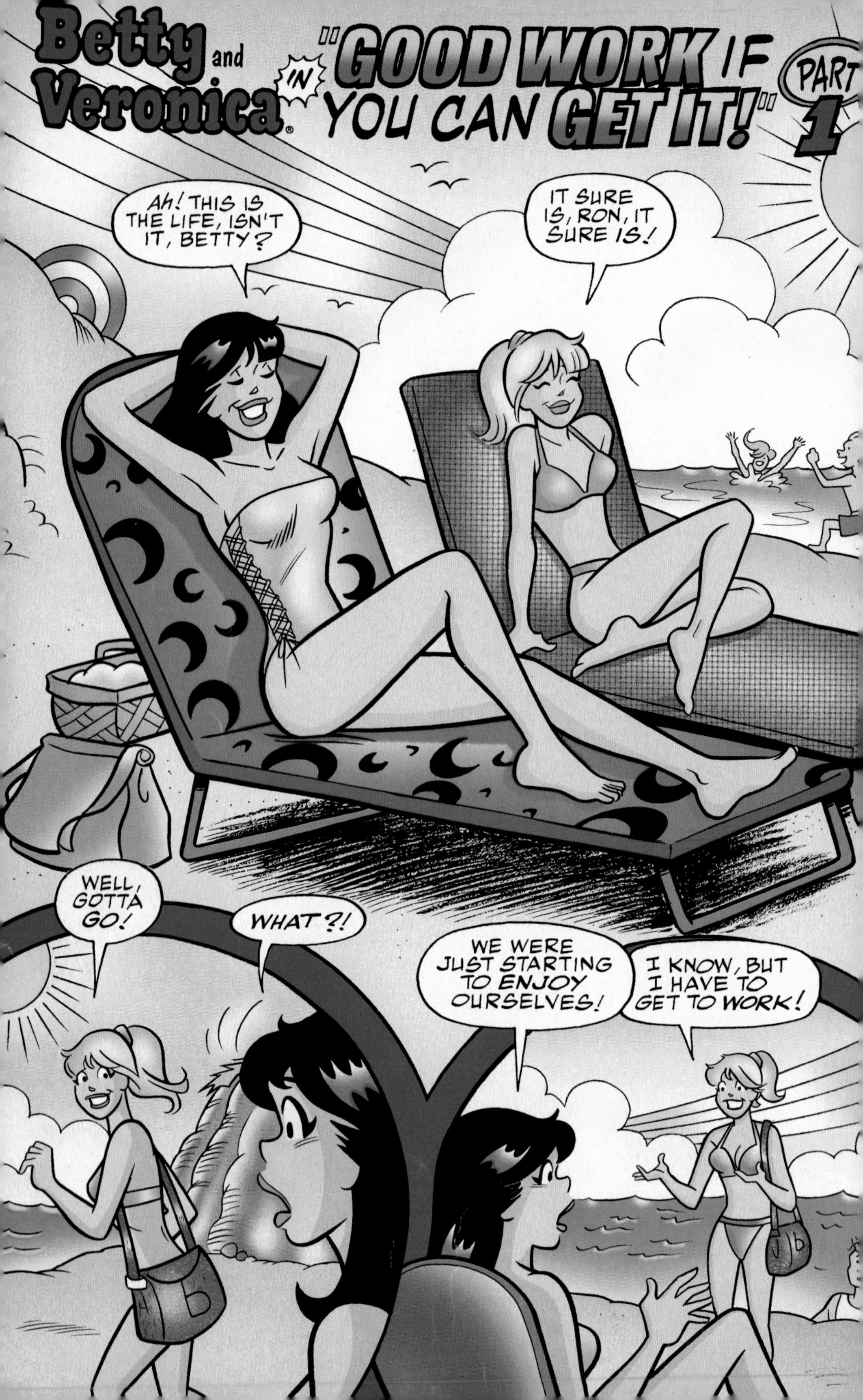
Betty and Veronica®
IN
"GOOD WORK IF YOU CAN GET IT!"
PART 1
Ah! THIS IS THE LIFE, ISN'T IT, BETTY?
IT SURE IS, RON, IT SURE IS!
WELL, GOTTA GO!
WHAT?!
WE WERE JUST STARTING TO ENJOY OURSELVES!
I KNOW, BUT I HAVE TO GET TO WORK!

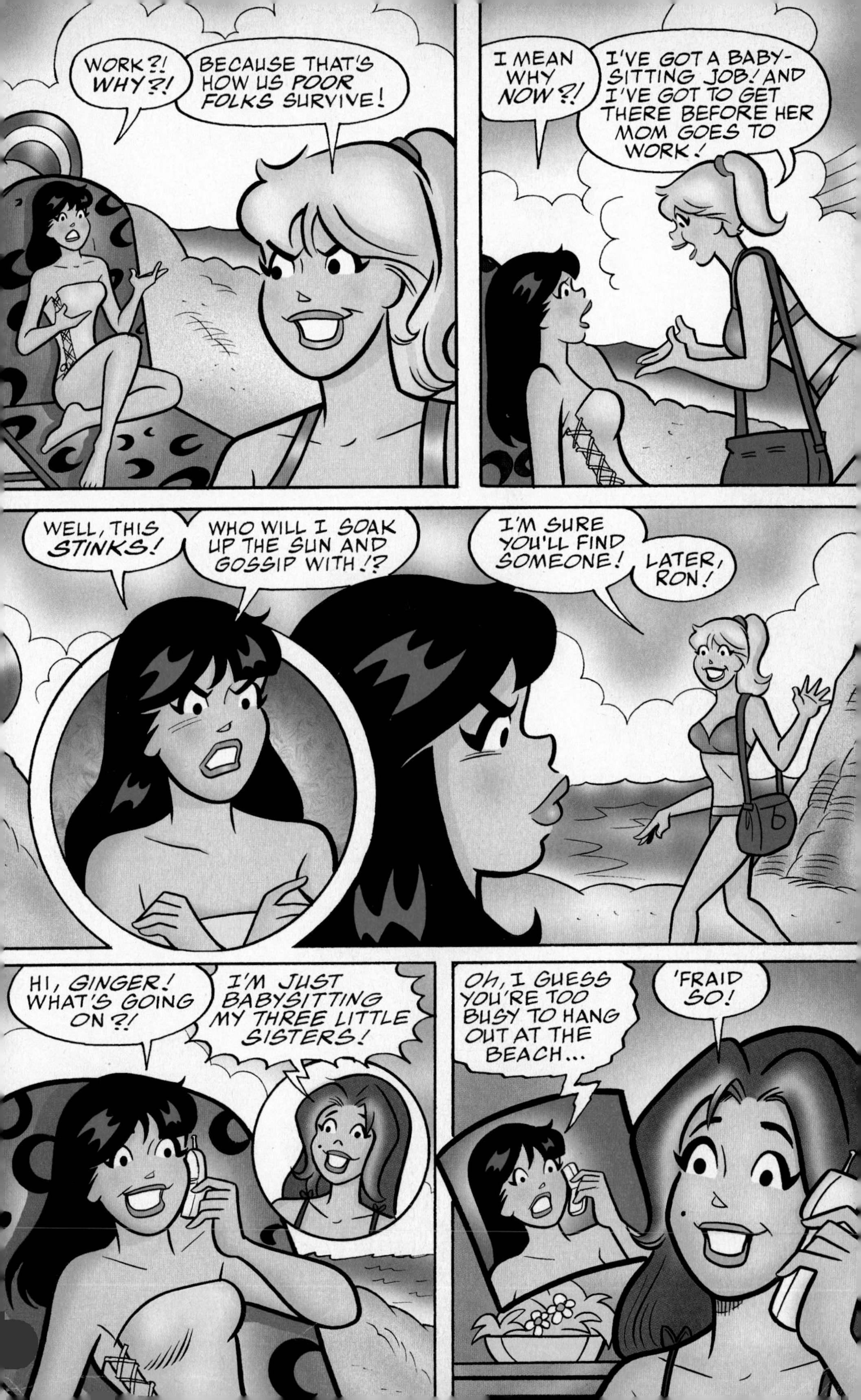
WORK?! WHY?!
BECAUSE THAT'S HOW US POOR FOLKS SURVIVE!
I MEAN WHY NOW?!
I'VE GOT A BABY-SITTING JOB! AND I'VE GOT TO GET THERE BEFORE HER MOM GOES TO WORK!
WELL, THIS STINKS!
WHO WILL I SOAK UP THE SUN AND GOSSIP WITH!?
I'M SURE YOU'LL FIND SOMEONE!
LATER, RON!
HI, GINGER! WHAT'S GOING ON?!
I'M JUST BABYSITTING MY THREE LITTLE SISTERS!
Oh, I GUESS YOU'RE TOO BUSY TO HANG OUT AT THE BEACH...
'FRAID SO!

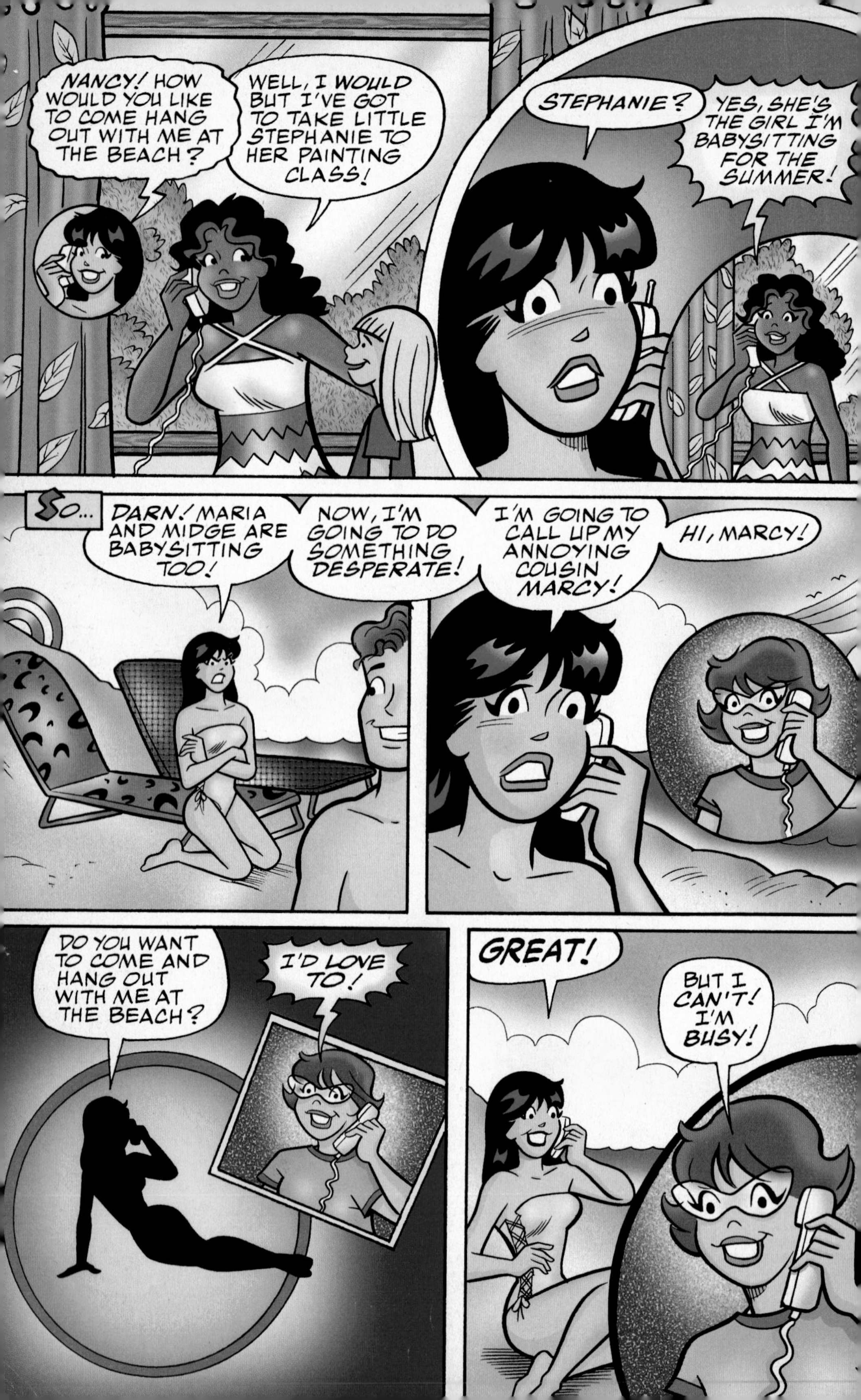
NANCY! HOW WOULD YOU LIKE TO COME HANG OUT WITH ME AT THE BEACH?
WELL, I WOULD BUT I'VE GOT TO TAKE LITTLE STEPHANIE TO HER PAINTING CLASS!
STEPHANIE?
YES, SHE'S THE GIRL I'M BABYSITTING FOR THE SUMMER!
SO...
DARN! MARIA AND MIDGE ARE BABYSITTING TOO!
NOW, I'M GOING TO DO SOMETHING DESPERATE!
I'M GOING TO CALL UP MY ANNOYING COUSIN MARCY!
HI, MARCY!
DO YOU WANT TO COME AND HANG OUT WITH ME AT THE BEACH?
I'D LOVE TO!
GREAT!
BUT I CAN'T! I'M BUSY!

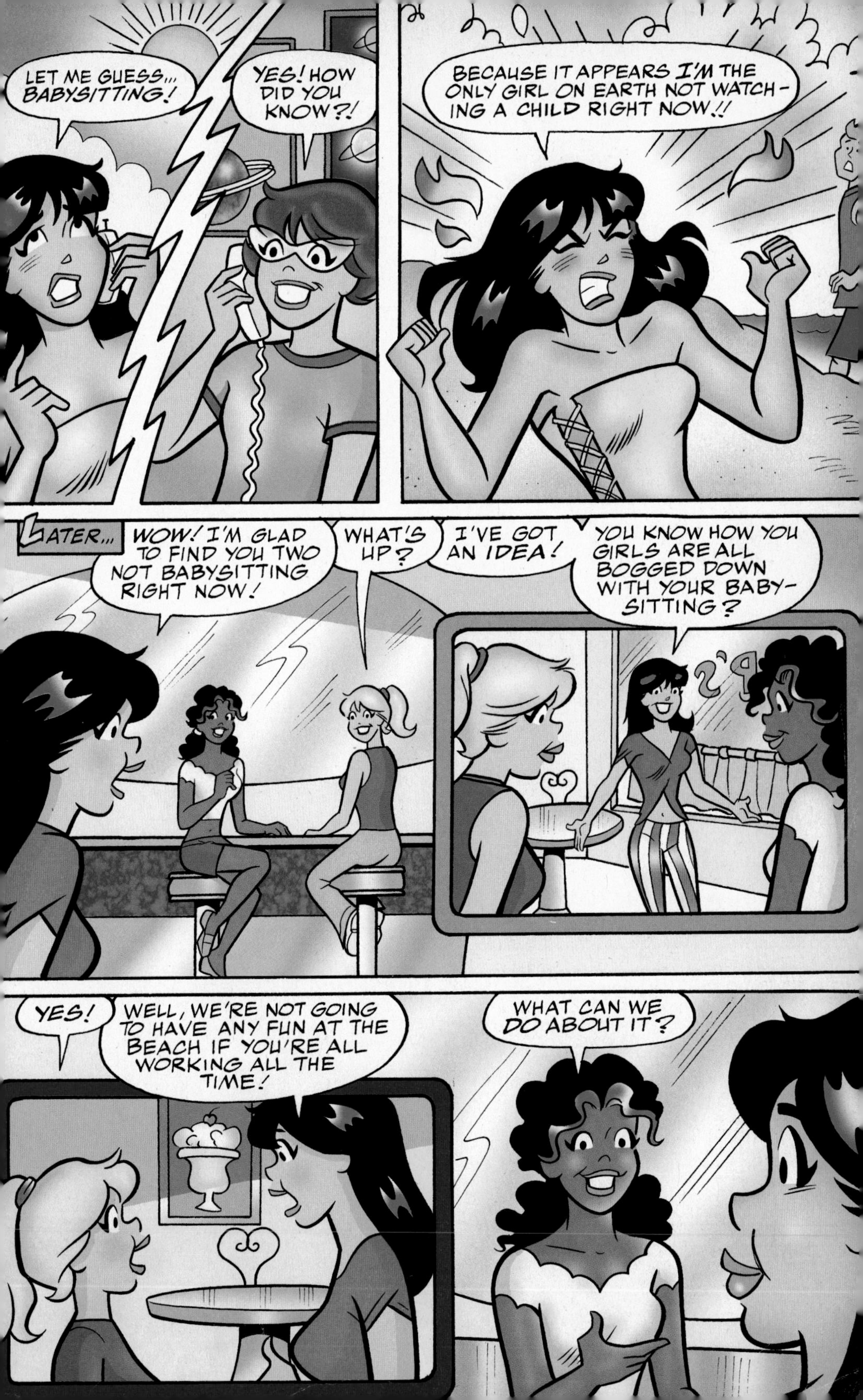
LET ME GUESS... BABYSITTING!
YES! HOW DID YOU KNOW?!
BECAUSE IT APPEARS I'M THE ONLY GIRL ON EARTH NOT WATCHING A CHILD RIGHT NOW!!
LATER...
WOW! I'M GLAD TO FIND YOU TWO NOT BABYSITTING RIGHT NOW!
WHAT'S UP?
I'VE GOT AN IDEA!
YOU KNOW HOW YOU GIRLS ARE ALL BOGGED DOWN WITH YOUR BABYSITTING?
YES!
WELL, WE'RE NOT GOING TO HAVE ANY FUN AT THE BEACH IF YOU'RE ALL WORKING ALL THE TIME!
WHAT CAN WE DO ABOUT IT?

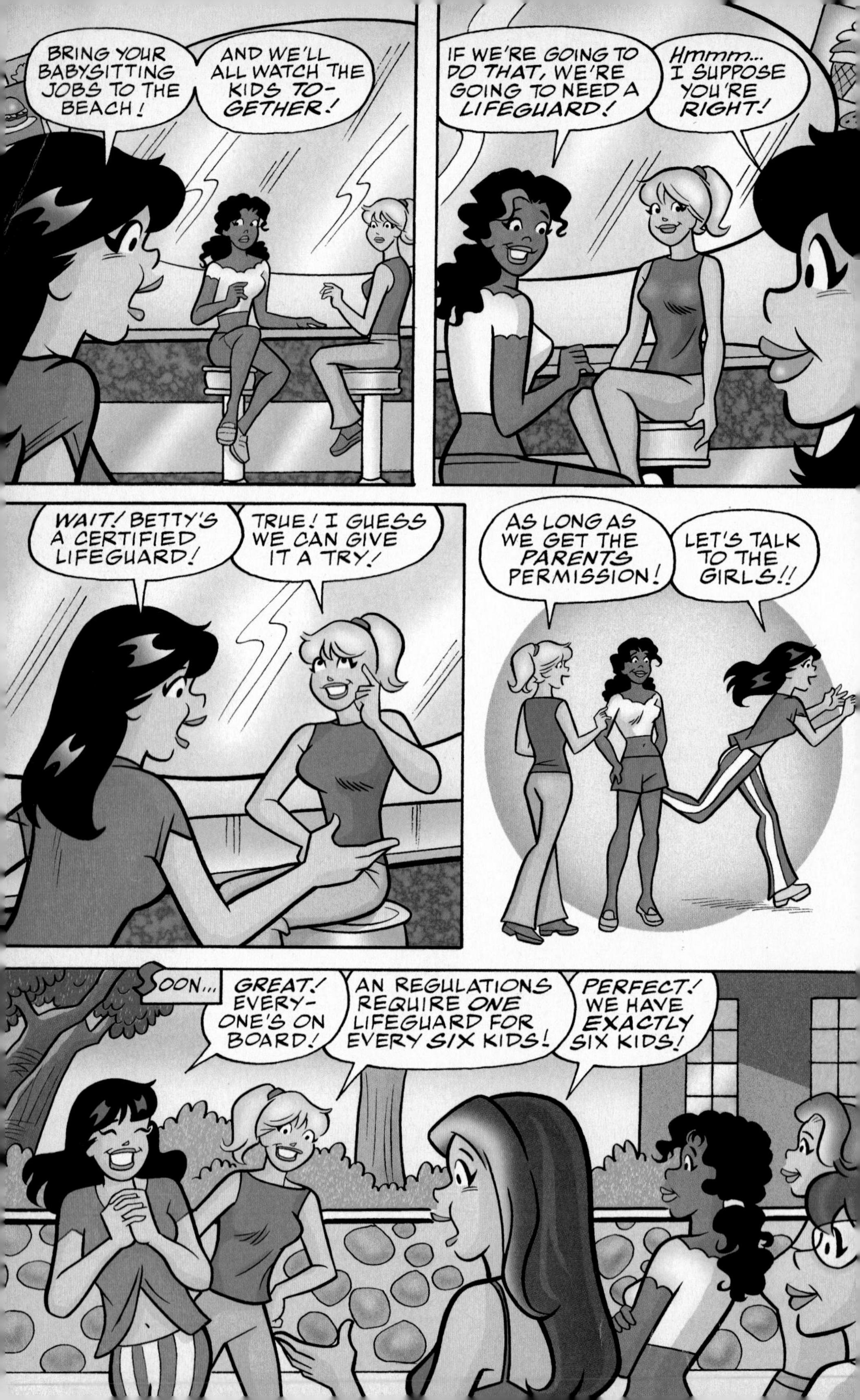
BRING YOUR BABYSITTING JOBS TO THE BEACH!
AND WE'LL ALL WATCH THE KIDS TO-GETHER!
IF WE'RE GOING TO DO THAT, WE'RE GOING TO NEED A LIFEGUARD!
Hmmm... I SUPPOSE YOU'RE RIGHT!
WAIT! BETTY'S A CERTIFIED LIFEGUARD!
TRUE! I GUESS WE CAN GIVE IT A TRY!
AS LONG AS WE GET THE PARENTS PERMISSION!
LET'S TALK TO THE GIRLS!!
SOON...
GREAT! EVERY-ONE'S ON BOARD!
AN REGULATIONS REQUIRE ONE LIFEGUARD FOR EVERY SIX KIDS!
PERFECT! WE HAVE EXACTLY SIX KIDS!

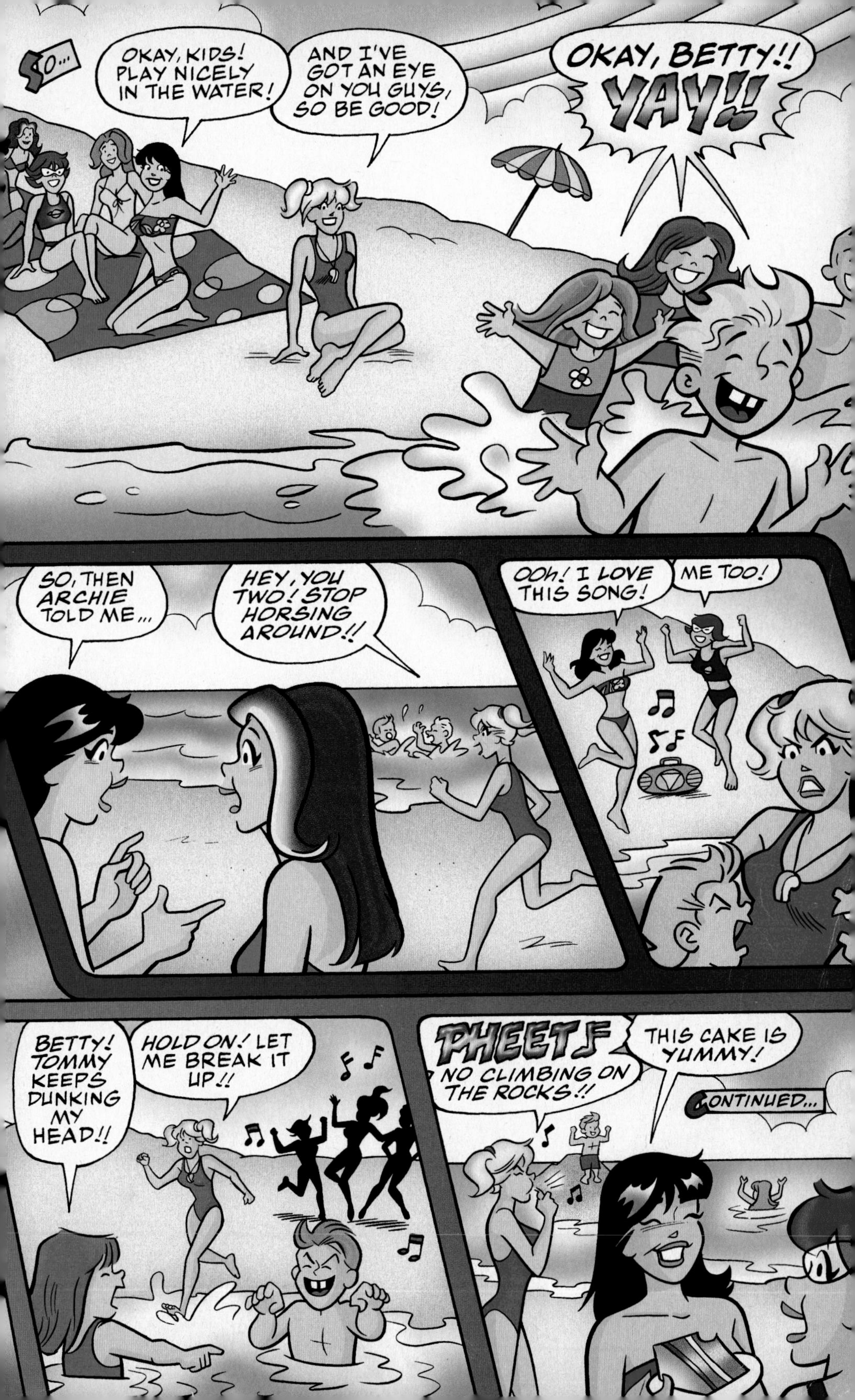
SO...
OKAY, KIDS! PLAY NICELY IN THE WATER!
AND I'VE GOT AN EYE ON YOU GUYS, SO BE GOOD!
OKAY, BETTY!! YAY!!
SO, THEN ARCHIE TOLD ME...
HEY, YOU TWO! STOP HORSING AROUND!!
OOH! I LOVE THIS SONG!
ME TOO!
BETTY! TOMMY KEEPS DUNKING MY HEAD!!
HOLD ON! LET ME BREAK IT UP!!
PHEET
NO CLIMBING ON THE ROCKS!!
THIS CAKE IS YUMMY!
CONTINUED...

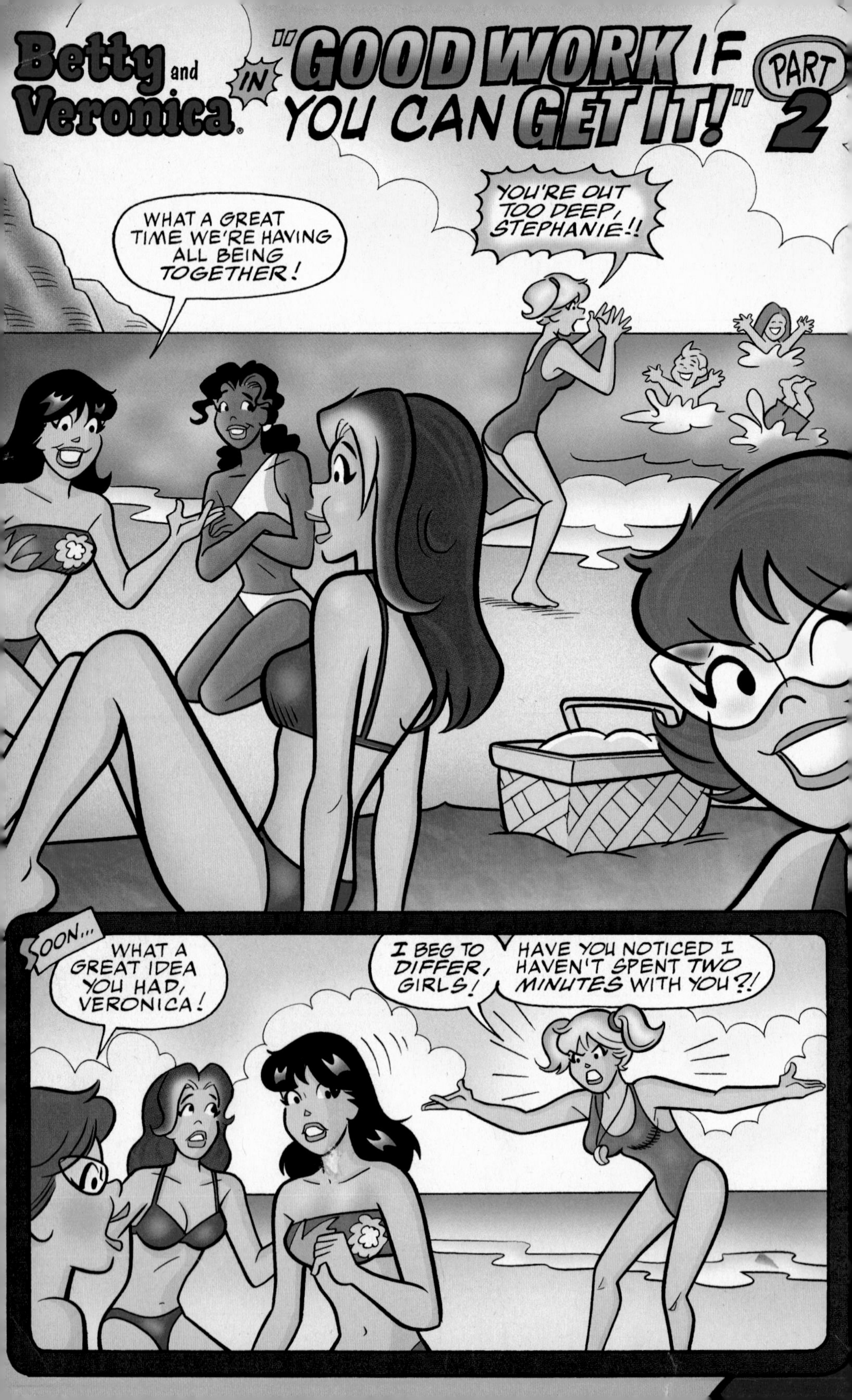
Betty and Veronica® IN "GOOD WORK IF YOU CAN GET IT!" PART 2
WHAT A GREAT TIME WE'RE HAVING ALL BEING TOGETHER!
YOU'RE OUT TOO DEEP, STEPHANIE!!
SOON...
WHAT A GREAT IDEA YOU HAD, VERONICA!
I BEG TO DIFFER, GIRLS!
HAVE YOU NOTICED I HAVEN'T SPENT TWO MINUTES WITH YOU?!

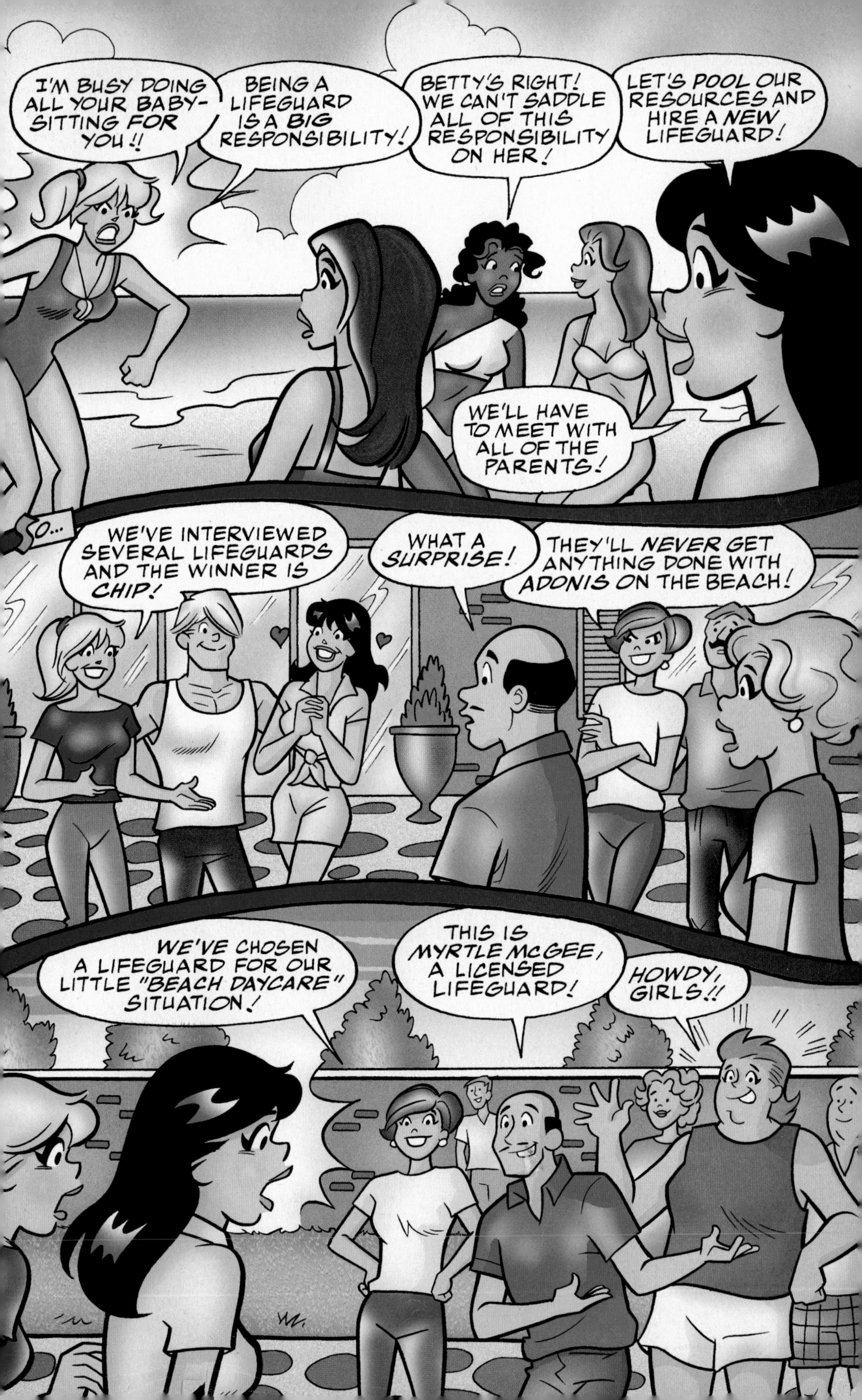
I'M BUSY DOING ALL YOUR BABY-SITTING FOR YOU!!
BEING A LIFEGUARD IS A BIG RESPONSIBILITY!
BETTY'S RIGHT! WE CAN'T SADDLE ALL OF THIS RESPONSIBILITY ON HER!
LET'S POOL OUR RESOURCES AND HIRE A NEW LIFEGUARD!
WE'LL HAVE TO MEET WITH ALL OF THE PARENTS!
SO...
WE'VE INTERVIEWED SEVERAL LIFEGUARDS AND THE WINNER IS CHIP!
WHAT A SURPRISE!
THEY'LL NEVER GET ANYTHING DONE WITH ADONIS ON THE BEACH!
WE'VE CHOSEN A LIFEGUARD FOR OUR LITTLE "BEACH DAYCARE" SITUATION!
THIS IS MYRTLE McGEE, A LICENSED LIFEGUARD!
HOWDY, GIRLS!!

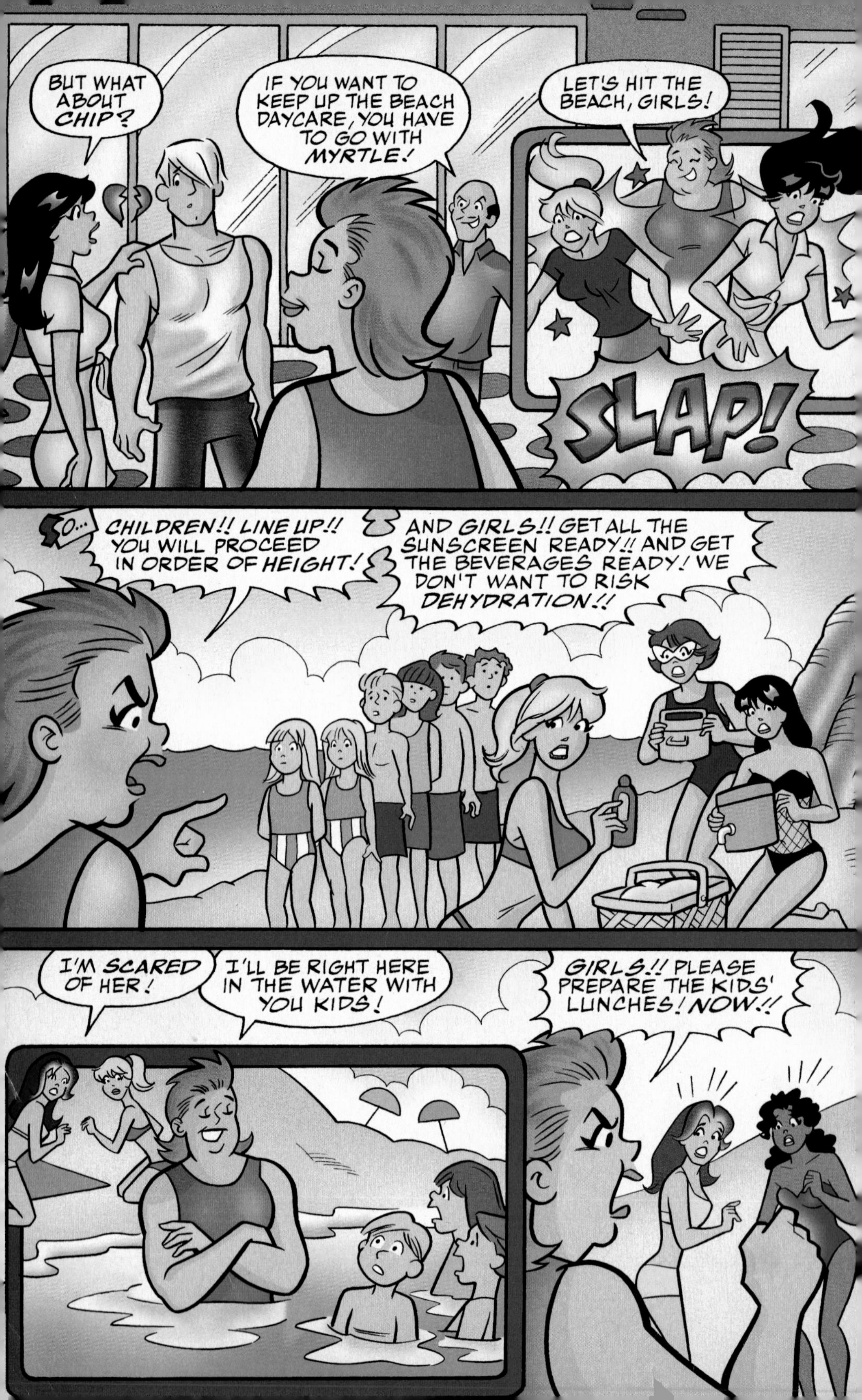
BUT WHAT ABOUT CHIP?
IF YOU WANT TO KEEP UP THE BEACH DAYCARE, YOU HAVE TO GO WITH MYRTLE!
LET'S HIT THE BEACH, GIRLS!
SLAP!
SO...
CHILDREN!! LINE UP!! YOU WILL PROCEED IN ORDER OF HEIGHT!
AND GIRLS!! GET ALL THE SUNSCREEN READY!! AND GET THE BEVERAGES READY! WE DON'T WANT TO RISK DEHYDRATION!!
I'M SCARED OF HER!
I'LL BE RIGHT HERE IN THE WATER WITH YOU KIDS!
GIRLS!! PLEASE PREPARE THE KIDS' LUNCHES! NOW!!

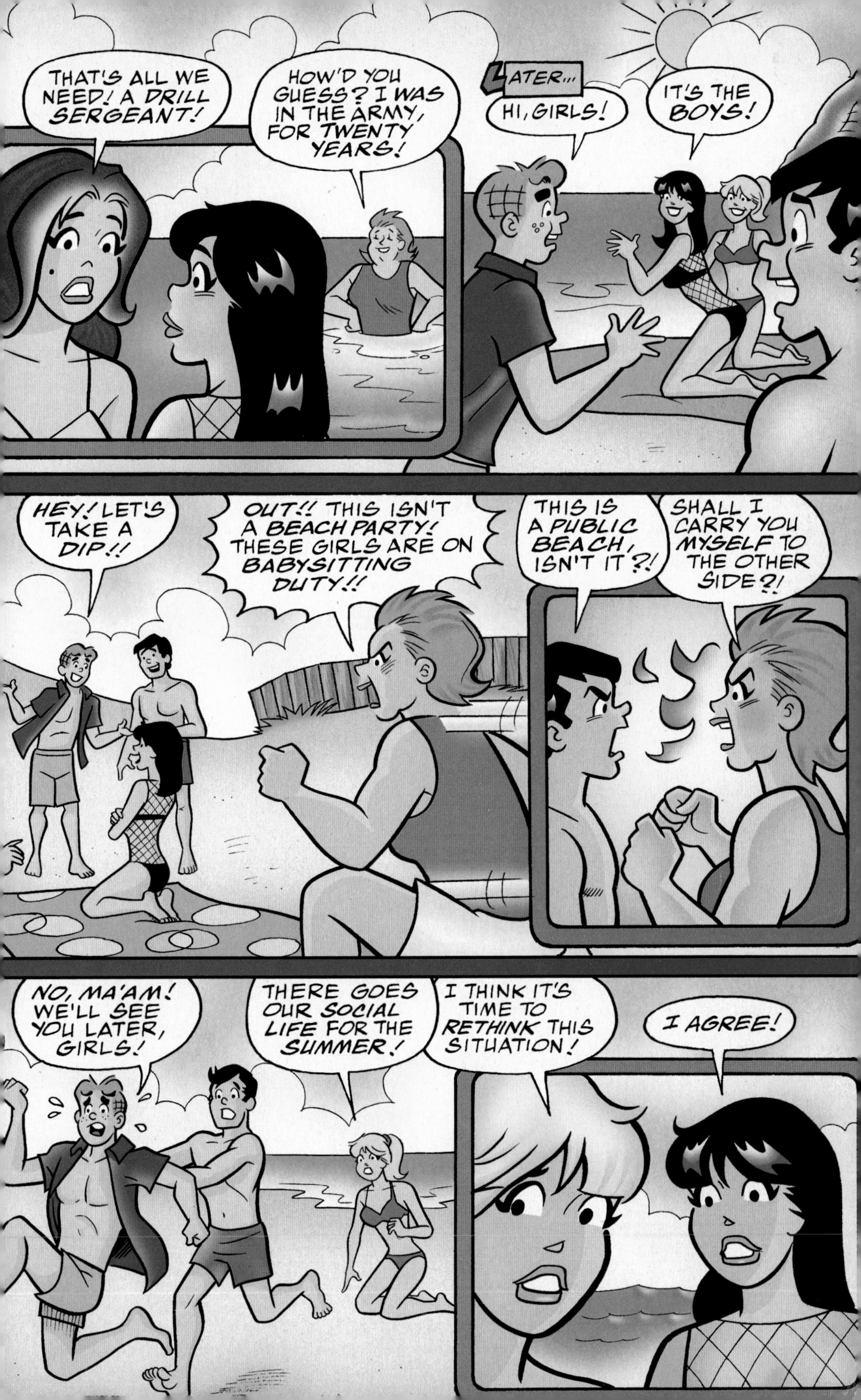
THAT'S ALL WE NEED! A DRILL SERGEANT!
HOW'D YOU GUESS? I WAS IN THE ARMY, FOR TWENTY YEARS!
LATER...
HI, GIRLS!
IT'S THE BOYS!
HEY! LET'S TAKE A DIP!!
OUT!! THIS ISN'T A BEACH PARTY! THESE GIRLS ARE ON BABYSITTING DUTY!!
THIS IS A PUBLIC BEACH, ISN'T IT?!
SHALL I CARRY YOU MYSELF TO THE OTHER SIDE?!
NO, MA'AM! WE'LL SEE YOU LATER, GIRLS!
THERE GOES OUR SOCIAL LIFE FOR THE SUMMER!
I THINK IT'S TIME TO RETHINK THIS SITUATION!
I AGREE!

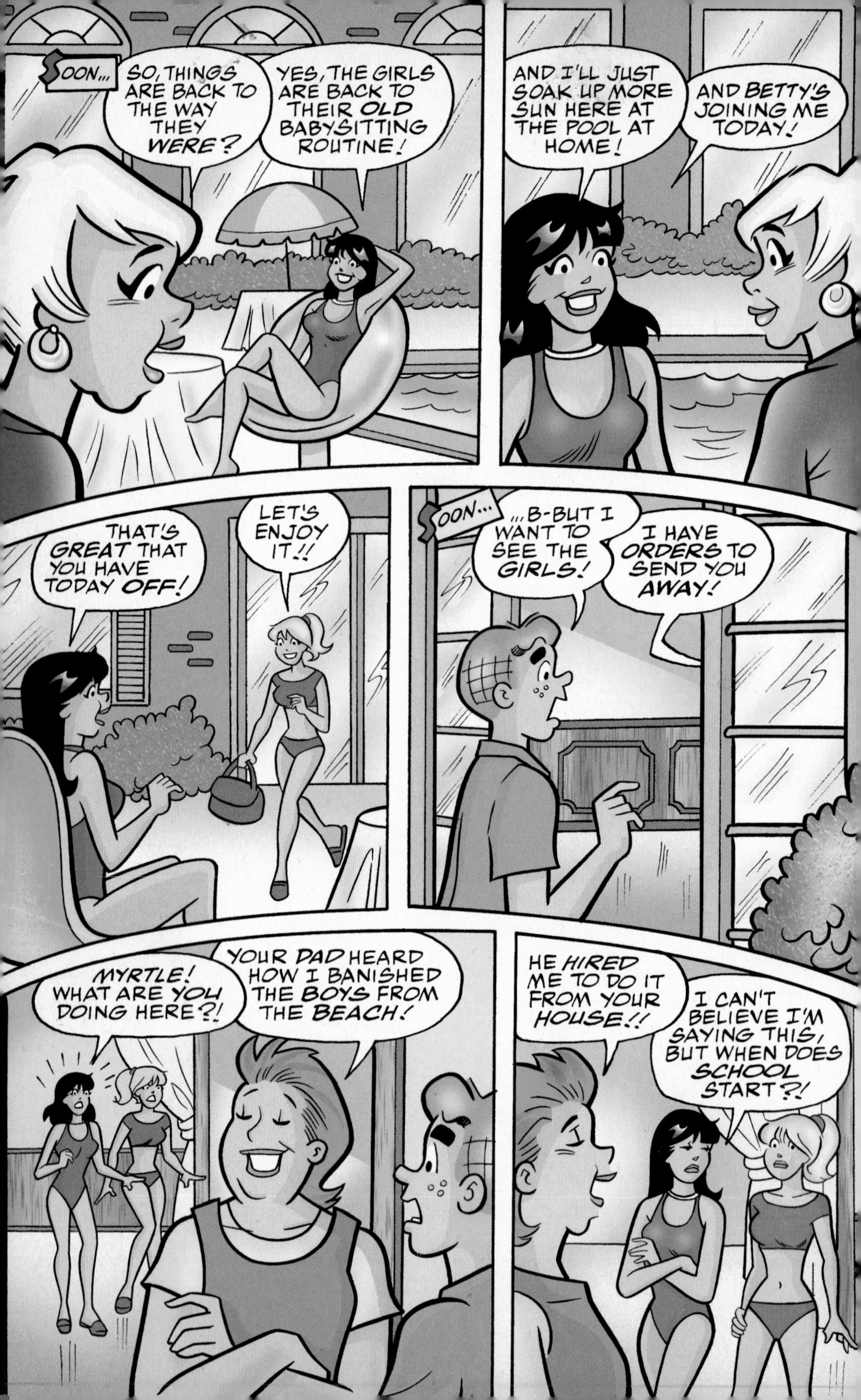
SOON...
SO, THINGS ARE BACK TO THE WAY THEY WERE?
YES, THE GIRLS ARE BACK TO THEIR OLD BABYSITTING ROUTINE!
AND I'LL JUST SOAK UP MORE SUN HERE AT THE POOL AT HOME!
AND BETTY'S JOINING ME TODAY!
THAT'S GREAT THAT YOU HAVE TODAY OFF!
LET'S ENJOY IT!!
SOON...
...B-BUT I WANT TO SEE THE GIRLS!
I HAVE ORDERS TO SEND YOU AWAY!
MYRTLE! WHAT ARE YOU DOING HERE?!
YOUR DAD HEARD HOW I BANISHED THE BOYS FROM THE BEACH!
HE HIRED ME TO DO IT FROM YOUR HOUSE!!
I CAN'T BELIEVE I'M SAYING THIS, BUT WHEN DOES SCHOOL START?!

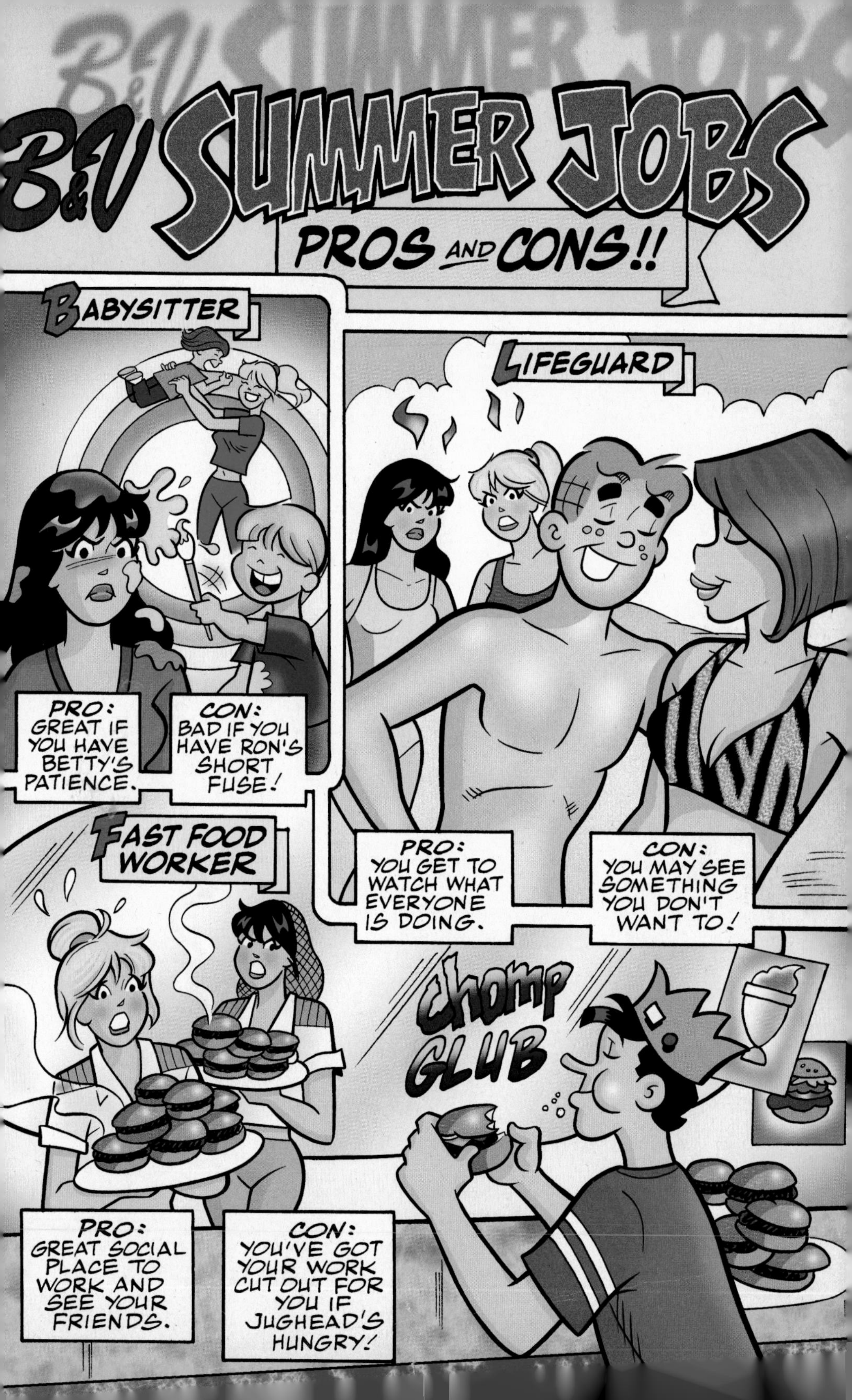
B&V SUMMER JOBS
PROS AND CONS!!
BABYSITTER
PRO: GREAT IF YOU HAVE BETTY'S PATIENCE.
CON: BAD IF YOU HAVE RON'S SHORT FUSE!
LIFEGUARD
PRO: YOU GET TO WATCH WHAT EVERYONE IS DOING.
CON: YOU MAY SEE SOMETHING YOU DON'T WANT TO!
FAST FOOD WORKER
CHOMP CLUB
PRO: GREAT SOCIAL PLACE TO WORK AND SEE YOUR FRIENDS.
CON: YOU'VE GOT YOUR WORK CUT OUT FOR YOU IF JUGHEAD'S HUNGRY!

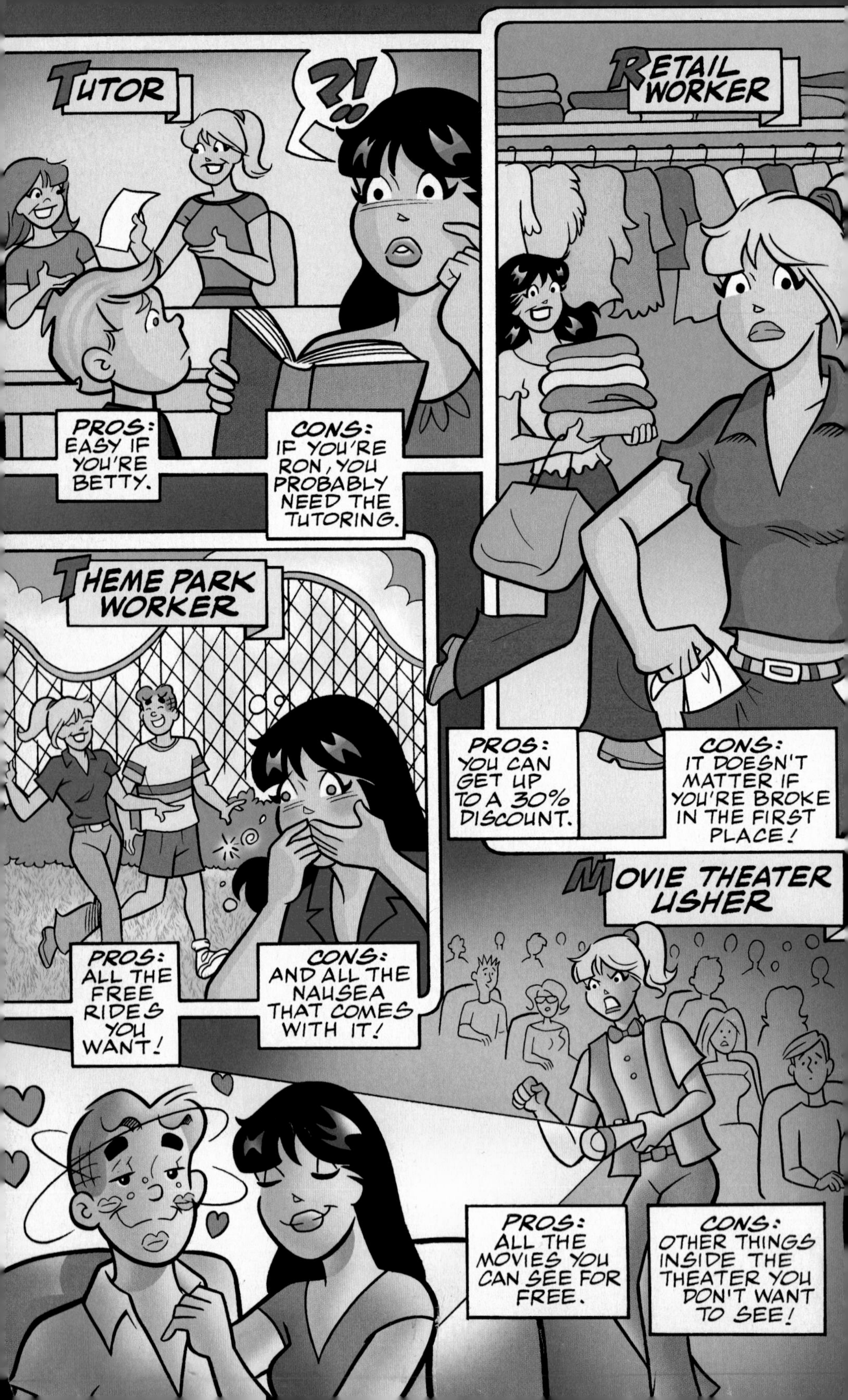
TUTOR
?!
PROS: EASY IF YOU'RE BETTY.
CONS: IF YOU'RE RON, YOU PROBABLY NEED THE TUTORING.
RETAIL WORKER
PROS: YOU CAN GET UP TO A 30% DISCOUNT.
CONS: IT DOESN'T MATTER IF YOU'RE BROKE IN THE FIRST PLACE!
THEME PARK WORKER
PROS: ALL THE FREE RIDES YOU WANT!
CONS: AND ALL THE NAUSEA THAT COMES WITH IT!
MOVIE THEATER USHER
PROS: ALL THE MOVIES YOU CAN SEE FOR FREE.
CONS: OTHER THINGS INSIDE THE THEATER YOU DON'T WANT TO SEE!

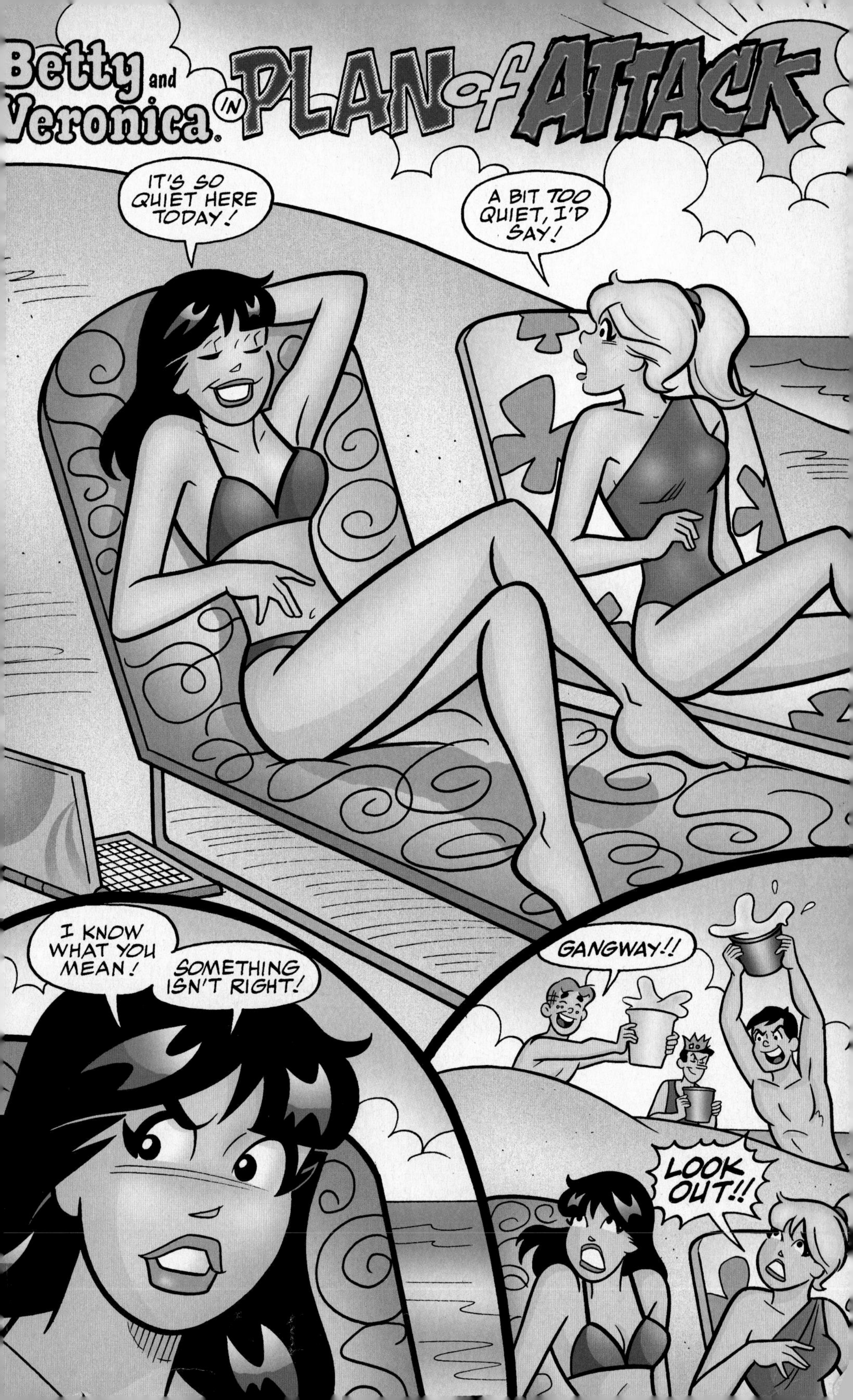
Betty and Veronica
IN
PLAN of ATTACK
IT'S SO QUIET HERE TODAY!
A BIT TOO QUIET, I'D SAY!
I KNOW WHAT YOU MEAN!
SOMETHING ISN'T RIGHT!
GANGWAY!!
LOOK OUT!!

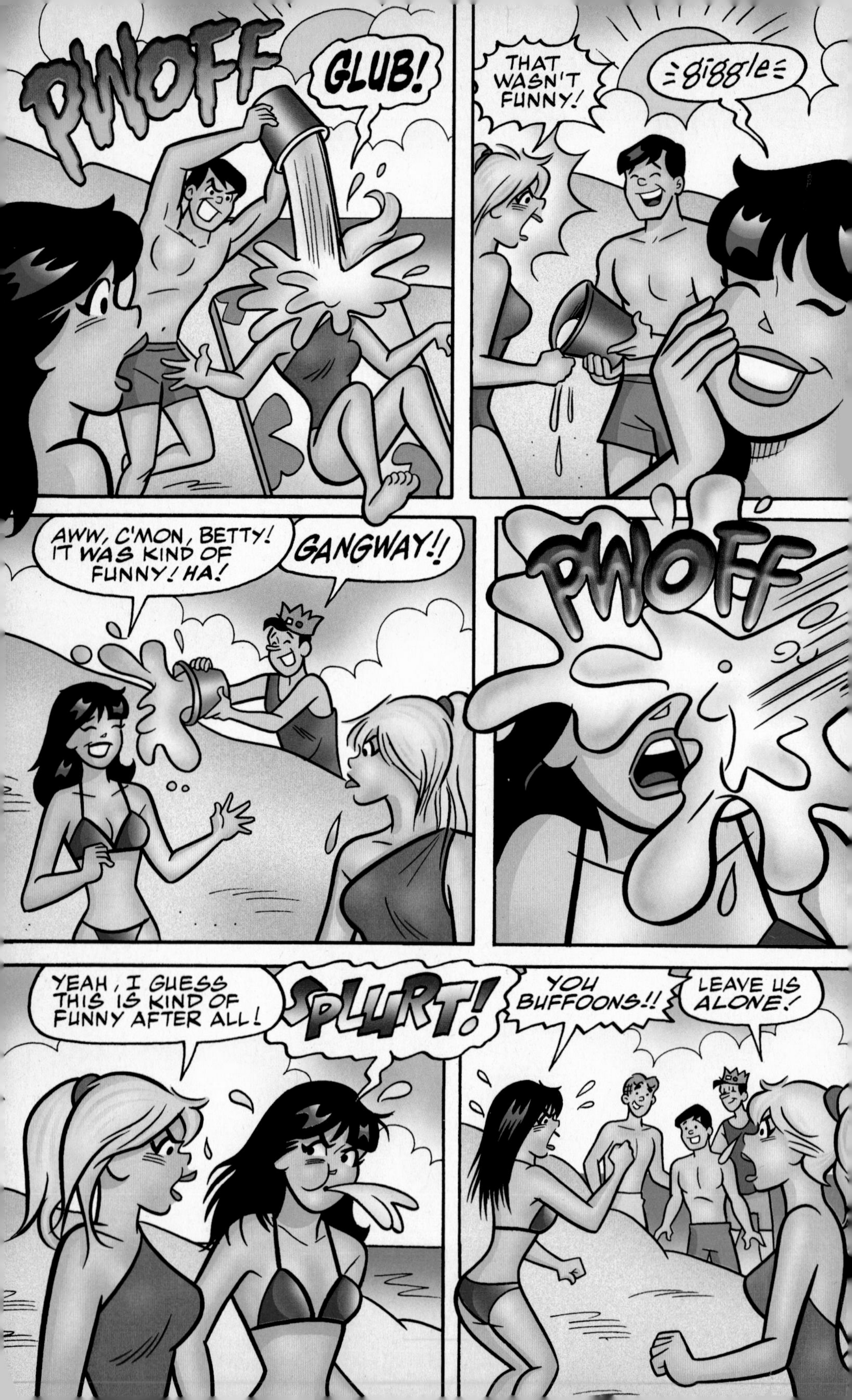
PWOFF
GLUB!
THAT WASN'T FUNNY!
giggle
AWW, C'MON, BETTY! IT WAS KIND OF FUNNY! HA!
GANGWAY!!
PWOFF
YEAH, I GUESS THIS IS KIND OF FUNNY AFTER ALL!
SPLURT!
YOU BUFFOONS!!
LEAVE US ALONE!

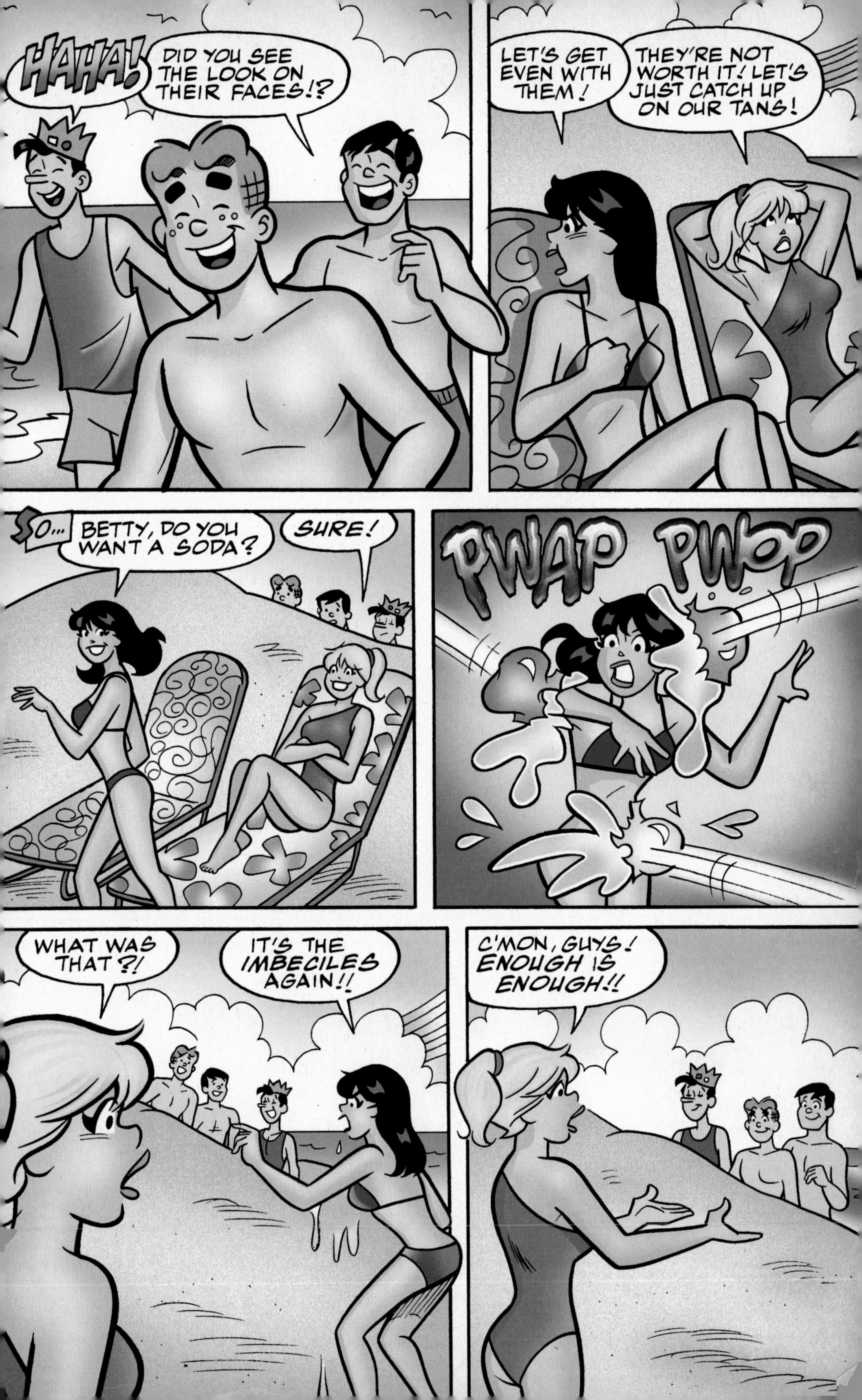
HAHA!
DID YOU SEE THE LOOK ON THEIR FACES!?
LET'S GET EVEN WITH THEM!
THEY'RE NOT WORTH IT! LET'S JUST CATCH UP ON OUR TANS!
SO...
BETTY, DO YOU WANT A SODA?
SURE!
PWAP PWOP
WHAT WAS THAT?!
IT'S THE IMBECILES AGAIN!!
C'MON, GUYS! ENOUGH IS ENOUGH!!

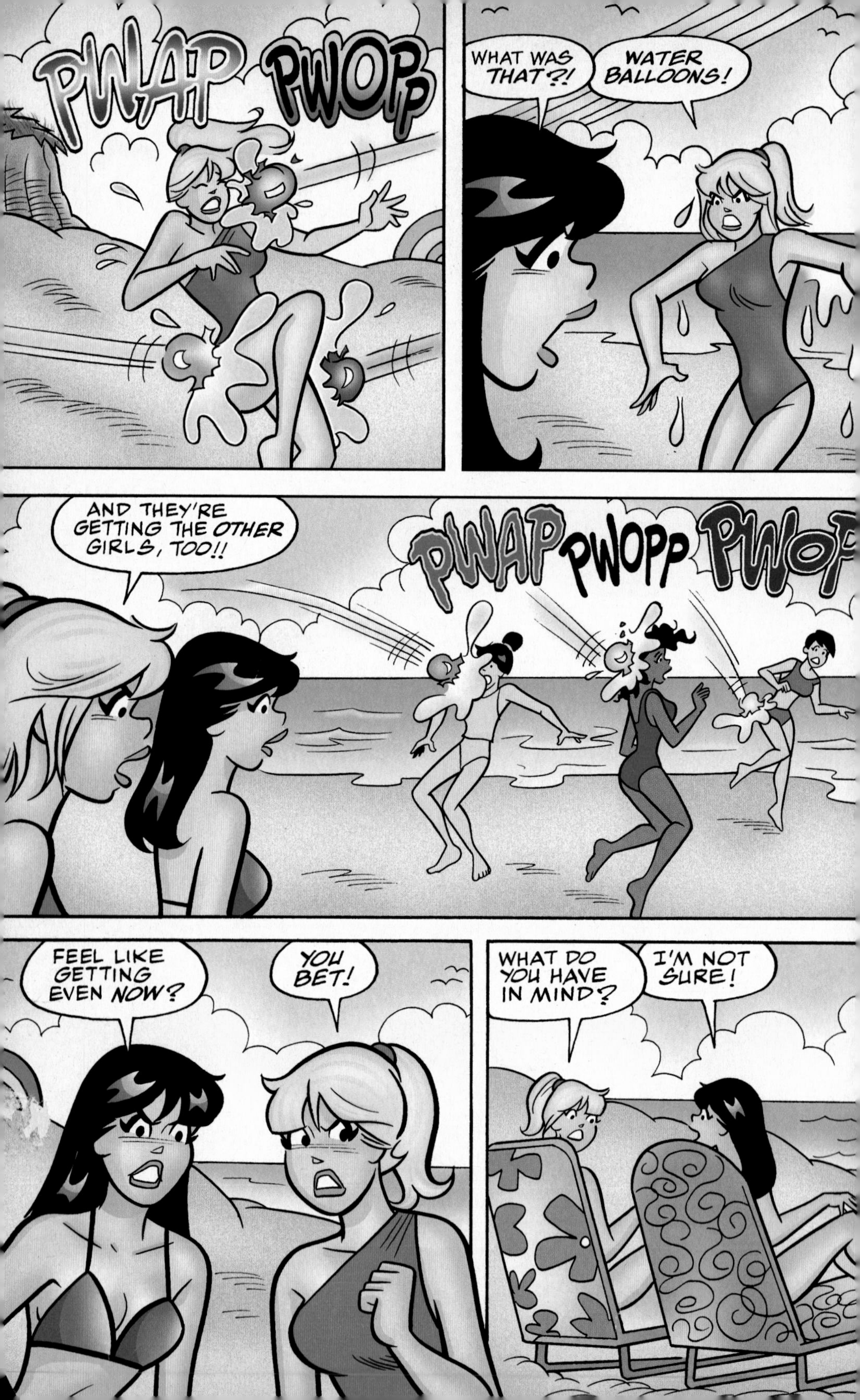
PWAP
PWOPP
WHAT WAS THAT?!
WATER BALLOONS!
AND THEY'RE GETTING THE OTHER GIRLS, TOO!!
PWAP
PWOPP
PWOP
FEEL LIKE GETTING EVEN NOW?
YOU BET!
WHAT DO YOU HAVE IN MIND?
I'M NOT SURE!

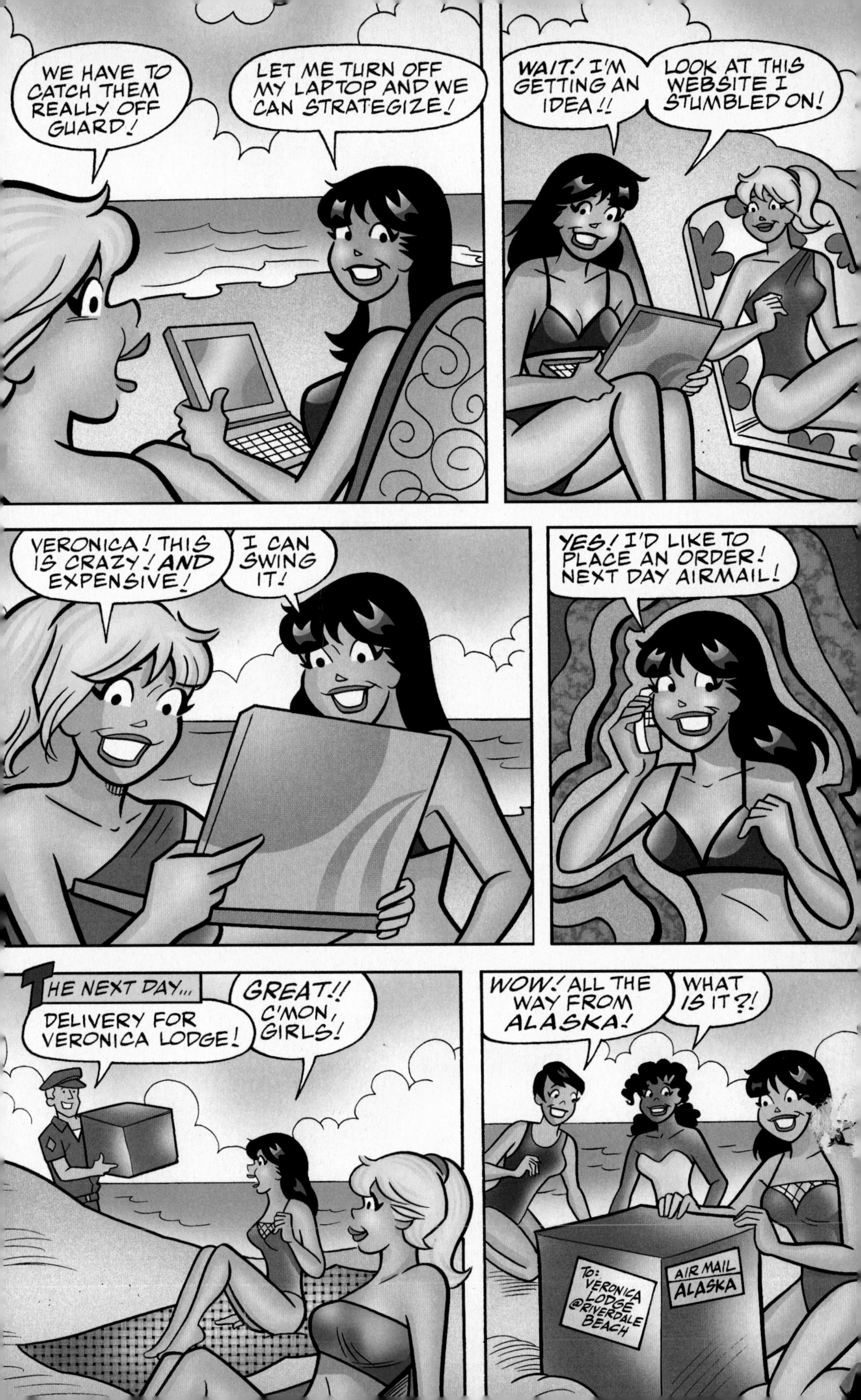
WE HAVE TO CATCH THEM REALLY OFF GUARD!
LET ME TURN OFF MY LAPTOP AND WE CAN STRATEGIZE!
WAIT! I'M GETTING AN IDEA!!
LOOK AT THIS WEBSITE I STUMBLED ON!
VERONICA! THIS IS CRAZY! AND EXPENSIVE!
I CAN SWING IT!
YES! I'D LIKE TO PLACE AN ORDER! NEXT DAY AIRMAIL!
THE NEXT DAY...
DELIVERY FOR VERONICA LODGE!
GREAT!! C'MON, GIRLS!
WOW! ALL THE WAY FROM ALASKA!
WHAT IS IT?!
TO: VERONICA LODGE @RIVERDALE BEACH
AIR MAIL
ALASKA

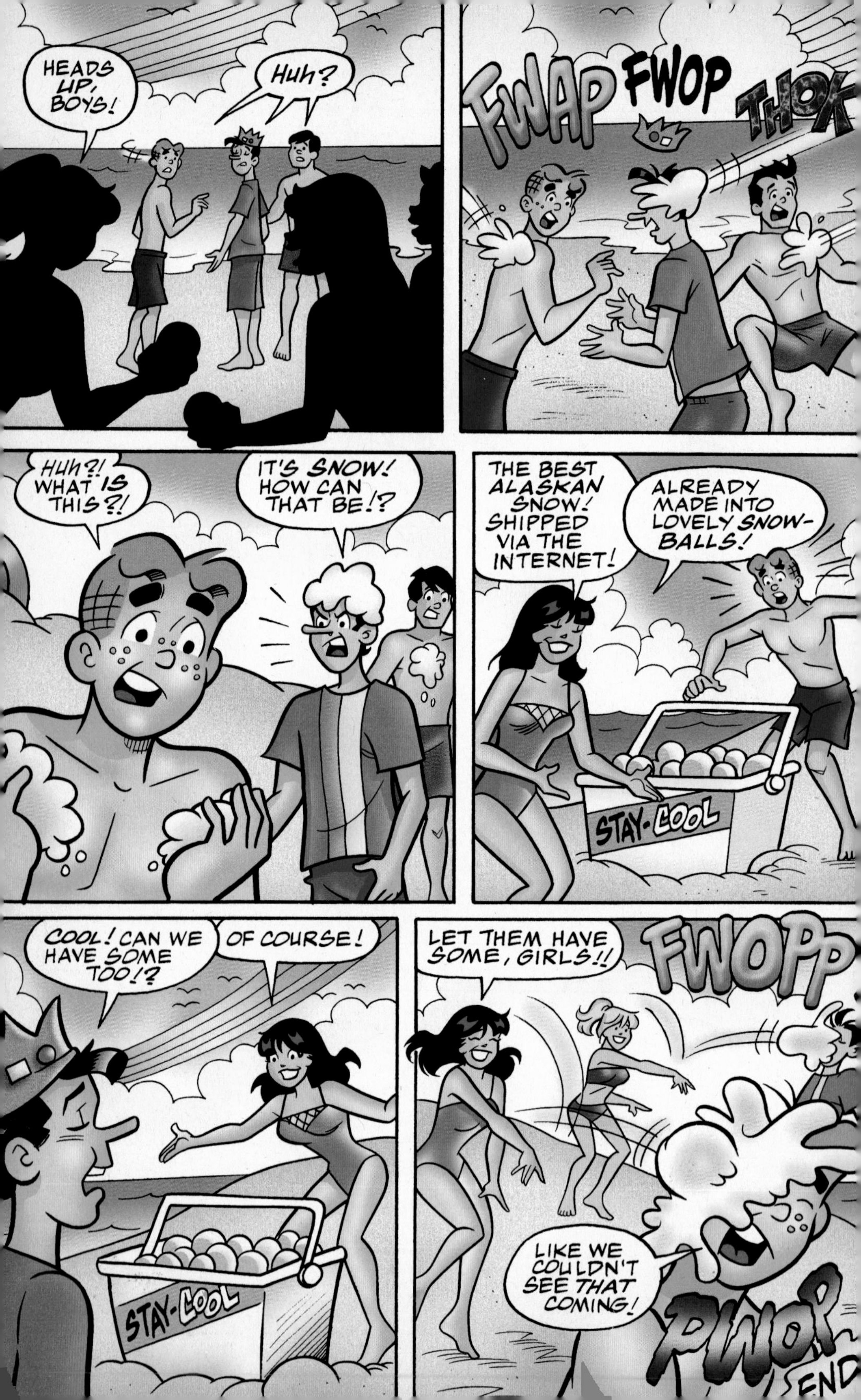
HEADS UP, BOYS!
Huh?
FWAP FWOP THOK
Huh?! WHAT IS THIS?!
IT'S SNOW! HOW CAN THAT BE!?
THE BEST ALASKAN SNOW! SHIPPED VIA THE INTERNET!
ALREADY MADE INTO LOVELY SNOW-BALLS!
STAY-COOL
COOL! CAN WE HAVE SOME TOO!?
OF COURSE!
STAY-COOL
LET THEM HAVE SOME, GIRLS!!
FWOPP
LIKE WE COULDN'T SEE THAT COMING!
PWOP
END

Betty and Veronica® in LUCK BEFORE YOU LEAP

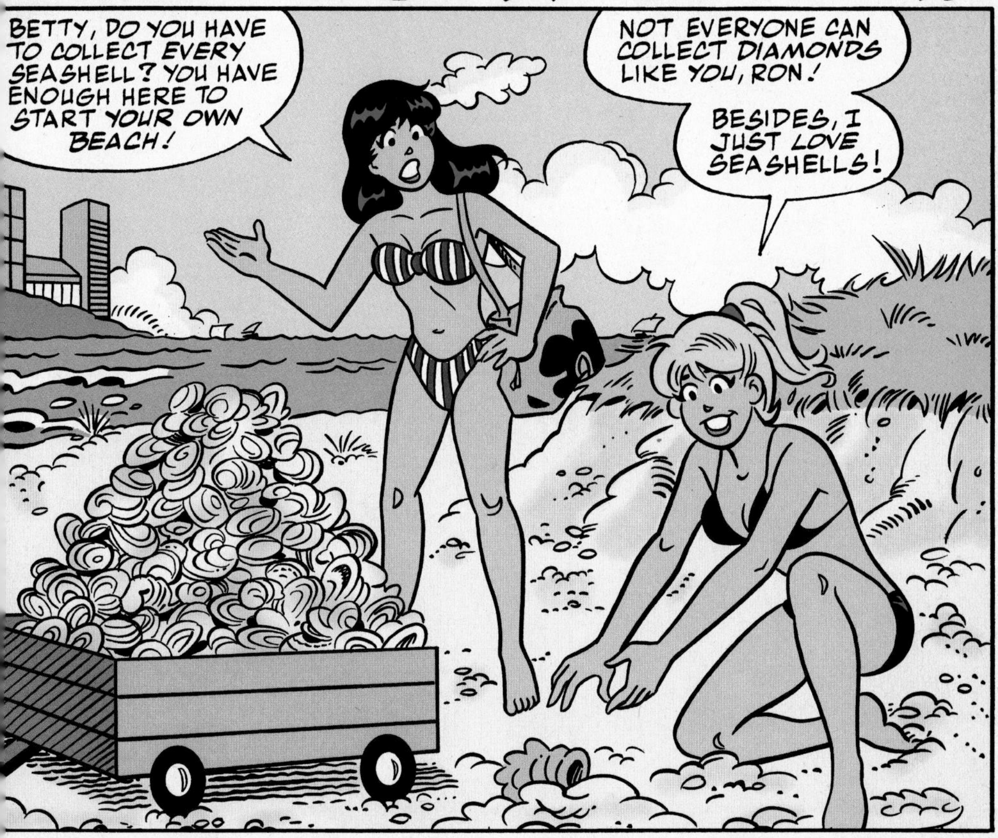
BETTY, DO YOU HAVE TO COLLECT EVERY SEASHELL? YOU HAVE ENOUGH HERE TO START YOUR OWN BEACH!
NOT EVERYONE CAN COLLECT DIAMONDS LIKE YOU, RON!
BESIDES, I JUST LOVE SEASHELLS!

SCRIPT: ANGELO DECESARE PENCILS: JEFF SHULTZ INKING: AL MILGROM LETTERING: JACK MORELLI COLORING: BARRY GROSSMAN EDITOR: VICTOR GORELICK EDITOR-IN-CHIEF: RICHARD GOLDWATER

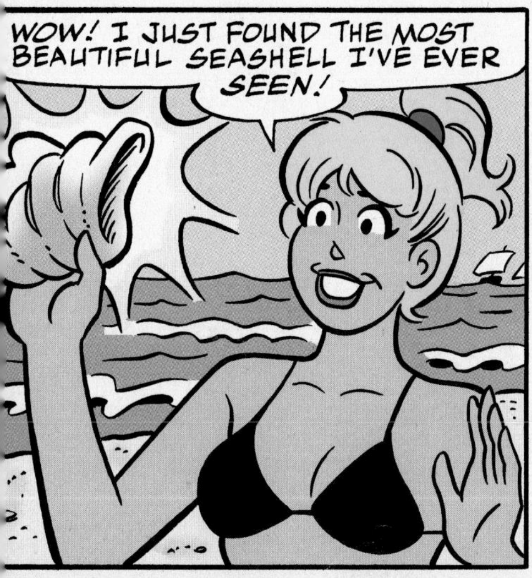
WOW! I JUST FOUND THE MOST BEAUTIFUL SEASHELL I'VE EVER SEEN!

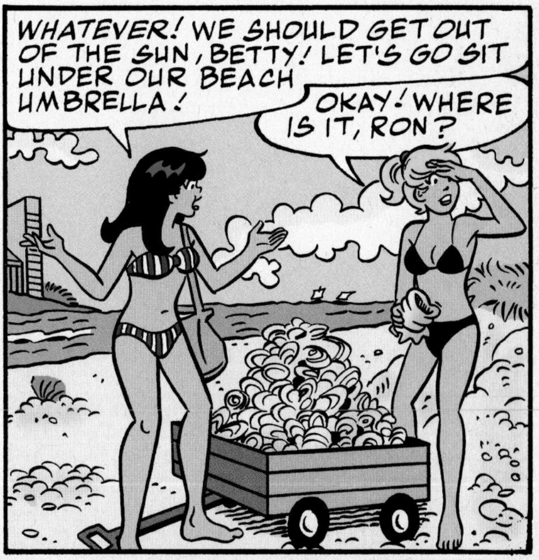
WHATEVER! WE SHOULD GET OUT OF THE SUN, BETTY! LET'S GO SIT UNDER OUR BEACH UMBRELLA!
OKAY! WHERE IS IT, RON?

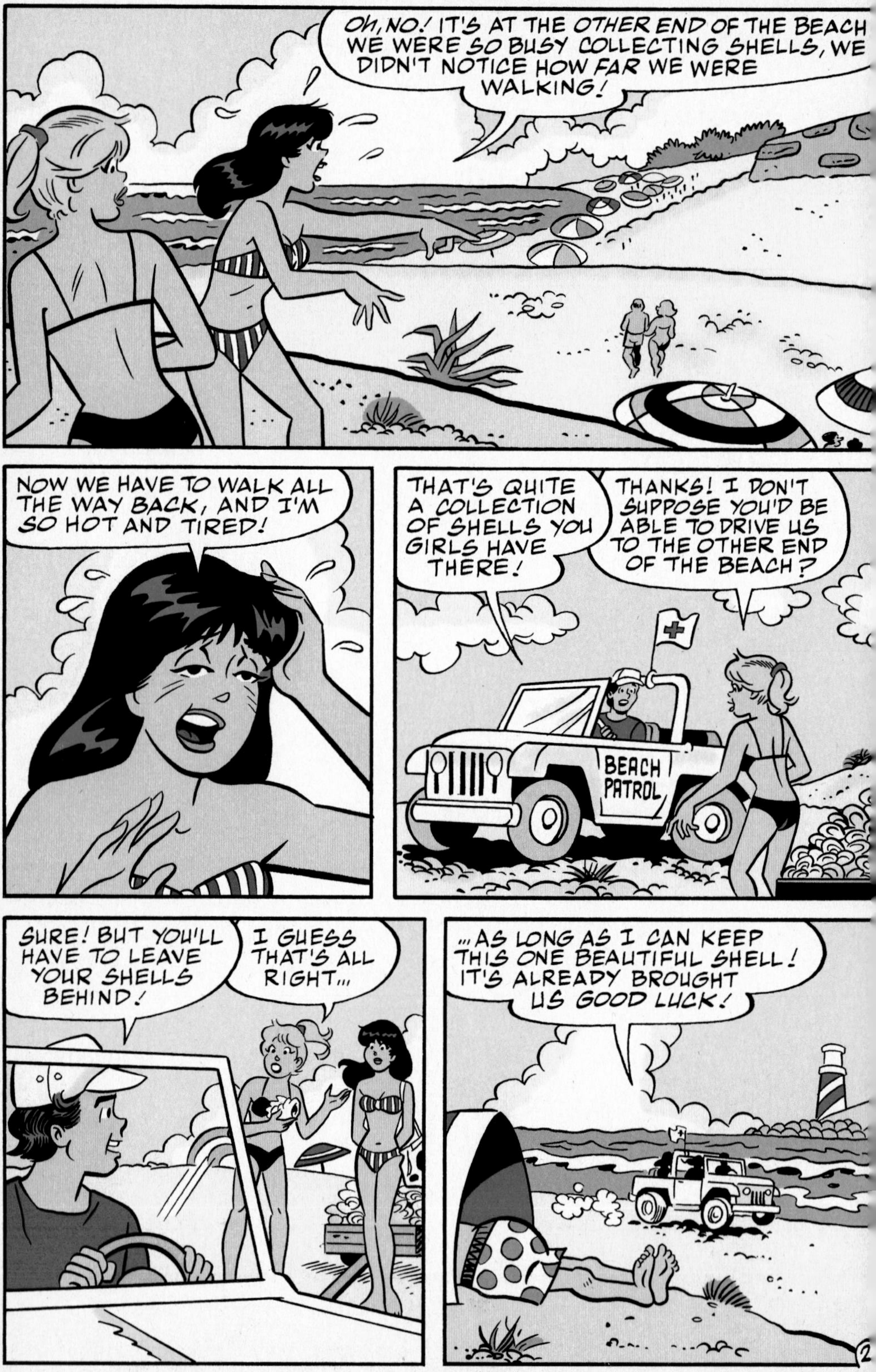
OH, NO! IT'S AT THE OTHER END OF THE BEACH WE WERE SO BUSY COLLECTING SHELLS, WE DIDN'T NOTICE HOW FAR WE WERE WALKING!
NOW WE HAVE TO WALK ALL THE WAY BACK, AND I'M SO HOT AND TIRED!
THAT'S QUITE A COLLECTION OF SHELLS YOU GIRLS HAVE THERE!
THANKS! I DON'T SUPPOSE YOU'D BE ABLE TO DRIVE US TO THE OTHER END OF THE BEACH?
BEACH PATROL
SURE! BUT YOU'LL HAVE TO LEAVE YOUR SHELLS BEHIND!
I GUESS THAT'S ALL RIGHT...
...AS LONG AS I CAN KEEP THIS ONE BEAUTIFUL SHELL! IT'S ALREADY BROUGHT US GOOD LUCK!

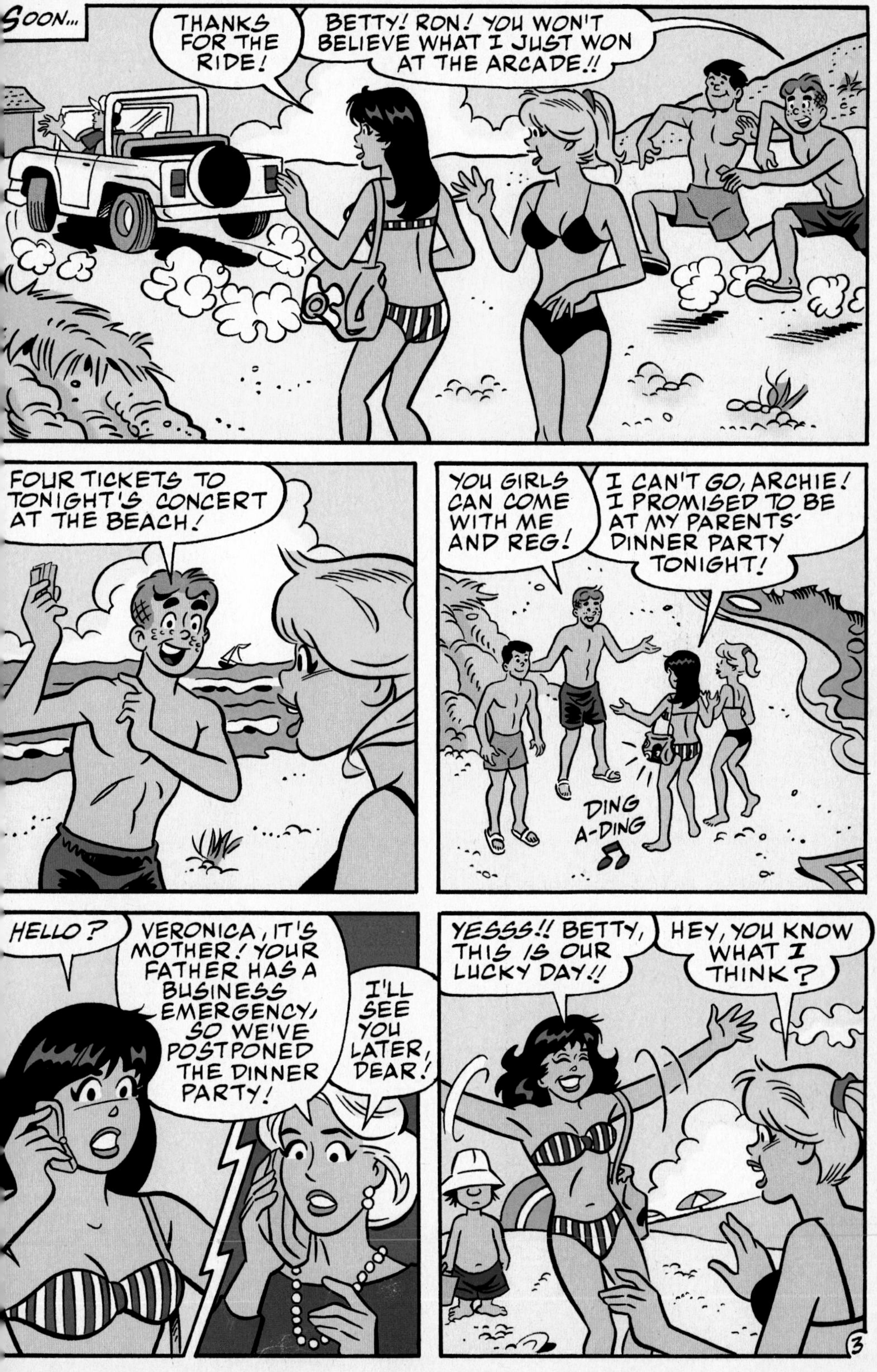
SOON...
THANKS FOR THE RIDE!
BETTY! RON! YOU WON'T BELIEVE WHAT I JUST WON AT THE ARCADE!!
FOUR TICKETS TO TONIGHT'S CONCERT AT THE BEACH!
YOU GIRLS CAN COME WITH ME AND REG!
I CAN'T GO, ARCHIE! I PROMISED TO BE AT MY PARENTS' DINNER PARTY TONIGHT!
DING A-DING
HELLO?
VERONICA, IT'S MOTHER! YOUR FATHER HAS A BUSINESS EMERGENCY, SO WE'VE POSTPONED THE DINNER PARTY!
I'LL SEE YOU LATER, DEAR!
YESSS!! BETTY, THIS IS OUR LUCKY DAY!!
HEY, YOU KNOW WHAT I THINK?
3

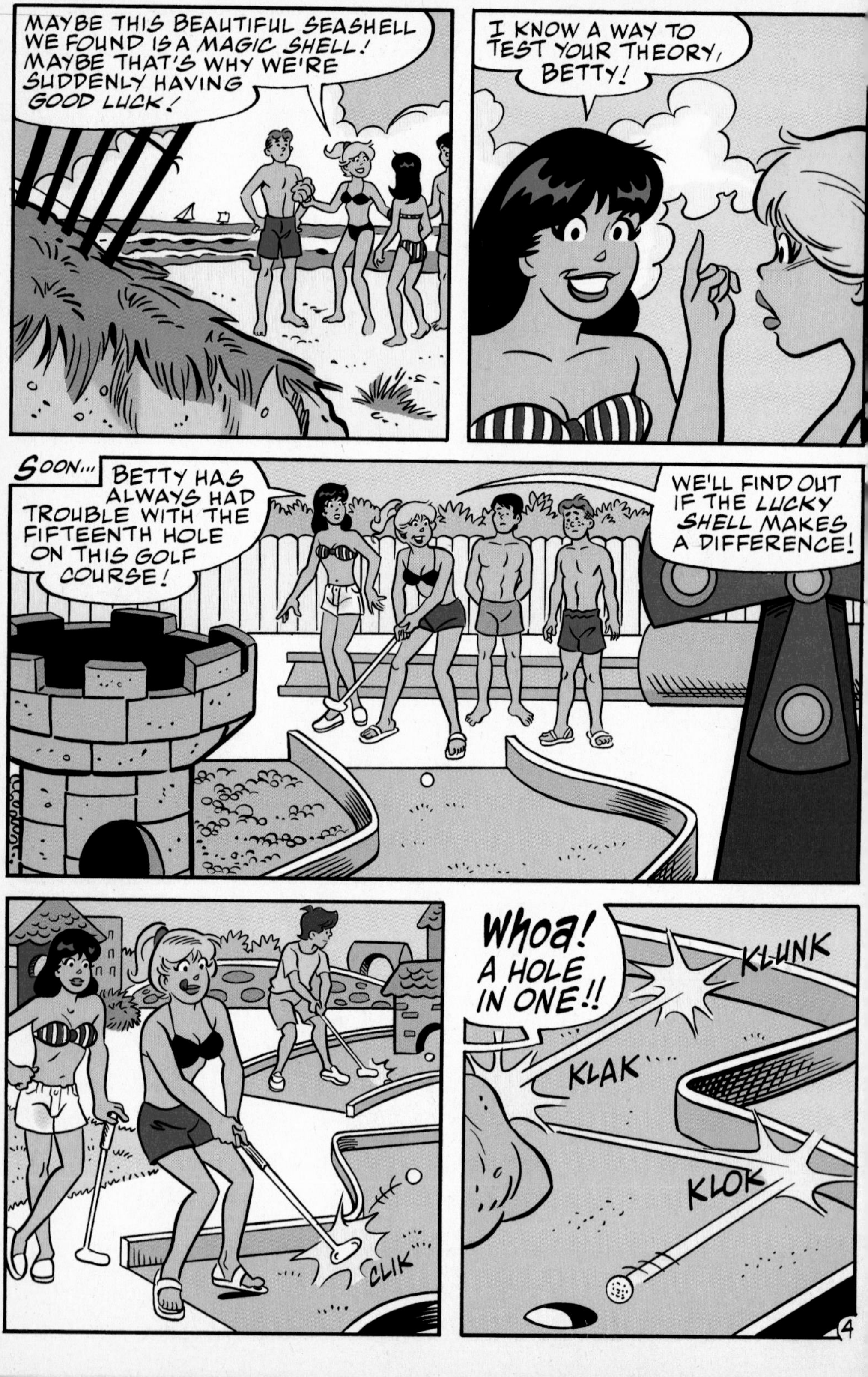
MAYBE THIS BEAUTIFUL SEASHELL WE FOUND IS A MAGIC SHELL! MAYBE THAT'S WHY WE'RE SUDDENLY HAVING GOOD LUCK!
I KNOW A WAY TO TEST YOUR THEORY, BETTY!
SOON...
BETTY HAS ALWAYS HAD TROUBLE WITH THE FIFTEENTH HOLE ON THIS GOLF COURSE!
WE'LL FIND OUT IF THE LUCKY SHELL MAKES A DIFFERENCE!
CLIK
Whoa! A HOLE IN ONE!!
KLUNK
KLAK
KLOK

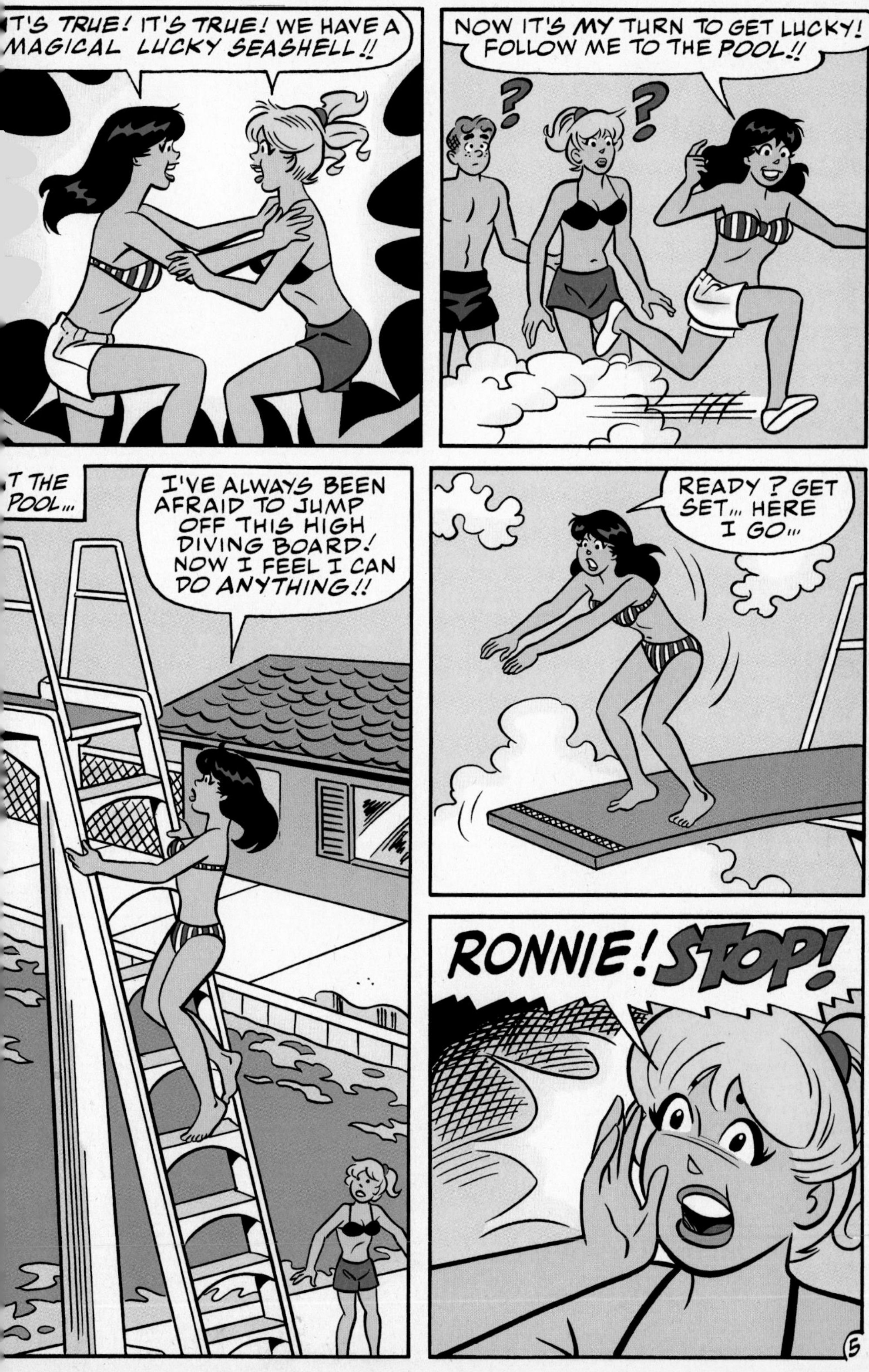

IT'S TRUE! IT'S TRUE! WE HAVE A MAGICAL LUCKY SEASHELL!!
NOW IT'S MY TURN TO GET LUCKY! FOLLOW ME TO THE POOL!!
?
?
T THE POOL...
I'VE ALWAYS BEEN AFRAID TO JUMP OFF THIS HIGH DIVING BOARD! NOW I FEEL I CAN DO ANYTHING!!
READY ? GET SET... HERE I GO...
RONNIE! STOP!

MAYBE THE SHELL *ISN'T* LUCKY! IT'S TRUE THAT GUY GAVE US A RIDE, BUT I HAD TO LEAVE ALL MY OTHER SHELLS BEHIND! AND I MADE THAT HOLE-IN-ONE 'CAUSE I'VE BEEN *PRACTICING!!*

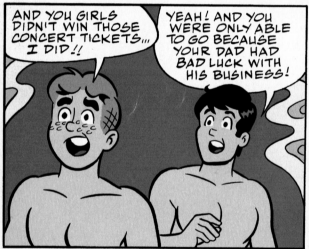

AND YOU GIRLS DIDN'T WIN THOSE CONCERT TICKETS... I DID*!!*

YEAH*!* AND YOU WERE ONLY ABLE TO GO BECAUSE YOUR DAD HAD BAD LUCK WITH HIS BUSINESS!

YOU'RE *RIGHT!* THERE'S NO SUCH THING AS A *LUCKY SEASHELL!*

MUCH LATER...

BUT, RON*!* I THOUGHT YOU SAID THERE'S NO SUCH *THING* AS A LUCKY SEASHELL*!*

THERE *ISN'T!* BUT I'M NOT GONNA TRY TO CLIMB DOWN TILL YOU GO GET MY *LUCKY HORSESHOE* AND A *FOUR LEAF CLOVER!*

THE END

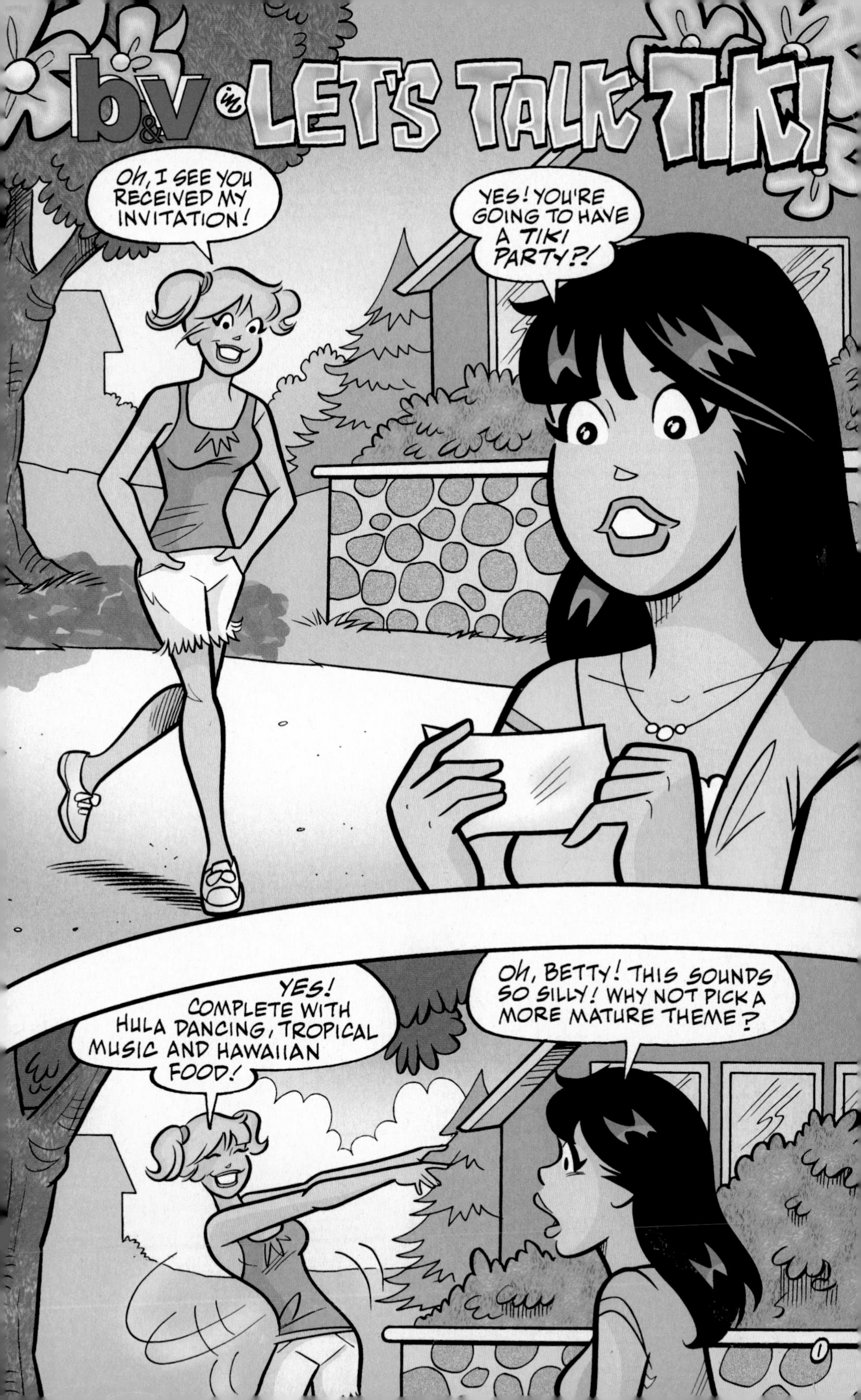
b&V in LET'S TALK TIKI!
OH, I SEE YOU RECEIVED MY INVITATION!
YES! YOU'RE GOING TO HAVE A TIKI PARTY?!
YES! COMPLETE WITH HULA DANCING, TROPICAL MUSIC AND HAWAIIAN FOOD!
OH, BETTY! THIS SOUNDS SO SILLY! WHY NOT PICK A MORE MATURE THEME?
1

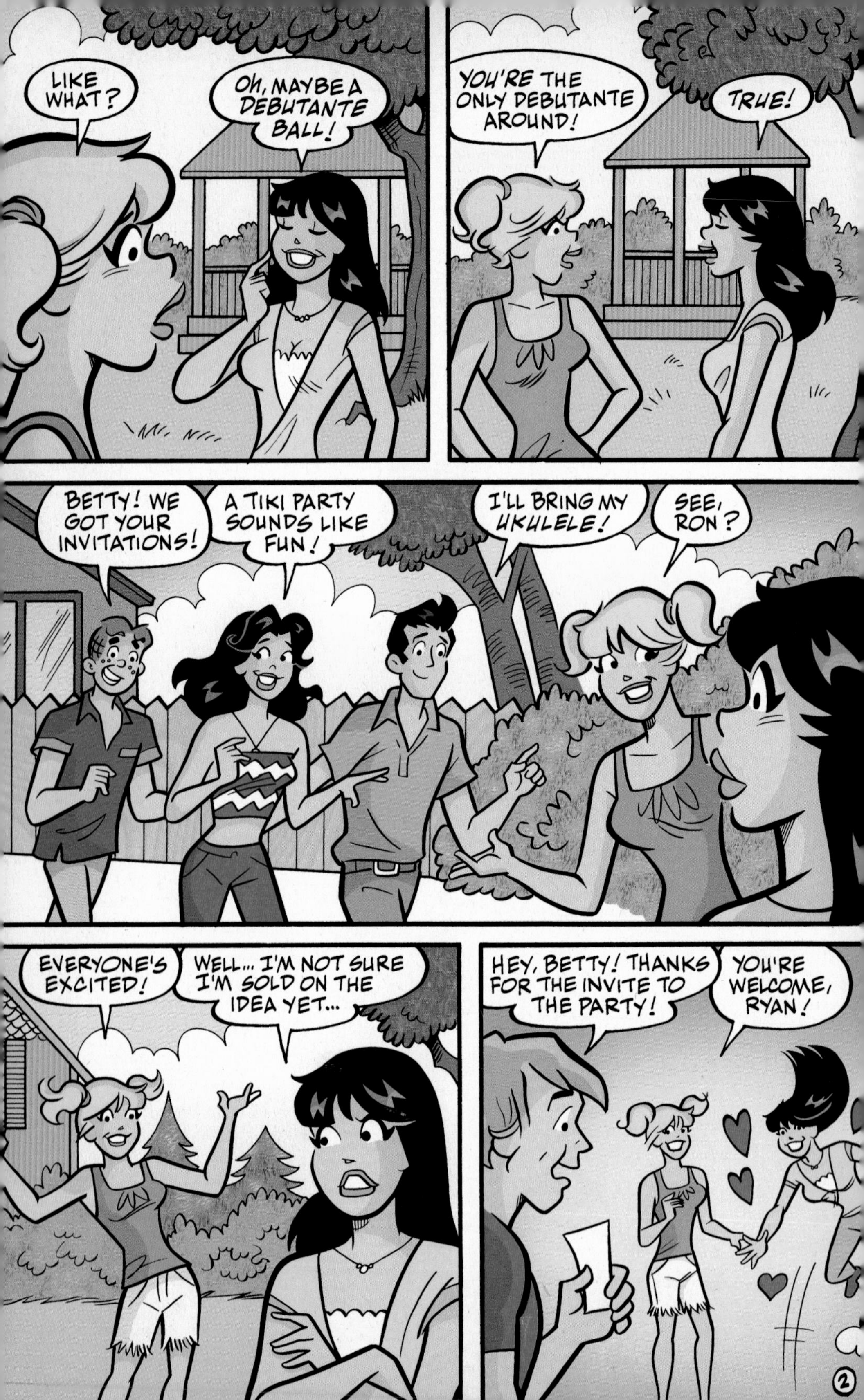
LIKE WHAT?
OH, MAYBE A DEBUTANTE BALL!
YOU'RE THE ONLY DEBUTANTE AROUND!
TRUE!
BETTY! WE GOT YOUR INVITATIONS!
A TIKI PARTY SOUNDS LIKE FUN!
I'LL BRING MY UKULELE!
SEE, RON?
EVERYONE'S EXCITED!
WELL... I'M NOT SURE I'M SOLD ON THE IDEA YET...
HEY, BETTY! THANKS FOR THE INVITE TO THE PARTY!
YOU'RE WELCOME, RYAN!

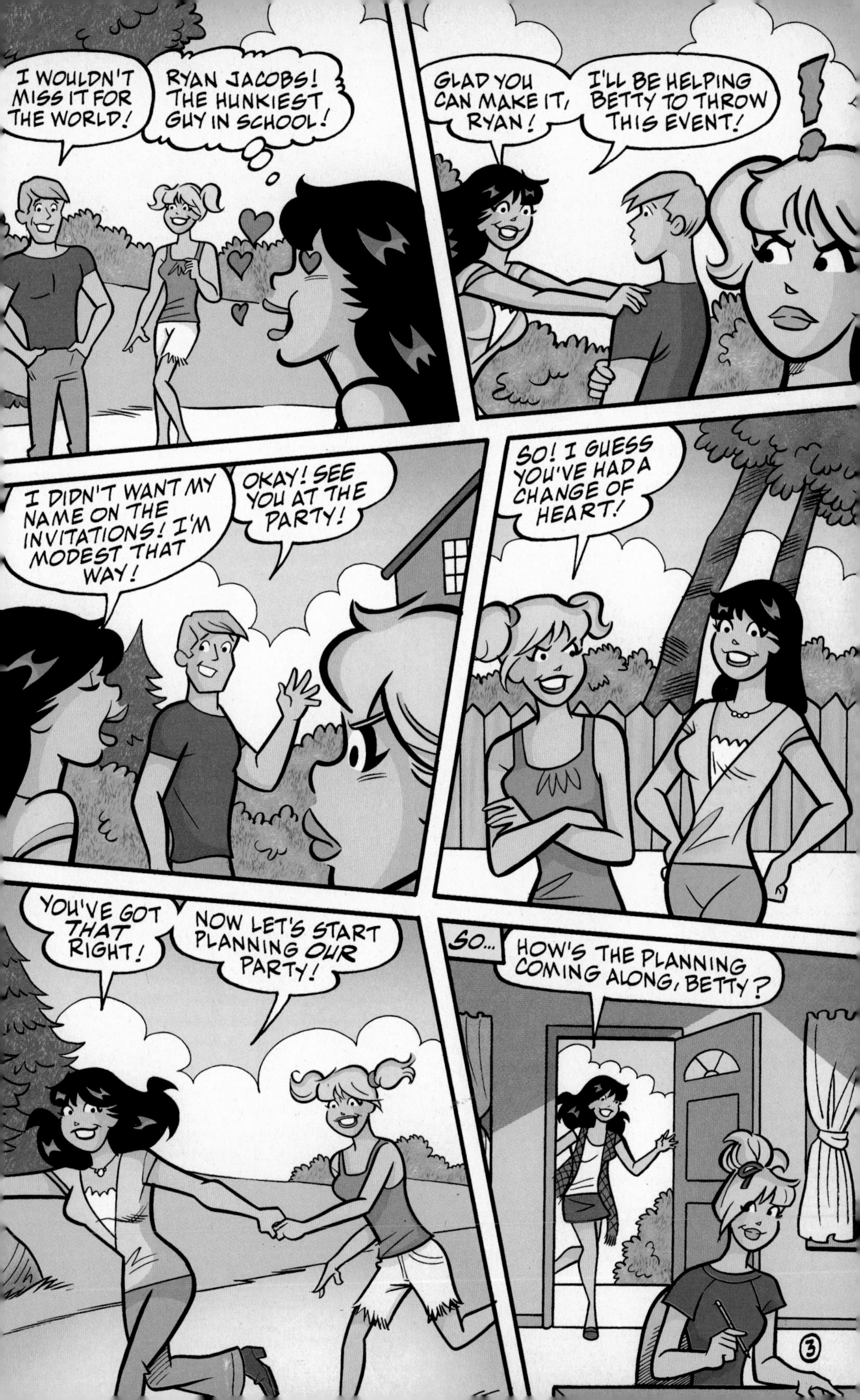
I WOULDN'T MISS IT FOR THE WORLD!
RYAN JACOBS! THE HUNKIEST GUY IN SCHOOL!
GLAD YOU CAN MAKE IT, RYAN!
I'LL BE HELPING BETTY TO THROW THIS EVENT!
!
I DIDN'T WANT MY NAME ON THE INVITATIONS! I'M MODEST THAT WAY!
OKAY! SEE YOU AT THE PARTY!
SO! I GUESS YOU'VE HAD A CHANGE OF HEART!
YOU'VE GOT THAT RIGHT!
NOW LET'S START PLANNING OUR PARTY!
SO...
HOW'S THE PLANNING COMING ALONG, BETTY?

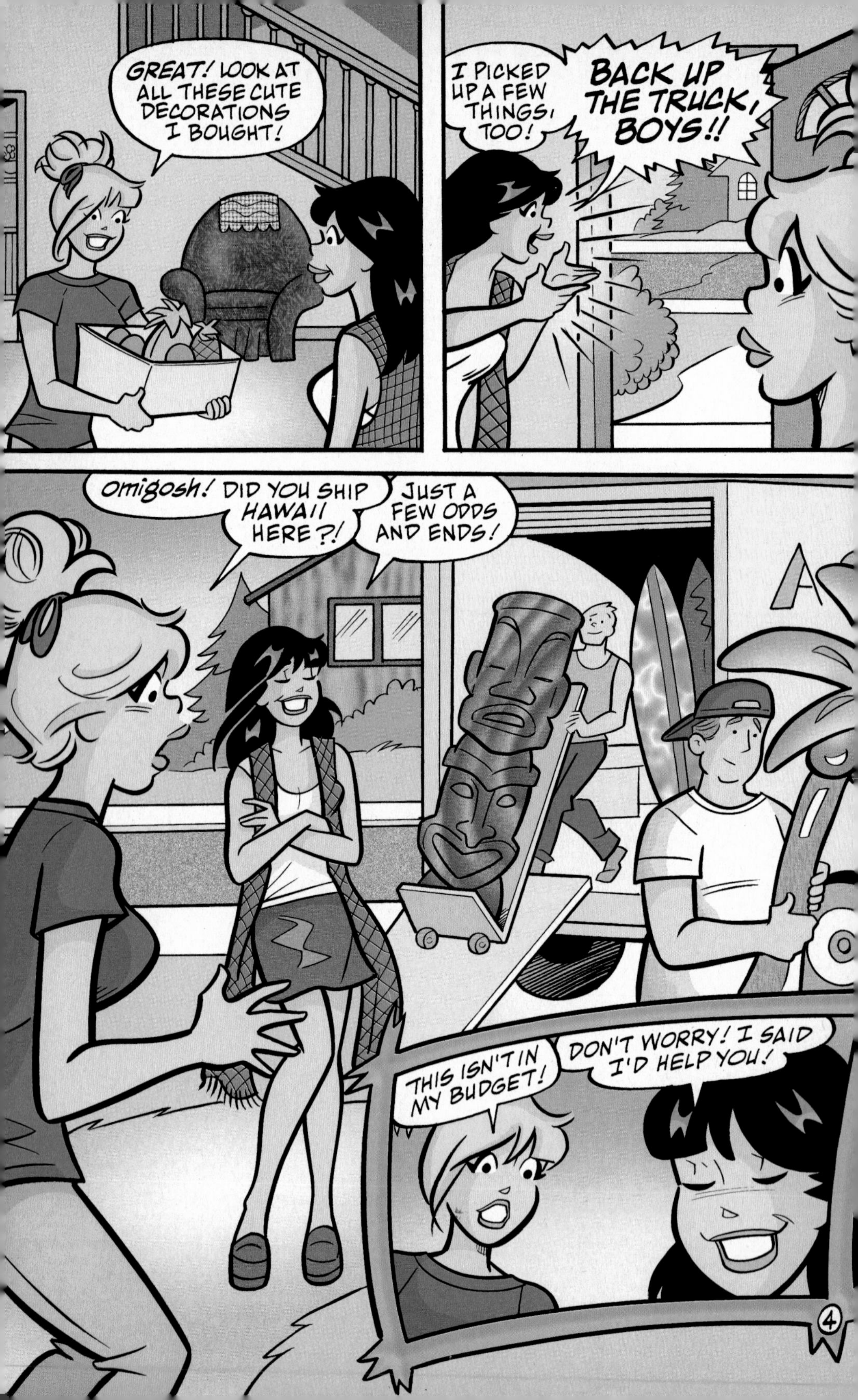
GREAT! LOOK AT ALL THESE CUTE DECORATIONS I BOUGHT!
I PICKED UP A FEW THINGS, TOO!
BACK UP THE TRUCK, BOYS!!
Omigosh! DID YOU SHIP HAWAII HERE?!
JUST A FEW ODDS AND ENDS!
THIS ISN'T IN MY BUDGET!
DON'T WORRY! I SAID I'D HELP YOU!
4

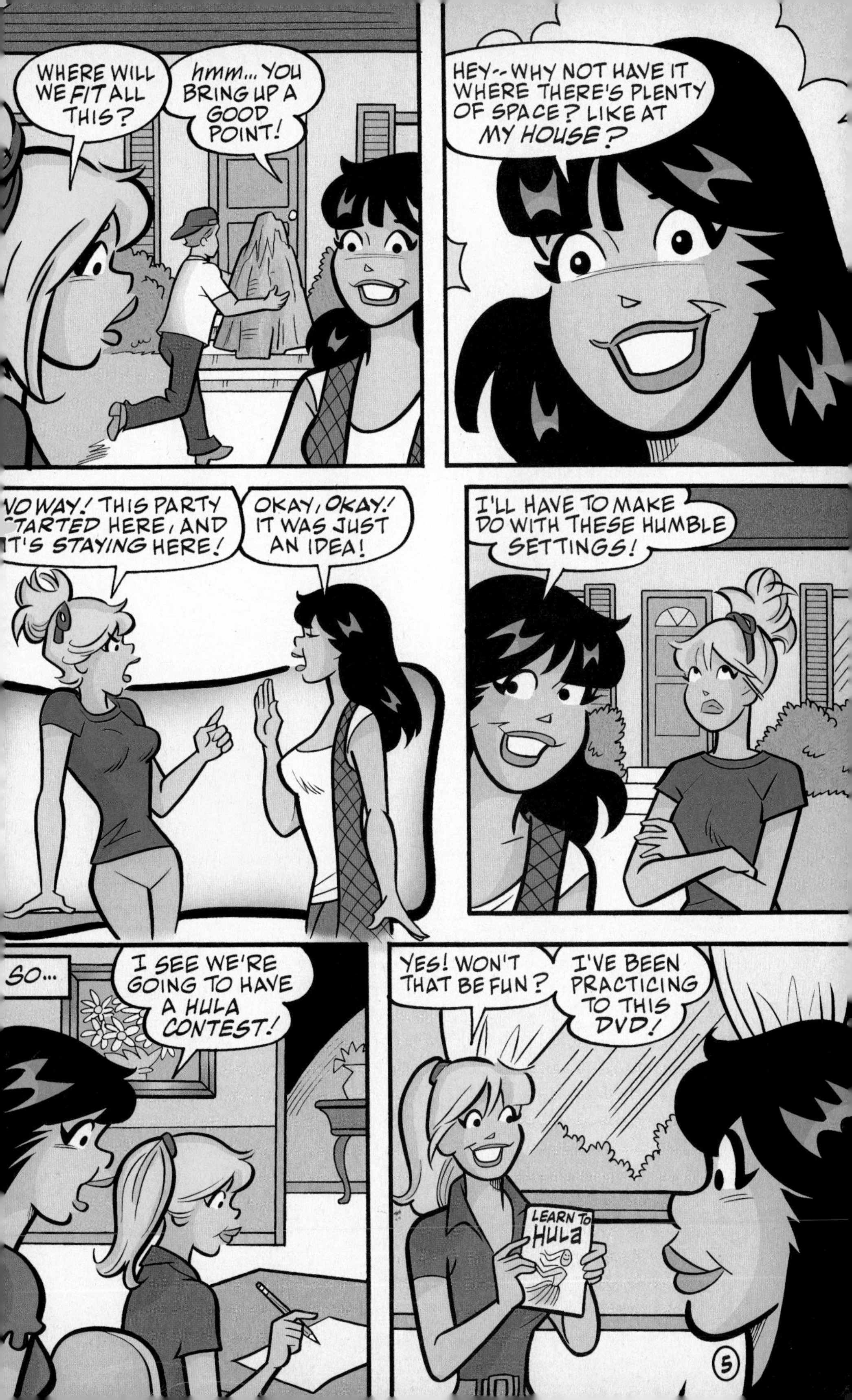
WHERE WILL WE FIT ALL THIS?
hmm... YOU BRING UP A GOOD POINT!
HEY-- WHY NOT HAVE IT WHERE THERE'S PLENTY OF SPACE? LIKE AT MY HOUSE?
NO WAY! THIS PARTY STARTED HERE, AND IT'S STAYING HERE!
OKAY, OKAY! IT WAS JUST AN IDEA!
I'LL HAVE TO MAKE DO WITH THESE HUMBLE SETTINGS!
SO...
I SEE WE'RE GOING TO HAVE A HULA CONTEST!
YES! WON'T THAT BE FUN?
I'VE BEEN PRACTICING TO THIS DVD!
LEARN TO HULA
5

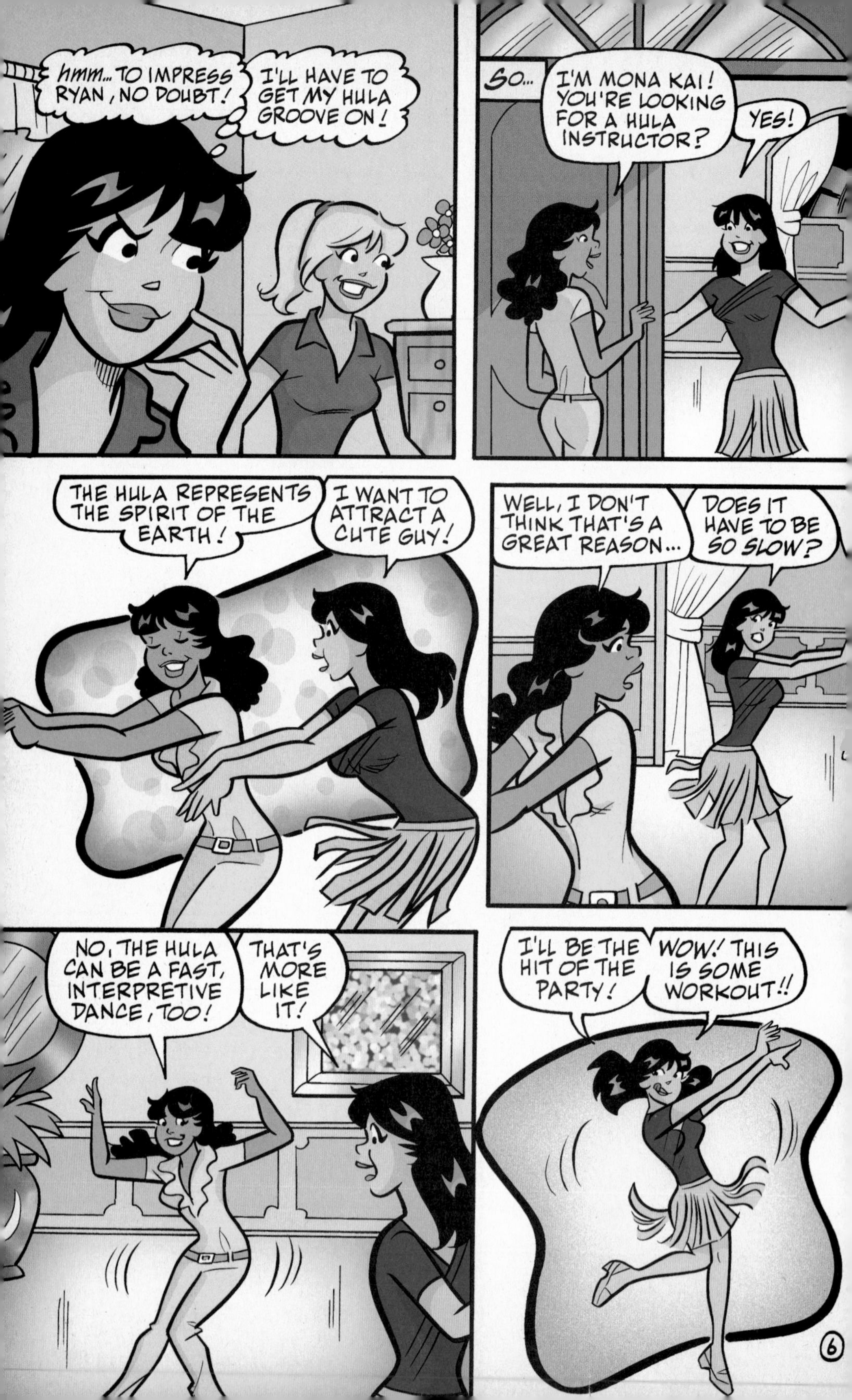

hmm... TO IMPRESS RYAN, NO DOUBT!
I'LL HAVE TO GET MY HULA GROOVE ON!
SO...
I'M MONA KAI! YOU'RE LOOKING FOR A HULA INSTRUCTOR?
YES!
THE HULA REPRESENTS THE SPIRIT OF THE EARTH!
I WANT TO ATTRACT A CUTE GUY!
WELL, I DON'T THINK THAT'S A GREAT REASON...
DOES IT HAVE TO BE SO SLOW?
NO, THE HULA CAN BE A FAST, INTERPRETIVE DANCE, TOO!
THAT'S MORE LIKE IT!
I'LL BE THE HIT OF THE PARTY!
WOW! THIS IS SOME WORKOUT!!

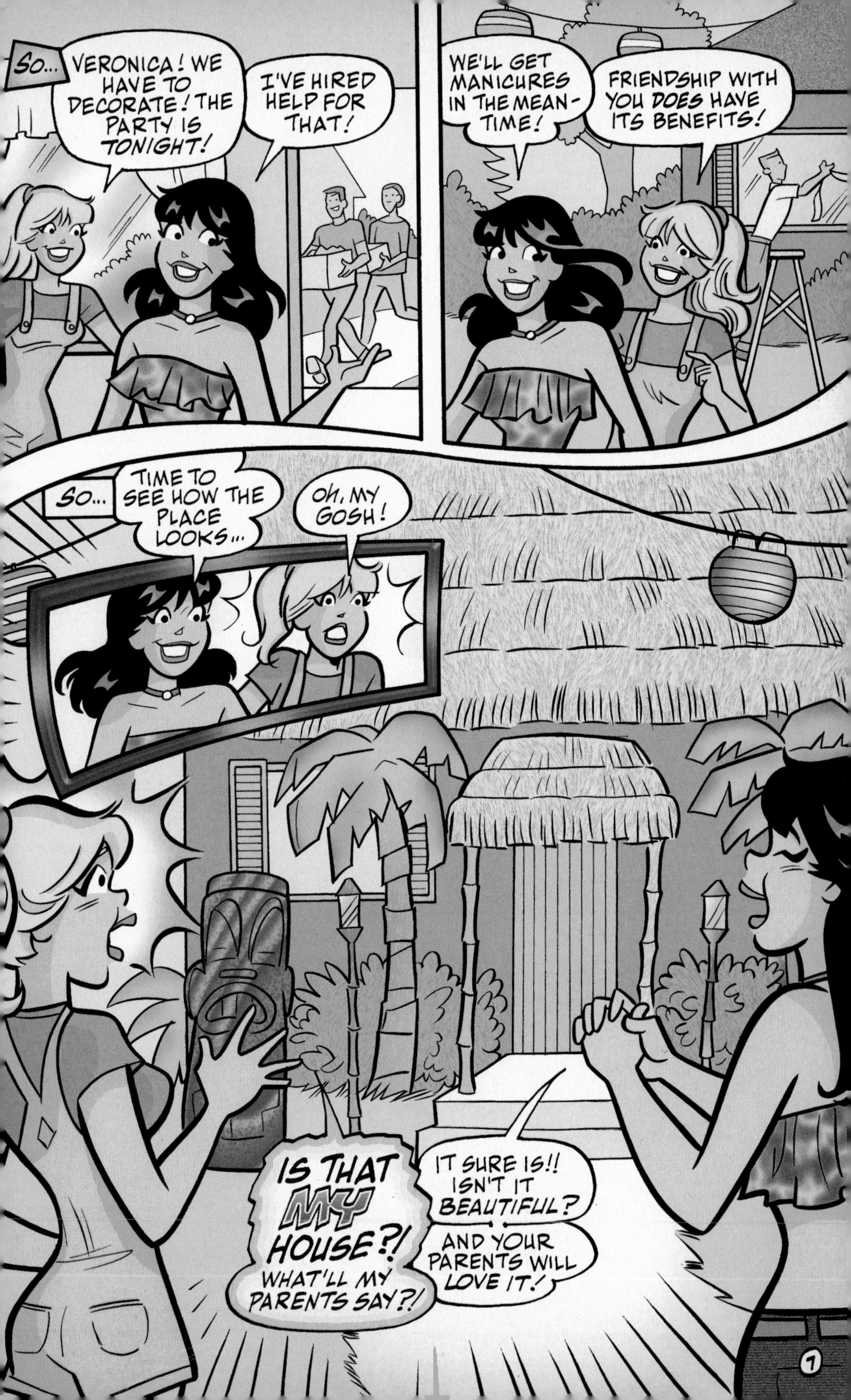

SO...
VERONICA! WE HAVE TO DECORATE! THE PARTY IS TONIGHT!
I'VE HIRED HELP FOR THAT!
WE'LL GET MANICURES IN THE MEAN-TIME!
FRIENDSHIP WITH YOU DOES HAVE ITS BENEFITS!
SO...
TIME TO SEE HOW THE PLACE LOOKS...
OH, MY GOSH!
IS THAT MY HOUSE?! WHAT'LL MY PARENTS SAY?!
IT SURE IS!! ISN'T IT BEAUTIFUL?
AND YOUR PARENTS WILL LOVE IT!

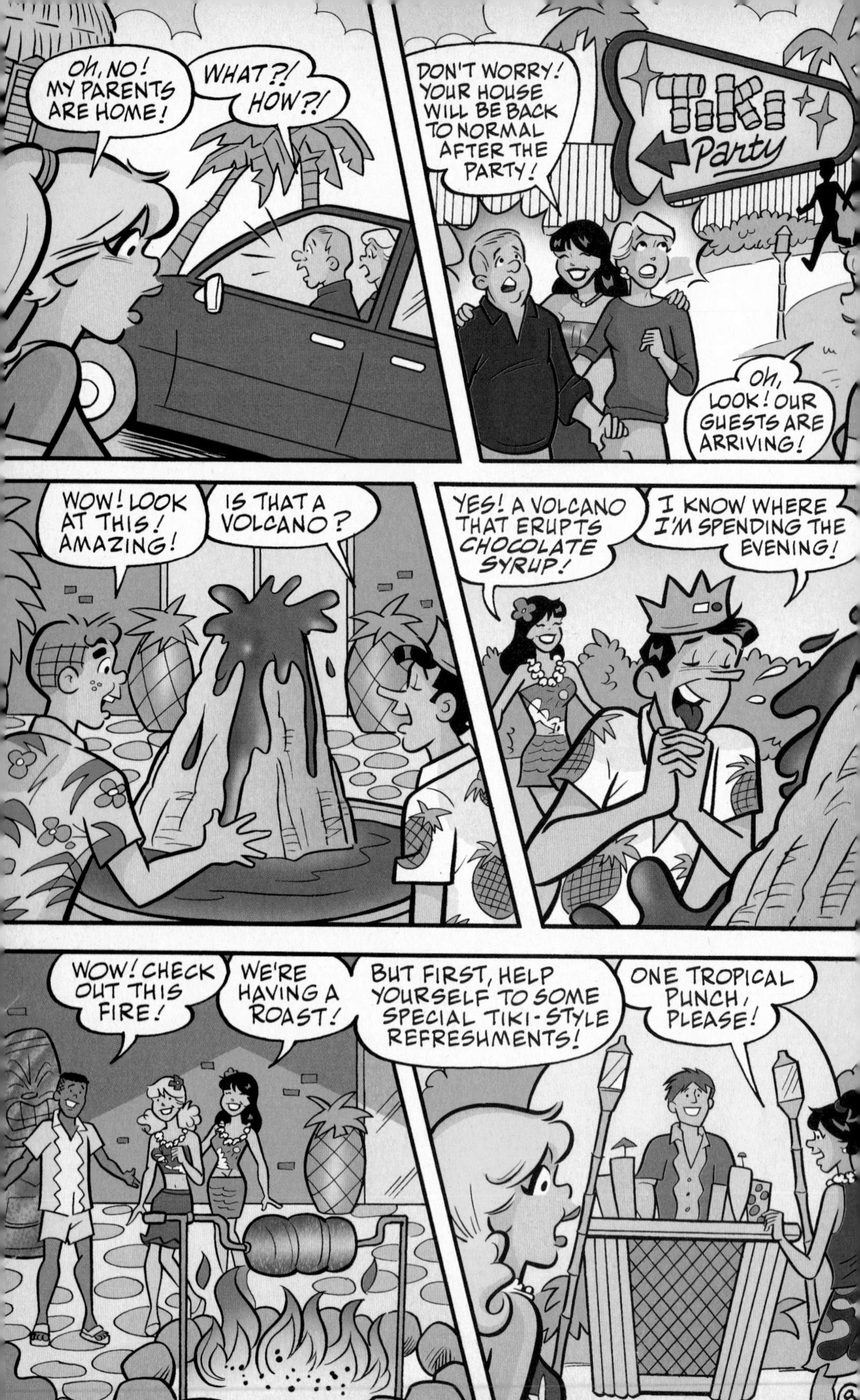

OH, NO! MY PARENTS ARE HOME!
WHAT?! HOW?!
DON'T WORRY! YOUR HOUSE WILL BE BACK TO NORMAL AFTER THE PARTY!
TIKI Party
OH, LOOK! OUR GUESTS ARE ARRIVING!
WOW! LOOK AT THIS! AMAZING!
IS THAT A VOLCANO?
YES! A VOLCANO THAT ERUPTS CHOCOLATE SYRUP!
I KNOW WHERE I'M SPENDING THE EVENING!
WOW! CHECK OUT THIS FIRE!
WE'RE HAVING A ROAST!
BUT FIRST, HELP YOURSELF TO SOME SPECIAL TIKI-STYLE REFRESHMENTS!
ONE TROPICAL PUNCH, PLEASE!

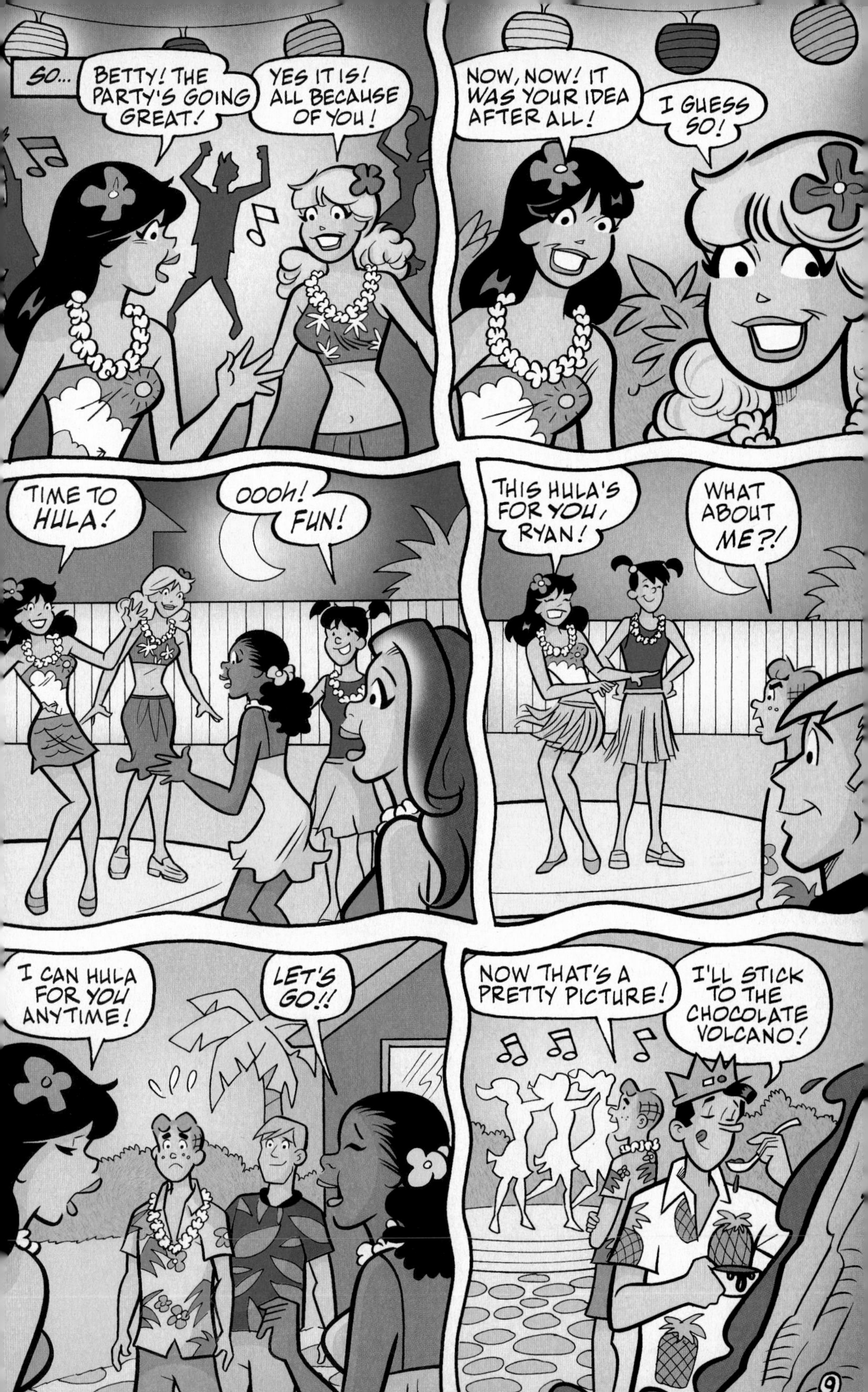
SO...
BETTY! THE PARTY'S GOING GREAT!
YES IT IS! ALL BECAUSE OF YOU!
NOW, NOW! IT WAS YOUR IDEA AFTER ALL!
I GUESS SO!
TIME TO HULA!
OOOH! FUN!
THIS HULA'S FOR YOU, RYAN!
WHAT ABOUT ME?!
I CAN HULA FOR YOU ANYTIME!
LET'S GO!!
NOW THAT'S A PRETTY PICTURE!
I'LL STICK TO THE CHOCOLATE VOLCANO!

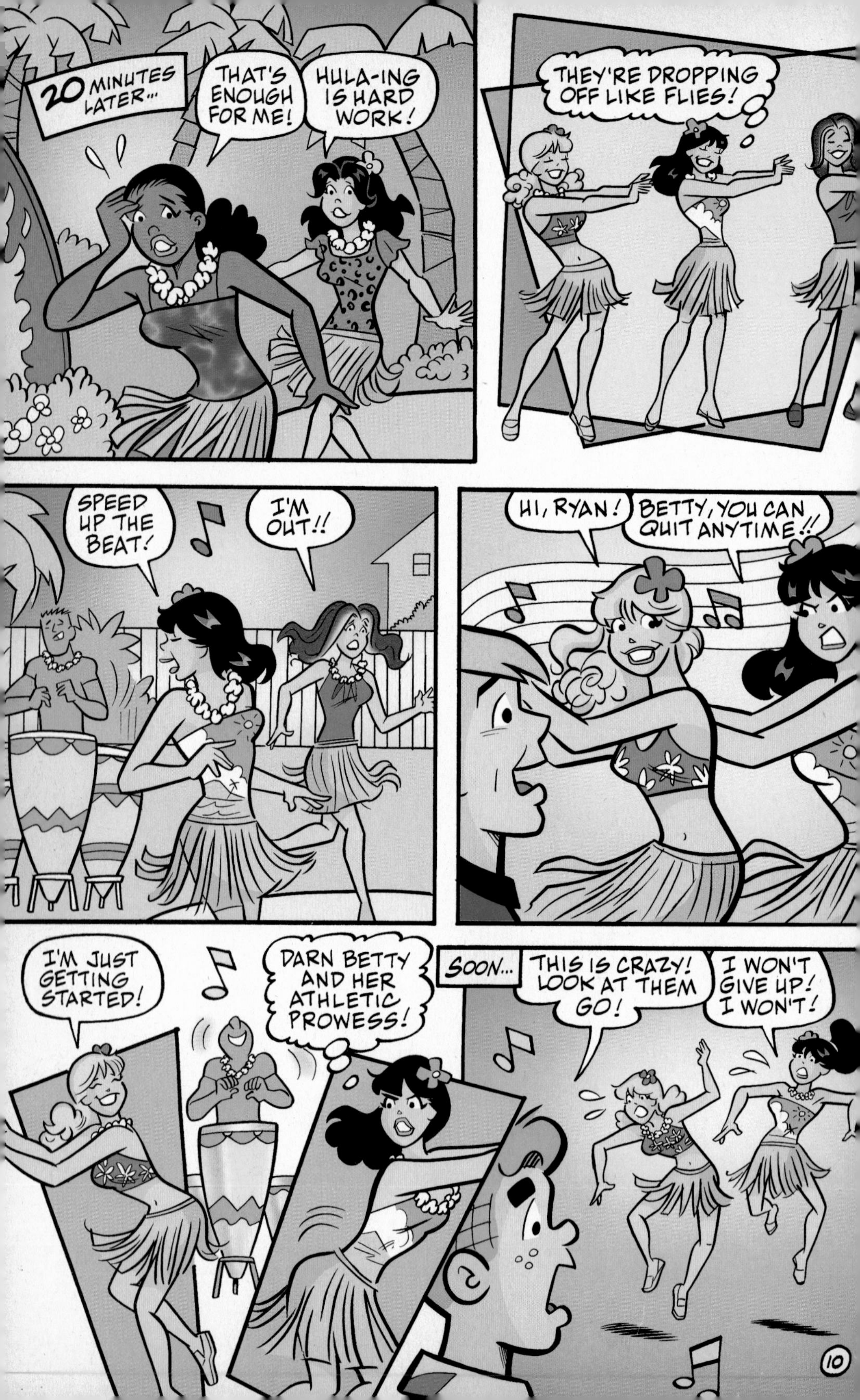

20 MINUTES LATER...
THAT'S ENOUGH FOR ME!
HULA-ING IS HARD WORK!
THEY'RE DROPPING OFF LIKE FLIES!
SPEED UP THE BEAT!
I'M OUT!!
HI, RYAN!
BETTY, YOU CAN QUIT ANYTIME!!
I'M JUST GETTING STARTED!
DARN BETTY AND HER ATHLETIC PROWESS!
SOON...
THIS IS CRAZY! LOOK AT THEM GO!
I WON'T GIVE UP! I WON'T!

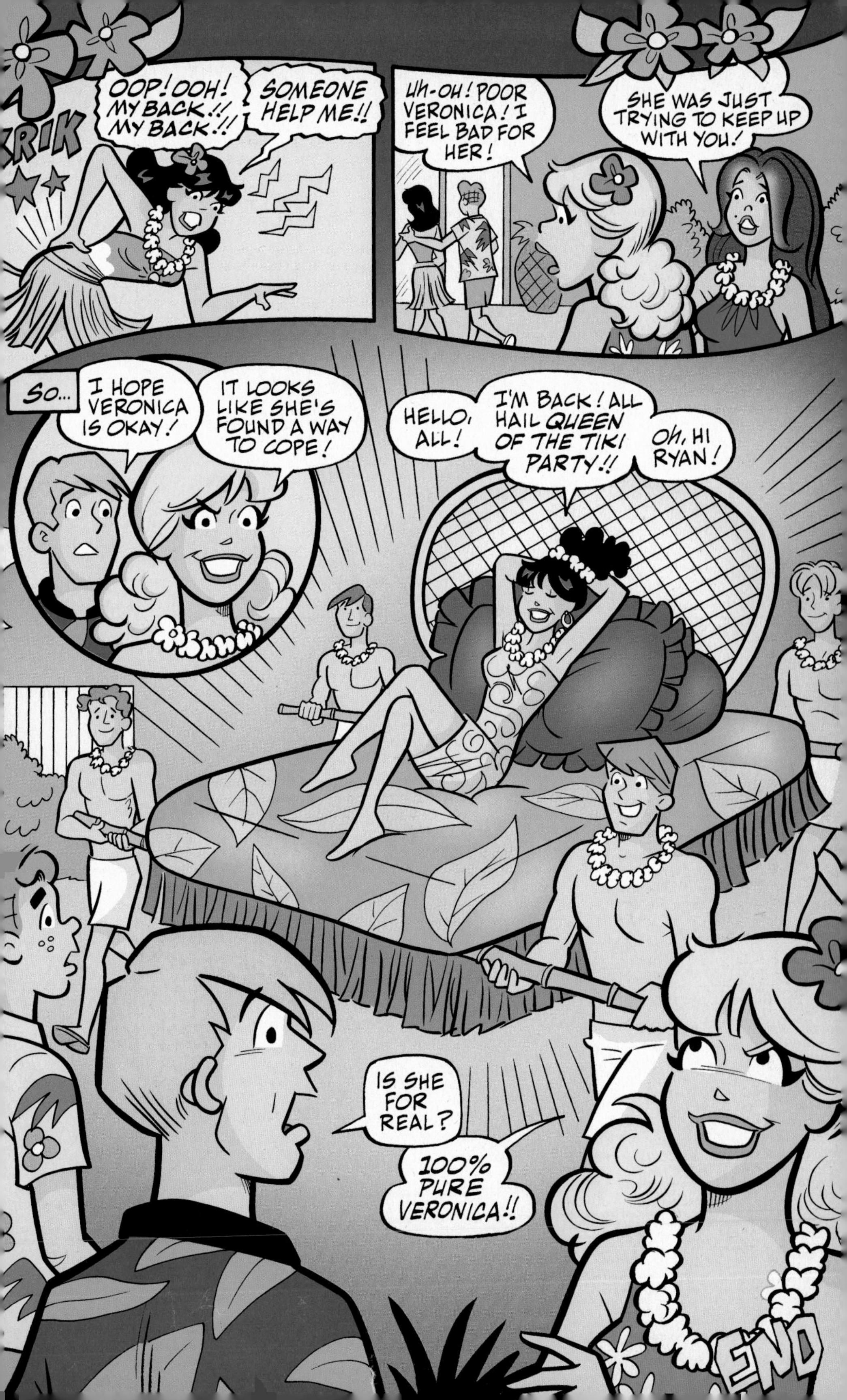

KRIK
OOP! OOH! MY BACK!! MY BACK!!
SOMEONE HELP ME!!
UH-OH! POOR VERONICA! I FEEL BAD FOR HER!
SHE WAS JUST TRYING TO KEEP UP WITH YOU!
SO...
I HOPE VERONICA IS OKAY!
IT LOOKS LIKE SHE'S FOUND A WAY TO COPE!
HELLO, ALL!
I'M BACK! ALL HAIL QUEEN OF THE TIKI PARTY!!
OH, HI RYAN!
IS SHE FOR REAL?
100% PURE VERONICA!!
END

Betty & Veronica present

HOW TO THROW A GREAT Tiki Party!

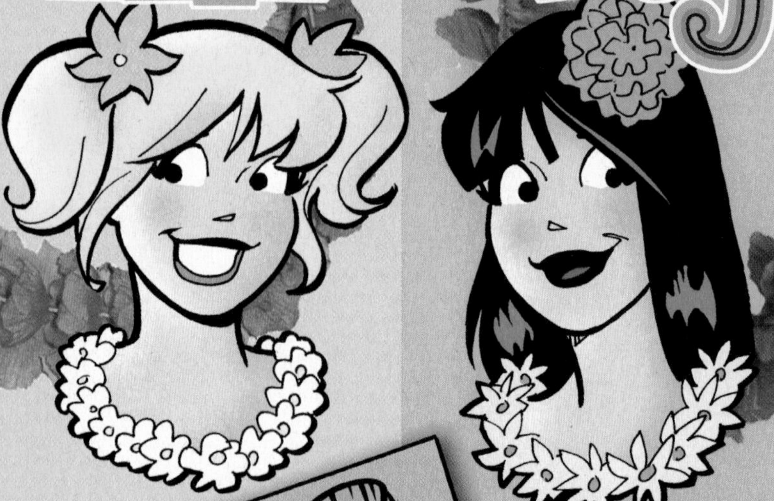

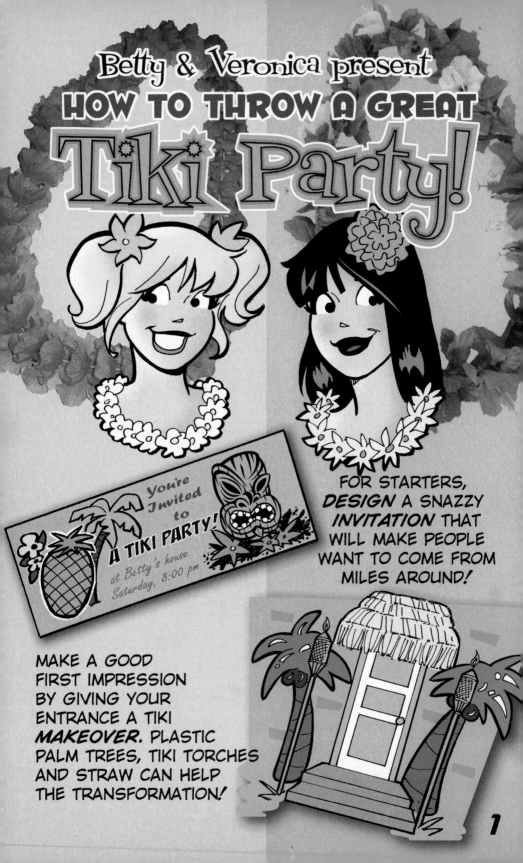

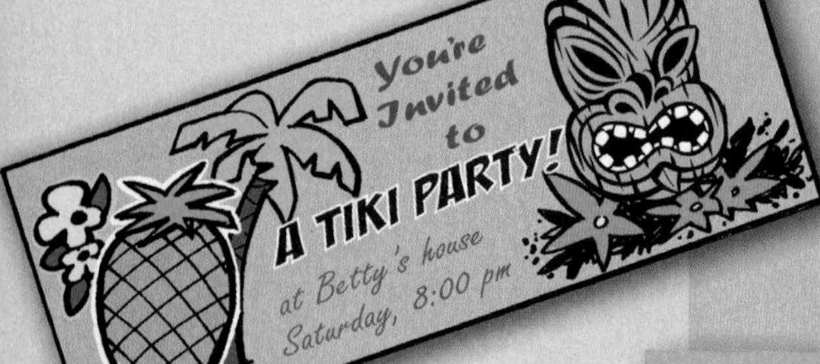
You're Invited to
A TIKI PARTY!
at Betty's house
Saturday, 8:00 pm

FOR STARTERS, ***DESIGN*** A SNAZZY ***INVITATION*** THAT WILL MAKE PEOPLE WANT TO COME FROM MILES AROUND!

MAKE A GOOD FIRST IMPRESSION BY GIVING YOUR ENTRANCE A TIKI ***MAKEOVER.*** PLASTIC PALM TREES, TIKI TORCHES AND STRAW CAN HELP THE TRANSFORMATION!

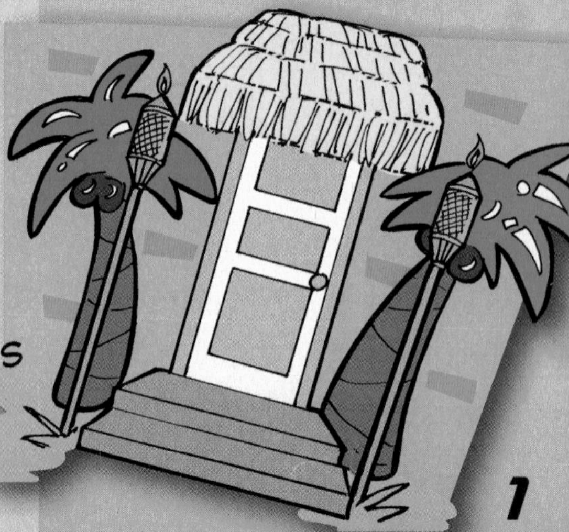

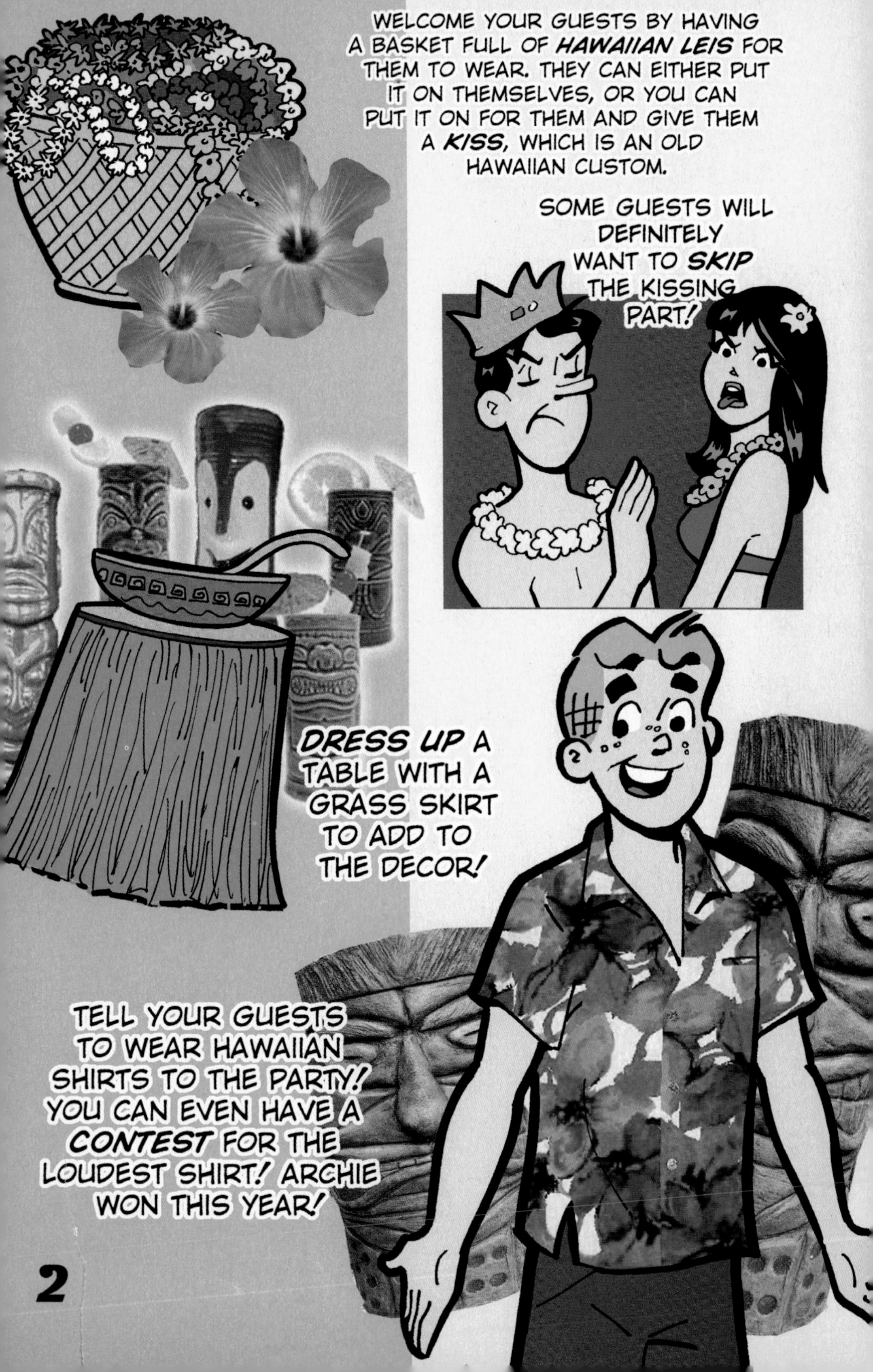
WELCOME YOUR GUESTS BY HAVING A BASKET FULL OF HAWAIIAN LEIS FOR THEM TO WEAR. THEY CAN EITHER PUT IT ON THEMSELVES, OR YOU CAN PUT IT ON FOR THEM AND GIVE THEM A KISS, WHICH IS AN OLD HAWAIIAN CUSTOM.
SOME GUESTS WILL DEFINITELY WANT TO SKIP THE KISSING PART!
DRESS UP A TABLE WITH A GRASS SKIRT TO ADD TO THE DECOR!
TELL YOUR GUESTS TO WEAR HAWAIIAN SHIRTS TO THE PARTY! YOU CAN EVEN HAVE A CONTEST FOR THE LOUDEST SHIRT! ARCHIE WON THIS YEAR!

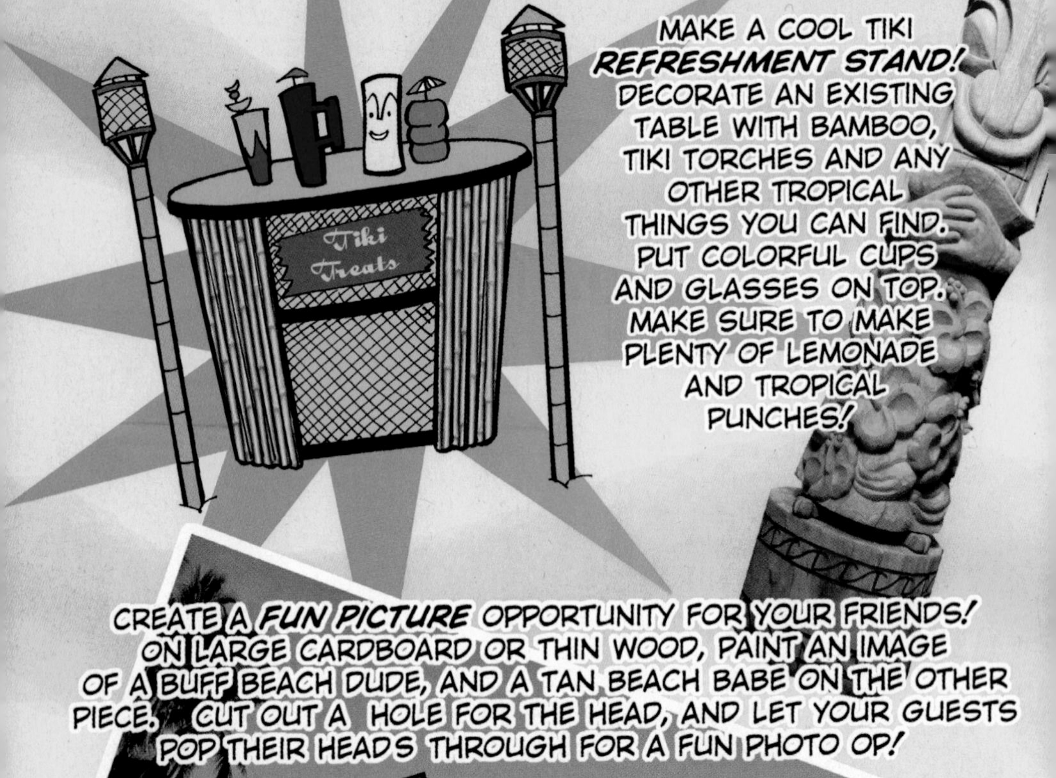
Tiki Treats

MAKE A COOL TIKI ***REFRESHMENT STAND!*** DECORATE AN EXISTING TABLE WITH BAMBOO, TIKI TORCHES AND ANY OTHER TROPICAL THINGS YOU CAN FIND. PUT COLORFUL CUPS AND GLASSES ON TOP. MAKE SURE TO MAKE PLENTY OF LEMONADE AND TROPICAL PUNCHES!

CREATE A ***FUN PICTURE*** OPPORTUNITY FOR YOUR FRIENDS! ON LARGE CARDBOARD OR THIN WOOD, PAINT AN IMAGE OF A BUFF BEACH DUDE, AND A TAN BEACH BABE ON THE OTHER PIECE. CUT OUT A HOLE FOR THE HEAD, AND LET YOUR GUESTS POP THEIR HEADS THROUGH FOR A FUN PHOTO OP!

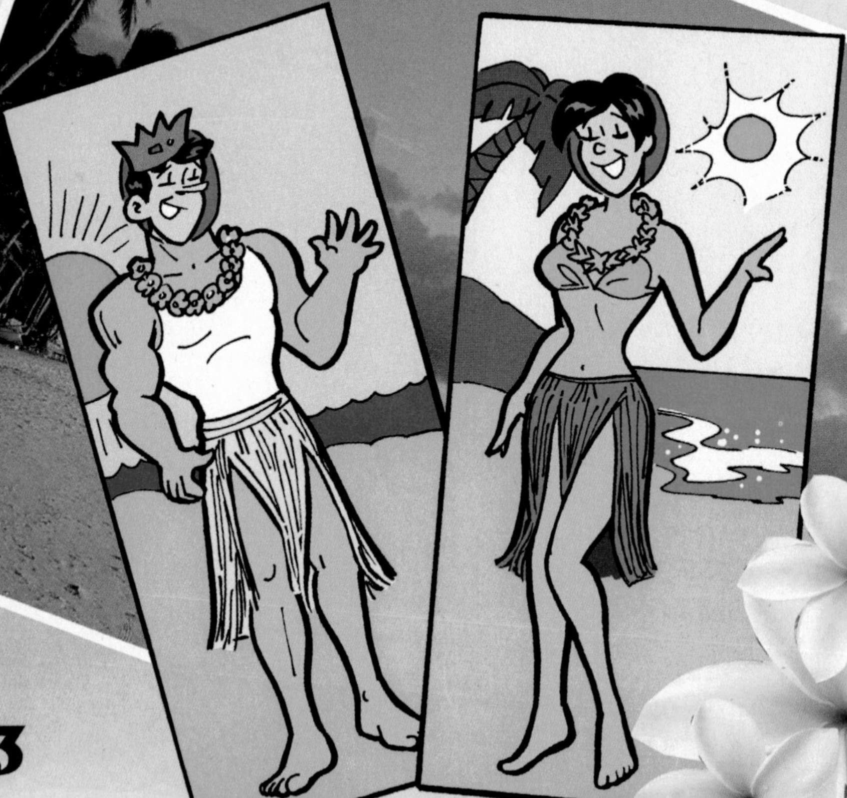

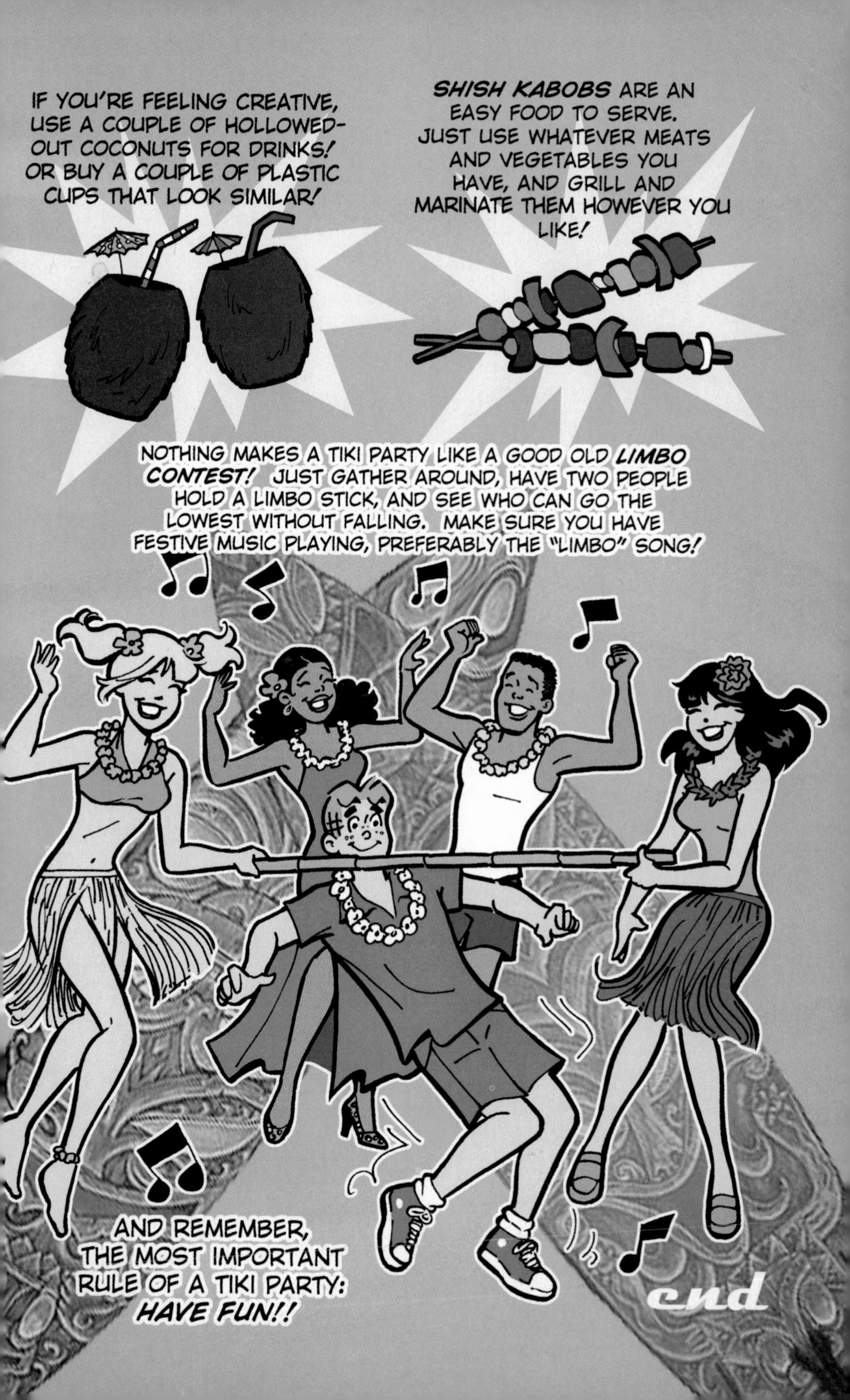
IF YOU'RE FEELING CREATIVE, USE A COUPLE OF HOLLOWED-OUT COCONUTS FOR DRINKS! OR BUY A COUPLE OF PLASTIC CUPS THAT LOOK SIMILAR!
SHISH KABOBS ARE AN EASY FOOD TO SERVE. JUST USE WHATEVER MEATS AND VEGETABLES YOU HAVE, AND GRILL AND MARINATE THEM HOWEVER YOU LIKE!
NOTHING MAKES A TIKI PARTY LIKE A GOOD OLD LIMBO CONTEST! JUST GATHER AROUND, HAVE TWO PEOPLE HOLD A LIMBO STICK, AND SEE WHO CAN GO THE LOWEST WITHOUT FALLING. MAKE SURE YOU HAVE FESTIVE MUSIC PLAYING, PREFERABLY THE "LIMBO" SONG!
AND REMEMBER, THE MOST IMPORTANT RULE OF A TIKI PARTY: HAVE FUN!!
end

Betty and Veronica® in IN A BLUE VEIN

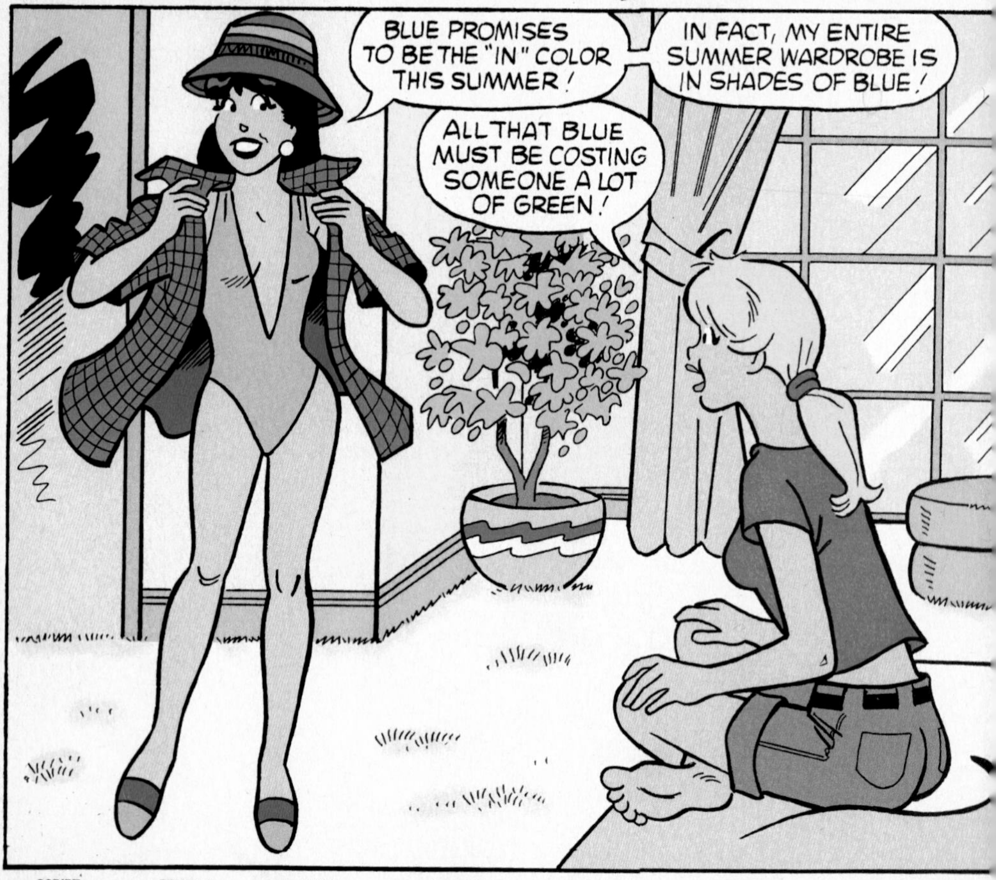
BLUE PROMISES TO BE THE "IN" COLOR THIS SUMMER!
IN FACT, MY ENTIRE SUMMER WARDROBE IS IN SHADES OF BLUE!
ALL THAT BLUE MUST BE COSTING SOMEONE A LOT OF GREEN!

SCRIPT: GEORGE GLADIR PENCILS: JEFF SHULTZ INKING: HENRY SCARPELLI LETTERING: BILL YOSHIDA COLORING: BARRY GROSSMAN EDITOR: VICTOR GORELICK EDITOR-IN-CHIEF: RICHARD GOLDWATER

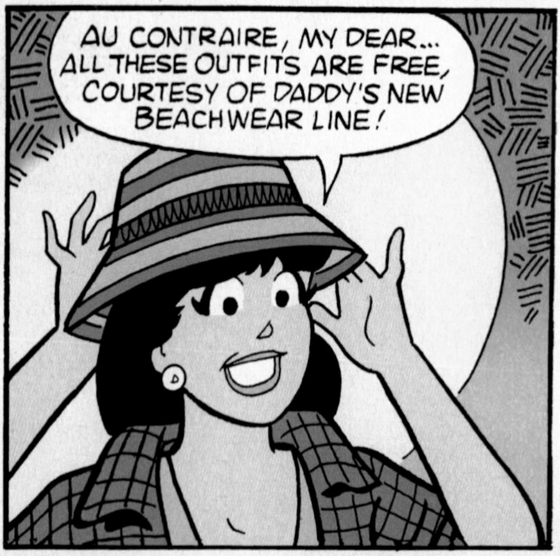
AU CONTRAIRE, MY DEAR... ALL THESE OUTFITS ARE FREE, COURTESY OF DADDY'S NEW BEACHWEAR LINE!

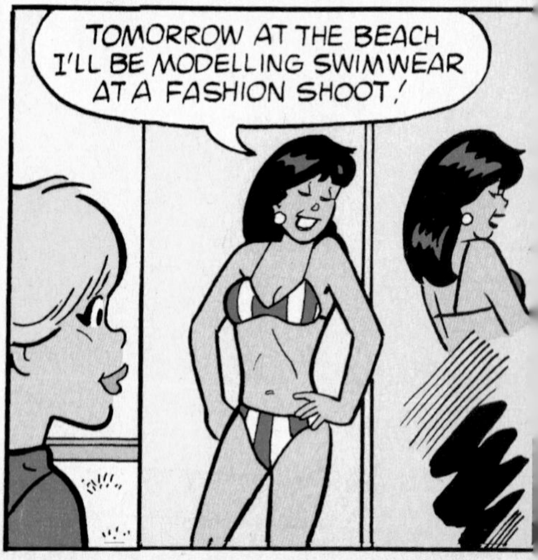
TOMORROW AT THE BEACH I'LL BE MODELLING SWIMWEAR AT A FASHION SHOOT!

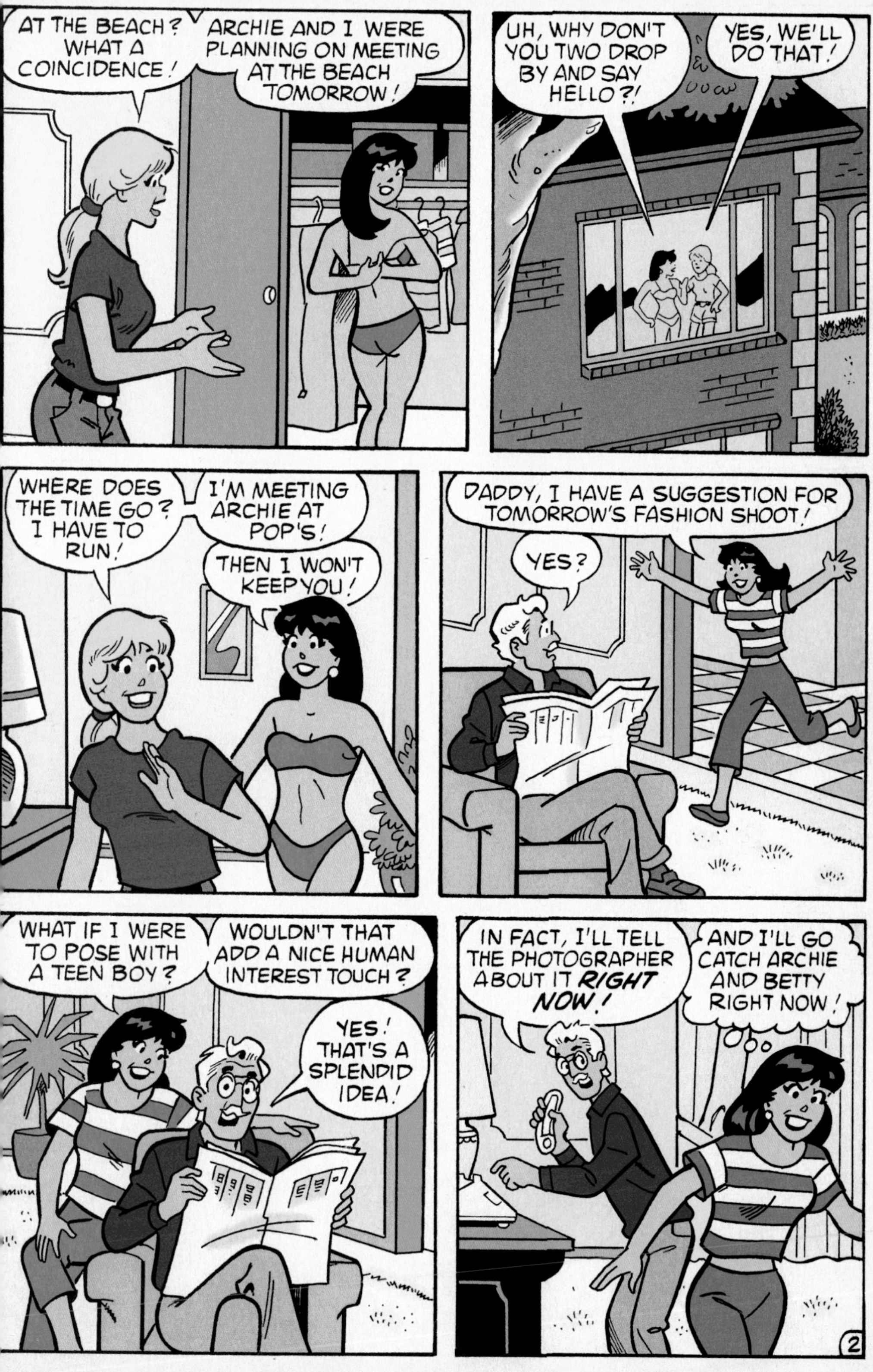
AT THE BEACH? WHAT A COINCIDENCE!
ARCHIE AND I WERE PLANNING ON MEETING AT THE BEACH TOMORROW!
UH, WHY DON'T YOU TWO DROP BY AND SAY HELLO?!
YES, WE'LL DO THAT!
WHERE DOES THE TIME GO? I HAVE TO RUN!
I'M MEETING ARCHIE AT POP'S!
THEN I WON'T KEEP YOU!
DADDY, I HAVE A SUGGESTION FOR TOMORROW'S FASHION SHOOT!
YES?
WHAT IF I WERE TO POSE WITH A TEEN BOY?
WOULDN'T THAT ADD A NICE HUMAN INTEREST TOUCH?
YES! THAT'S A SPLENDID IDEA!
IN FACT, I'LL TELL THE PHOTOGRAPHER ABOUT IT **RIGHT NOW**!
AND I'LL GO CATCH ARCHIE AND BETTY RIGHT NOW!
2

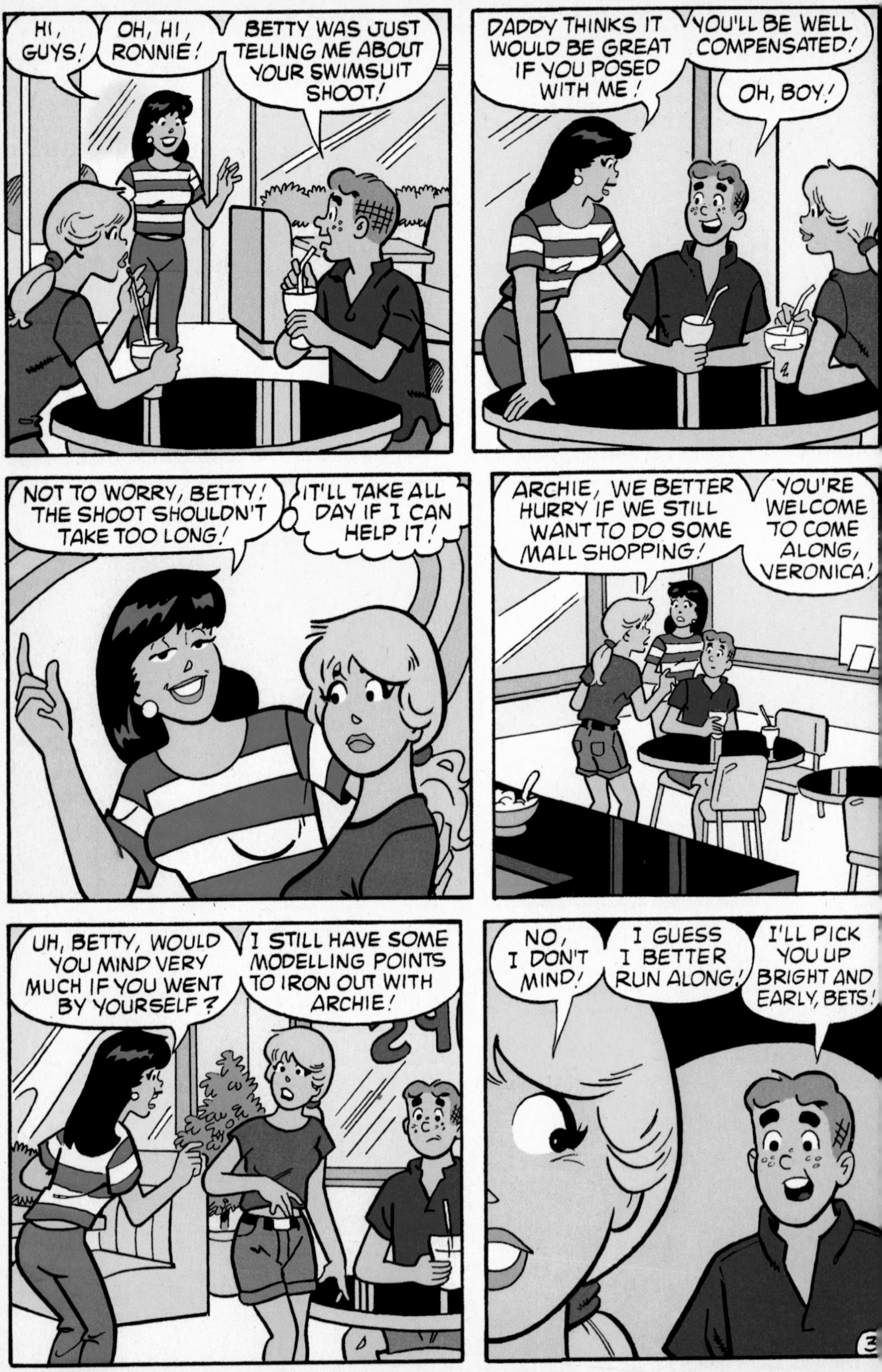
HI, GUYS!
OH, HI, RONNIE!
BETTY WAS JUST TELLING ME ABOUT YOUR SWIMSUIT SHOOT!
DADDY THINKS IT WOULD BE GREAT IF YOU POSED WITH ME!
YOU'LL BE WELL COMPENSATED!
OH, BOY!
NOT TO WORRY, BETTY! THE SHOOT SHOULDN'T TAKE TOO LONG!
IT'LL TAKE ALL DAY IF I CAN HELP IT!
ARCHIE, WE BETTER HURRY IF WE STILL WANT TO DO SOME MALL SHOPPING!
YOU'RE WELCOME TO COME ALONG, VERONICA!
UH, BETTY, WOULD YOU MIND VERY MUCH IF YOU WENT BY YOURSELF?
I STILL HAVE SOME MODELLING POINTS TO IRON OUT WITH ARCHIE!
NO, I DON'T MIND!
I GUESS I BETTER RUN ALONG!
I'LL PICK YOU UP BRIGHT AND EARLY, BETS!
3

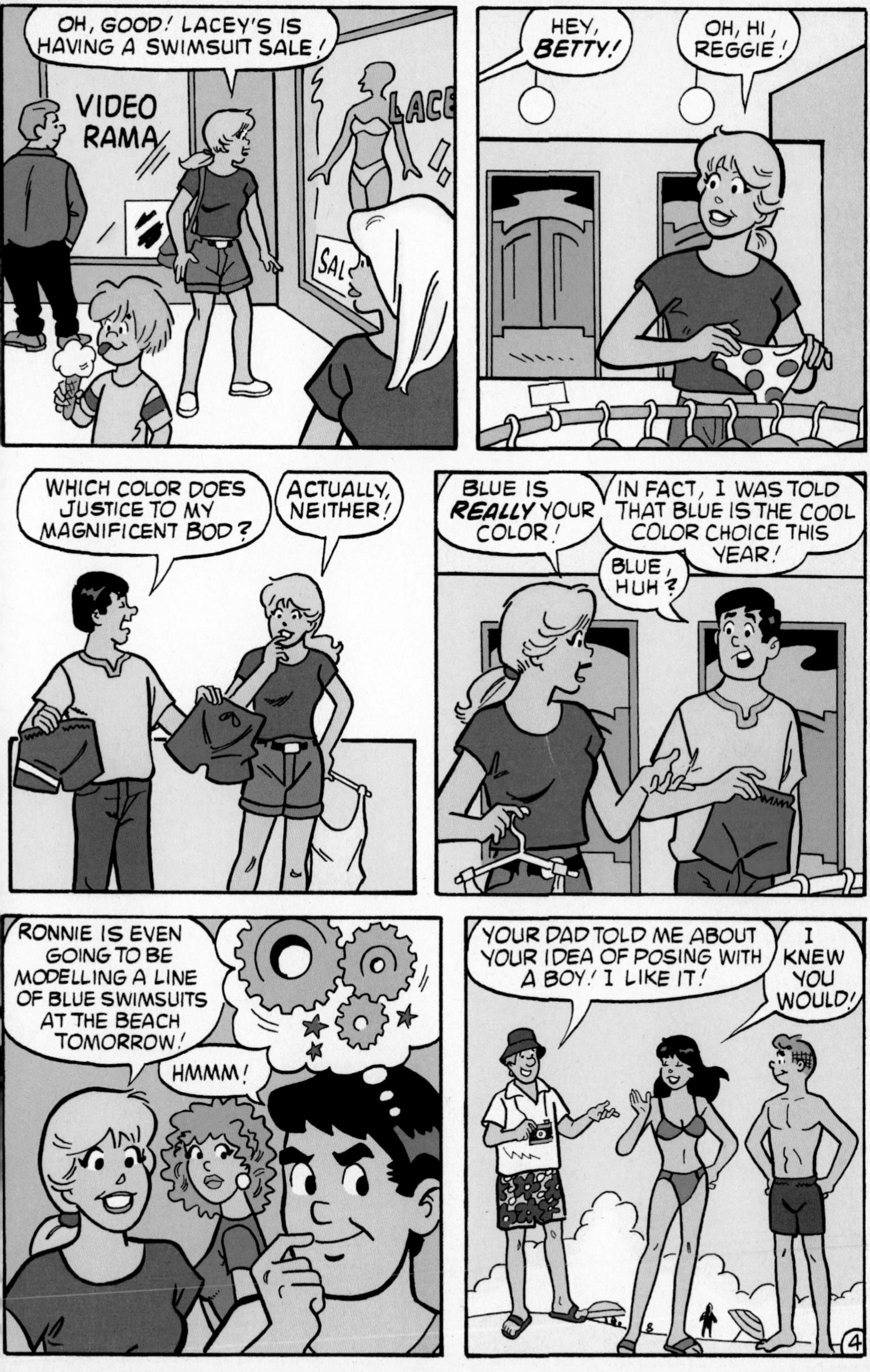
OH, GOOD! LACEY'S IS HAVING A SWIMSUIT SALE!
VIDEO RAMA
HEY, BETTY!
OH, HI, REGGIE!
WHICH COLOR DOES JUSTICE TO MY MAGNIFICENT BOD?
ACTUALLY, NEITHER!
BLUE IS REALLY YOUR COLOR!
IN FACT, I WAS TOLD THAT BLUE IS THE COOL COLOR CHOICE THIS YEAR!
BLUE, HUH?
RONNIE IS EVEN GOING TO BE MODELLING A LINE OF BLUE SWIMSUITS AT THE BEACH TOMORROW!
HMMM!
YOUR DAD TOLD ME ABOUT YOUR IDEA OF POSING WITH A BOY! I LIKE IT!
I KNEW YOU WOULD!
4

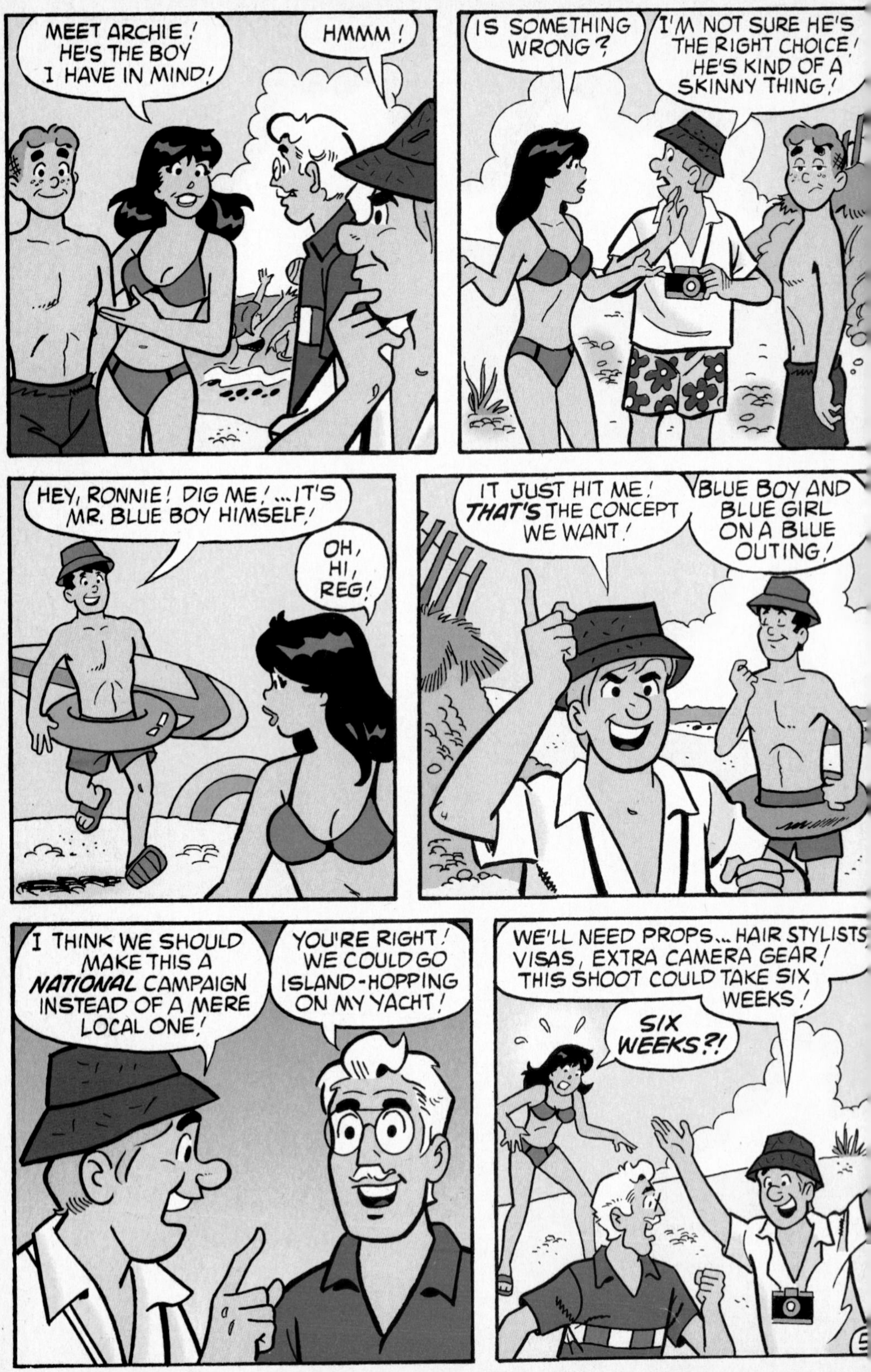
MEET ARCHIE! HE'S THE BOY I HAVE IN MIND!
HMMM!
IS SOMETHING WRONG?
I'M NOT SURE HE'S THE RIGHT CHOICE! HE'S KIND OF A SKINNY THING!
HEY, RONNIE! DIG ME! ...IT'S MR. BLUE BOY HIMSELF!
OH, HI, REG!
IT JUST HIT ME! THAT'S THE CONCEPT WE WANT!
BLUE BOY AND BLUE GIRL ON A BLUE OUTING!
I THINK WE SHOULD MAKE THIS A NATIONAL CAMPAIGN INSTEAD OF A MERE LOCAL ONE!
YOU'RE RIGHT! WE COULD GO ISLAND-HOPPING ON MY YACHT!
WE'LL NEED PROPS... HAIR STYLISTS, VISAS, EXTRA CAMERA GEAR! THIS SHOOT COULD TAKE SIX WEEKS!
SIX WEEKS?!
5

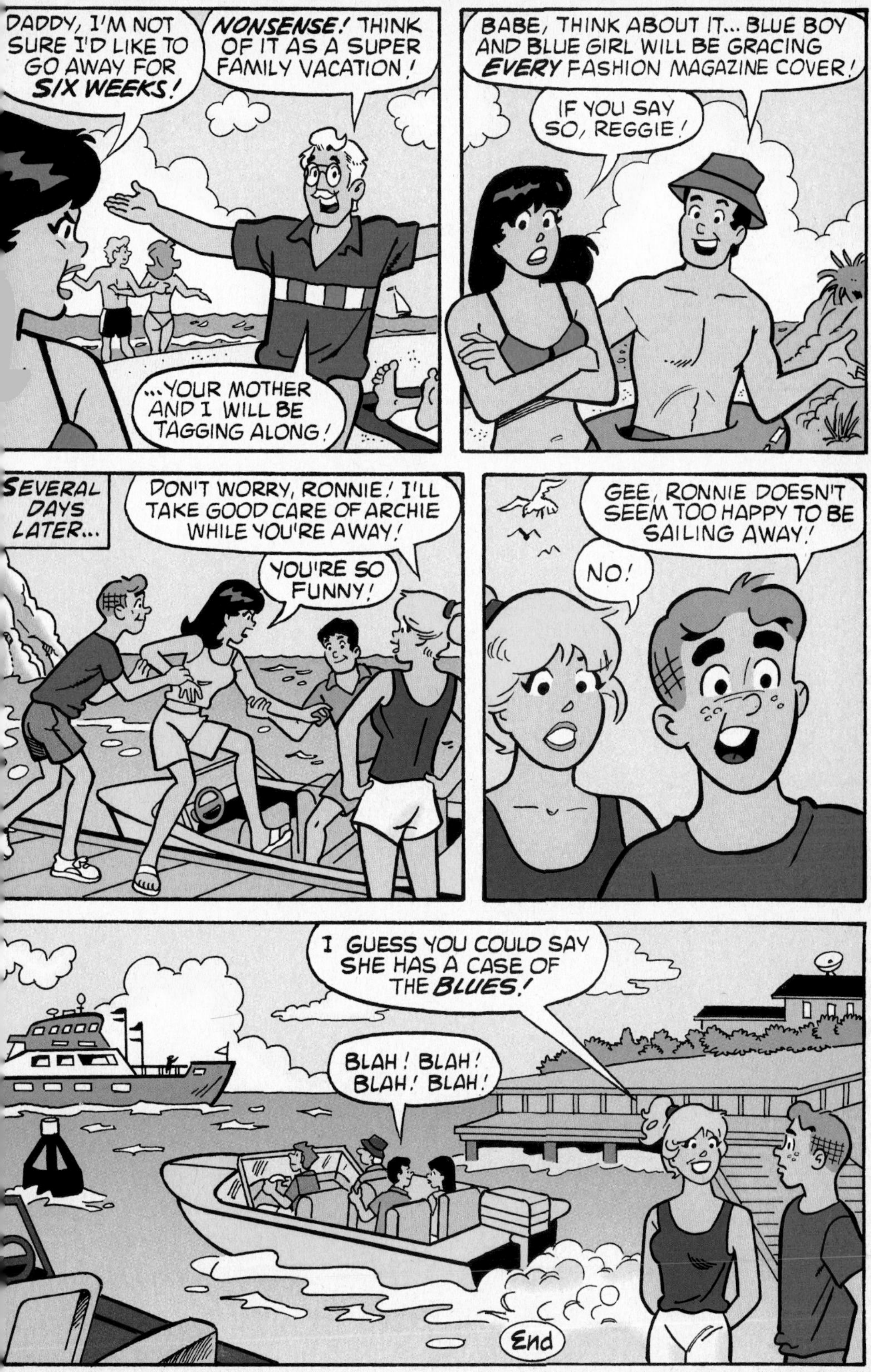
DADDY, I'M NOT SURE I'D LIKE TO GO AWAY FOR SIX WEEKS!
NONSENSE! THINK OF IT AS A SUPER FAMILY VACATION!
...YOUR MOTHER AND I WILL BE TAGGING ALONG!
BABE, THINK ABOUT IT... BLUE BOY AND BLUE GIRL WILL BE GRACING EVERY FASHION MAGAZINE COVER!
IF YOU SAY SO, REGGIE!
SEVERAL DAYS LATER...
DON'T WORRY, RONNIE! I'LL TAKE GOOD CARE OF ARCHIE WHILE YOU'RE AWAY!
YOU'RE SO FUNNY!
GEE, RONNIE DOESN'T SEEM TOO HAPPY TO BE SAILING AWAY!
NO!
I GUESS YOU COULD SAY SHE HAS A CASE OF THE BLUES!
BLAH! BLAH! BLAH! BLAH!
End

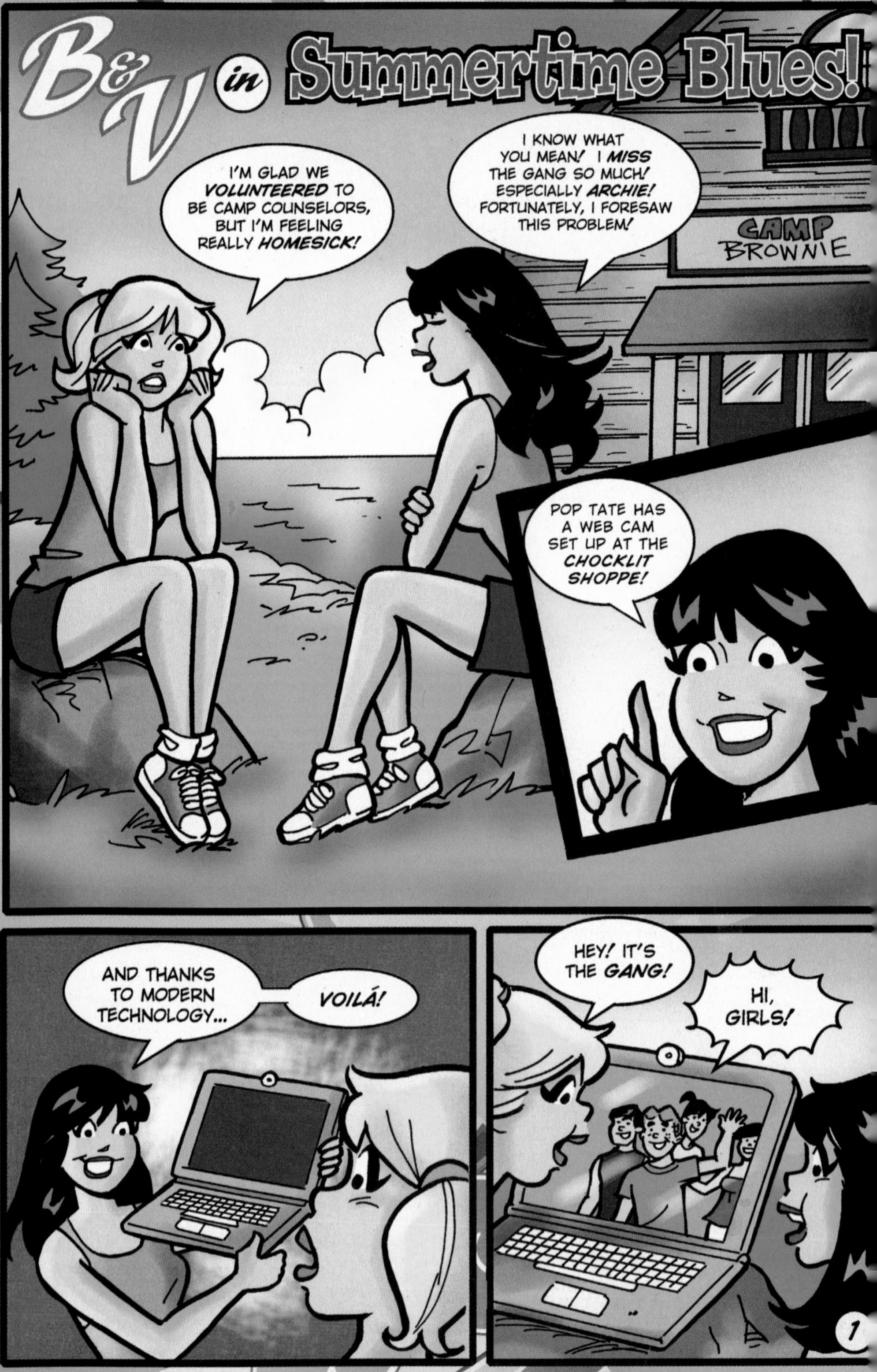
B&V in Summertime Blues!
I'M GLAD WE VOLUNTEERED TO BE CAMP COUNSELORS, BUT I'M FEELING REALLY HOMESICK!
I KNOW WHAT YOU MEAN! I MISS THE GANG SO MUCH! ESPECIALLY ARCHIE! FORTUNATELY, I FORESAW THIS PROBLEM!
CAMP BROWNIE
POP TATE HAS A WEB CAM SET UP AT THE CHOCKLIT SHOPPE!
AND THANKS TO MODERN TECHNOLOGY...
VOILÁ!
HEY! IT'S THE GANG!
HI, GIRLS!

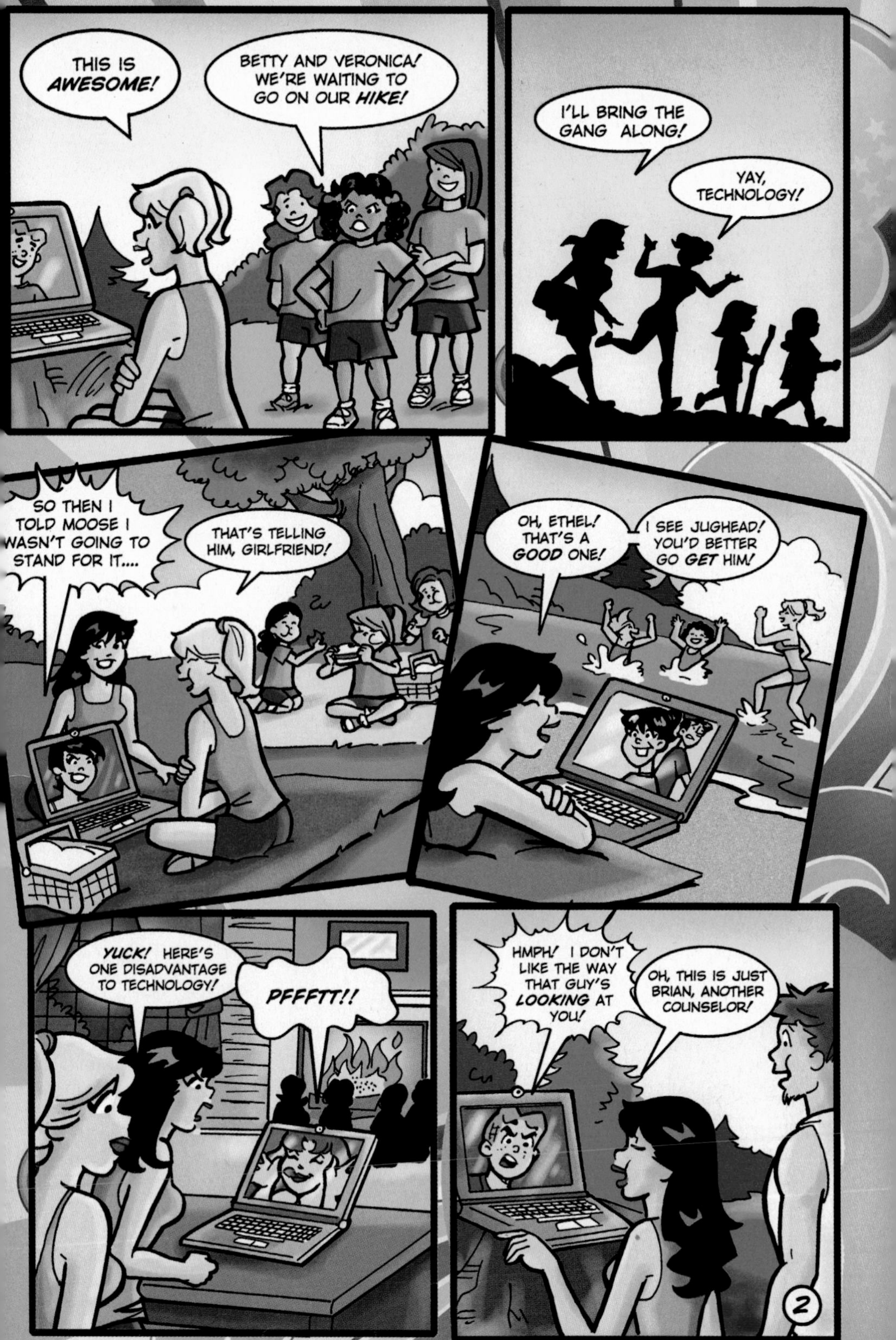
THIS IS AWESOME!
BETTY AND VERONICA! WE'RE WAITING TO GO ON OUR HIKE!
I'LL BRING THE GANG ALONG!
YAY, TECHNOLOGY!
SO THEN I TOLD MOOSE I WASN'T GOING TO STAND FOR IT....
THAT'S TELLING HIM, GIRLFRIEND!
OH, ETHEL! THAT'S A GOOD ONE!
I SEE JUGHEAD! YOU'D BETTER GO GET HIM!
YUCK! HERE'S ONE DISADVANTAGE TO TECHNOLOGY!
PFFFTT!!
HMPH! I DON'T LIKE THE WAY THAT GUY'S LOOKING AT YOU!
OH, THIS IS JUST BRIAN, ANOTHER COUNSELOR!
2

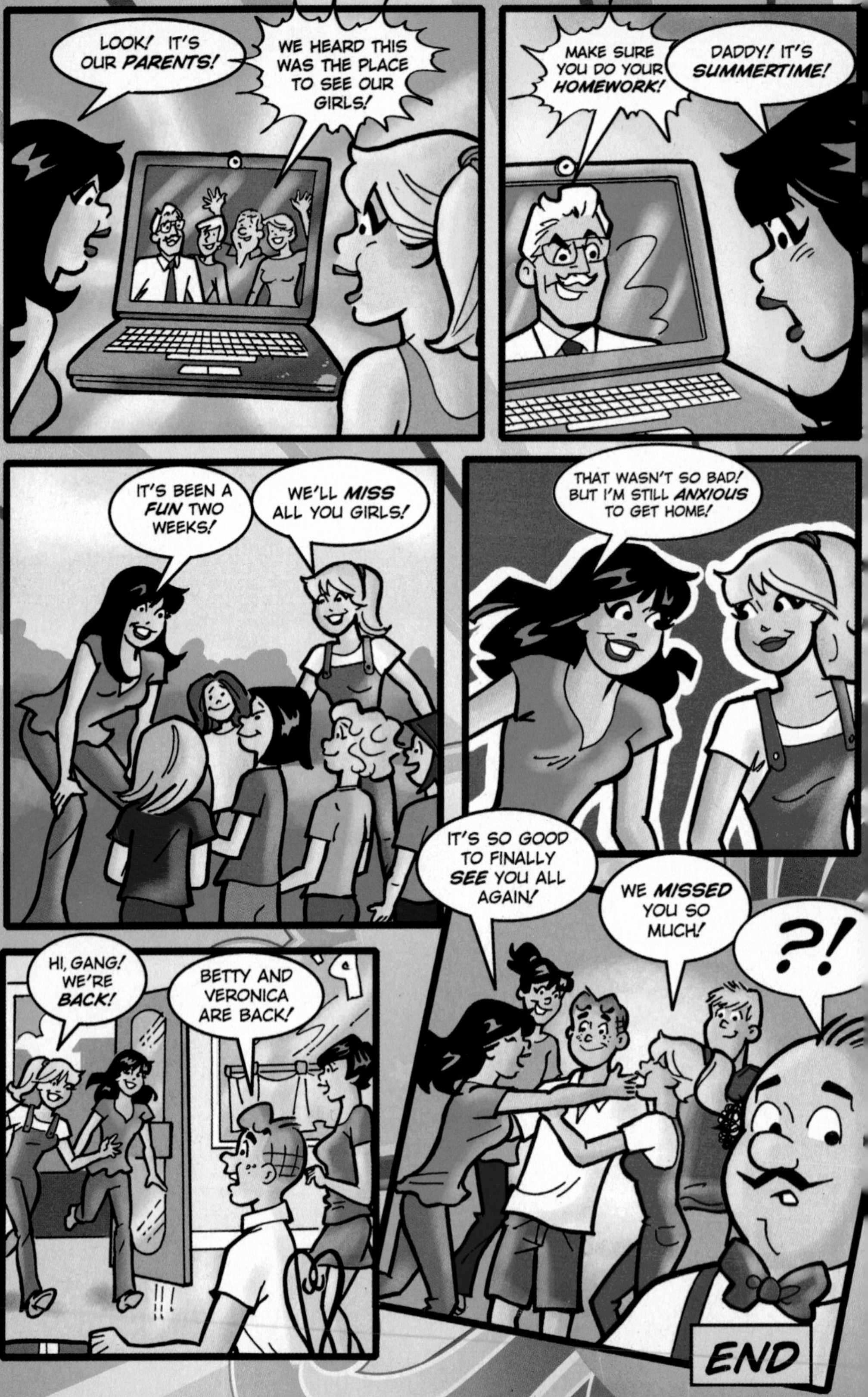
LOOK! IT'S OUR PARENTS!
WE HEARD THIS WAS THE PLACE TO SEE OUR GIRLS!
MAKE SURE YOU DO YOUR HOMEWORK!
DADDY! IT'S SUMMERTIME!
IT'S BEEN A FUN TWO WEEKS!
WE'LL MISS ALL YOU GIRLS!
THAT WASN'T SO BAD! BUT I'M STILL ANXIOUS TO GET HOME!
HI, GANG! WE'RE BACK!
BETTY AND VERONICA ARE BACK!
IT'S SO GOOD TO FINALLY SEE YOU ALL AGAIN!
WE MISSED YOU SO MUCH!
?!
END

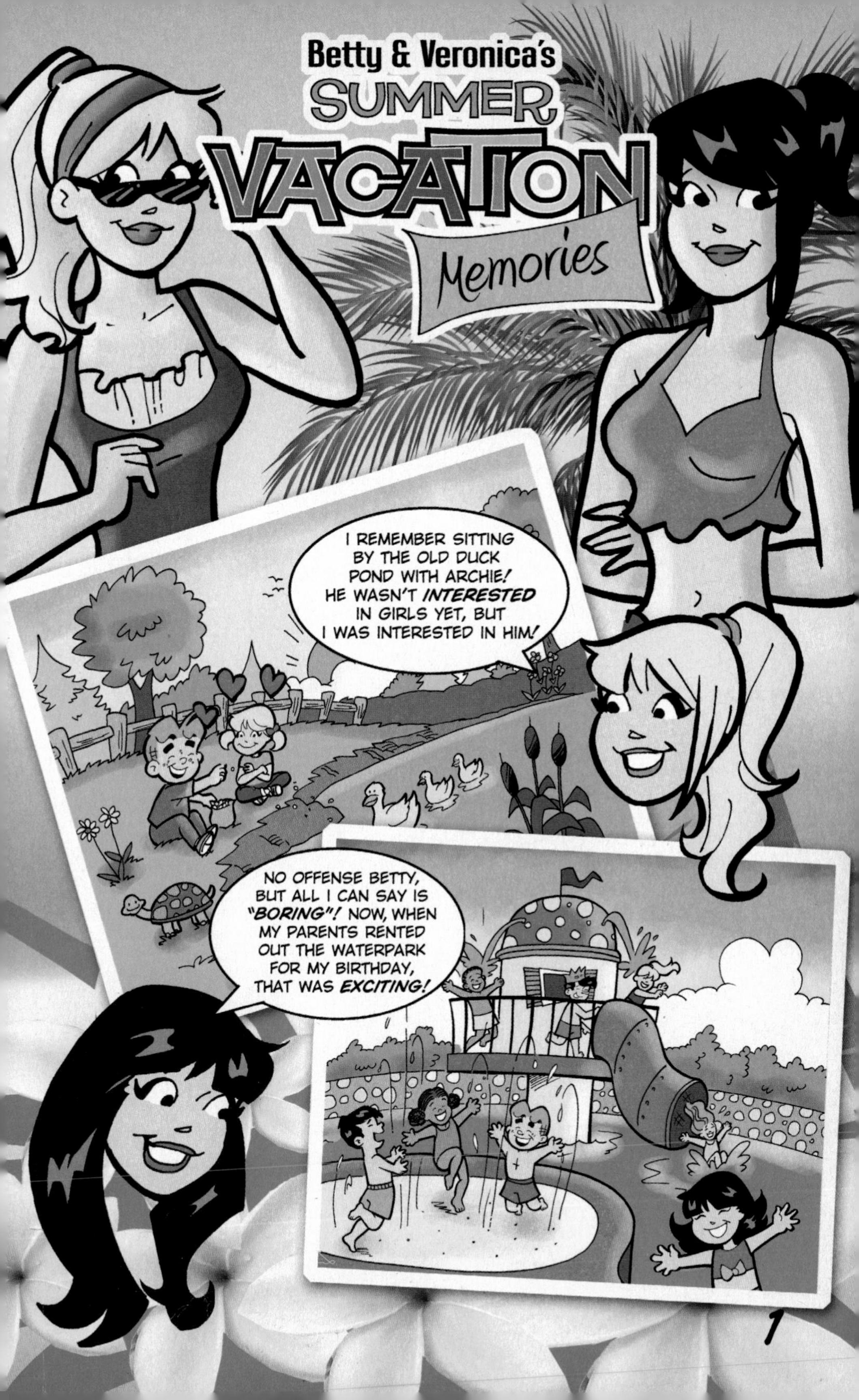
Betty & Veronica's
SUMMER VACATION
Memories
I REMEMBER SITTING BY THE OLD DUCK POND WITH ARCHIE! HE WASN'T INTERESTED IN GIRLS YET, BUT I WAS INTERESTED IN HIM!
NO OFFENSE BETTY, BUT ALL I CAN SAY IS "BORING"! NOW, WHEN MY PARENTS RENTED OUT THE WATERPARK FOR MY BIRTHDAY, THAT WAS EXCITING!

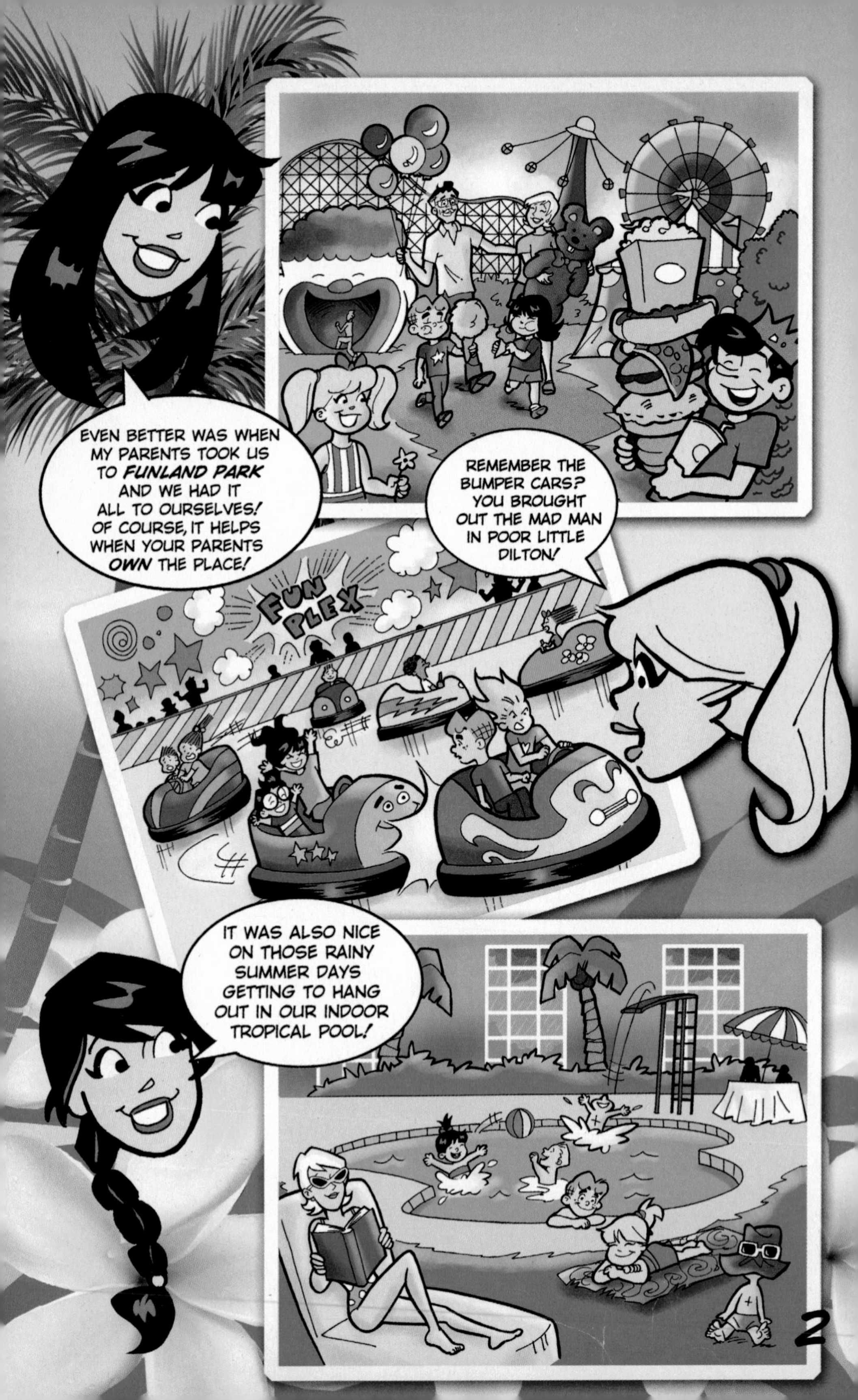

EVEN BETTER WAS WHEN MY PARENTS TOOK US TO FUNLAND PARK AND WE HAD IT ALL TO OURSELVES! OF COURSE, IT HELPS WHEN YOUR PARENTS OWN THE PLACE!
REMEMBER THE BUMPER CARS? YOU BROUGHT OUT THE MAD MAN IN POOR LITTLE DILTON!
FUN PLEX
IT WAS ALSO NICE ON THOSE RAINY SUMMER DAYS GETTING TO HANG OUT IN OUR INDOOR TROPICAL POOL!

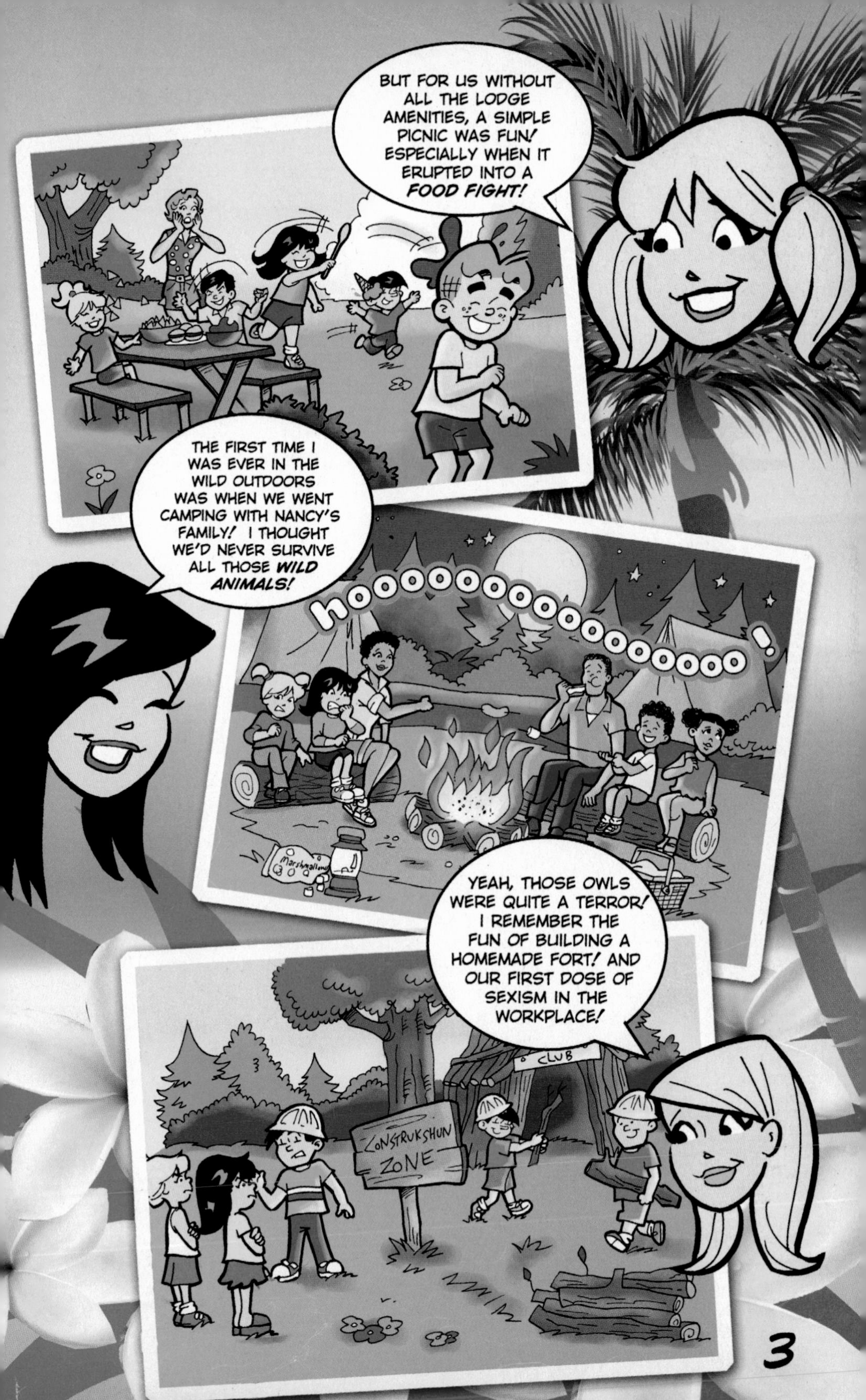
BUT FOR US WITHOUT ALL THE LODGE AMENITIES, A SIMPLE PICNIC WAS FUN! ESPECIALLY WHEN IT ERUPTED INTO A FOOD FIGHT!
THE FIRST TIME I WAS EVER IN THE WILD OUTDOORS WAS WHEN WE WENT CAMPING WITH NANCY'S FAMILY! I THOUGHT WE'D NEVER SURVIVE ALL THOSE WILD ANIMALS!
hooooooooooooooooo!
Marshmallows
YEAH, THOSE OWLS WERE QUITE A TERROR! I REMEMBER THE FUN OF BUILDING A HOMEMADE FORT! AND OUR FIRST DOSE OF SEXISM IN THE WORKPLACE!
CLUB
CONSTRUKSHUN ZONE

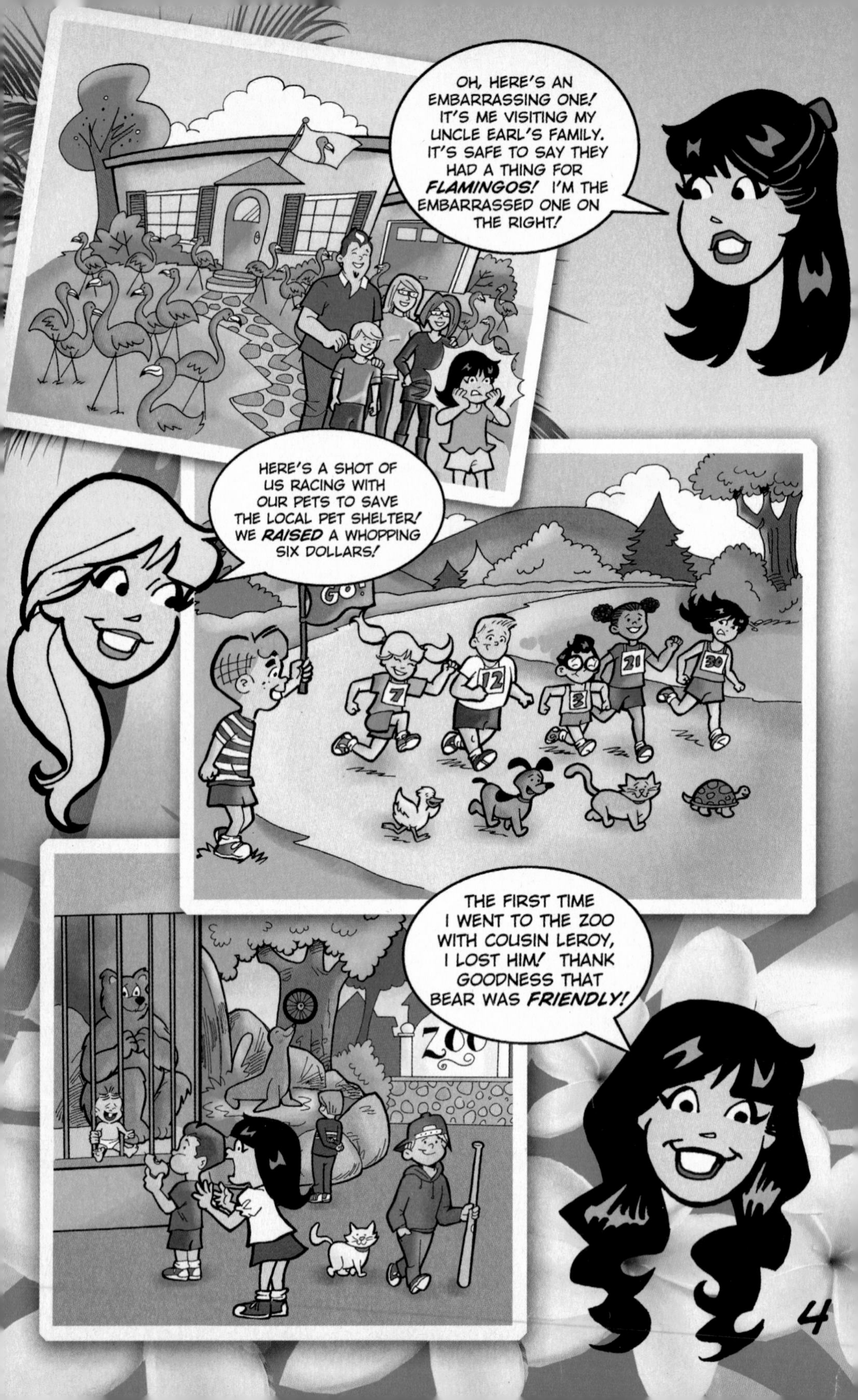
OH, HERE'S AN EMBARRASSING ONE! IT'S ME VISITING MY UNCLE EARL'S FAMILY. IT'S SAFE TO SAY THEY HAD A THING FOR *FLAMINGOS!* I'M THE EMBARRASSED ONE ON THE RIGHT!
HERE'S A SHOT OF US RACING WITH OUR PETS TO SAVE THE LOCAL PET SHELTER! WE *RAISED* A WHOPPING SIX DOLLARS!
GO!
THE FIRST TIME I WENT TO THE ZOO WITH COUSIN LEROY, I LOST HIM! THANK GOODNESS THAT BEAR WAS *FRIENDLY!*
ZOO

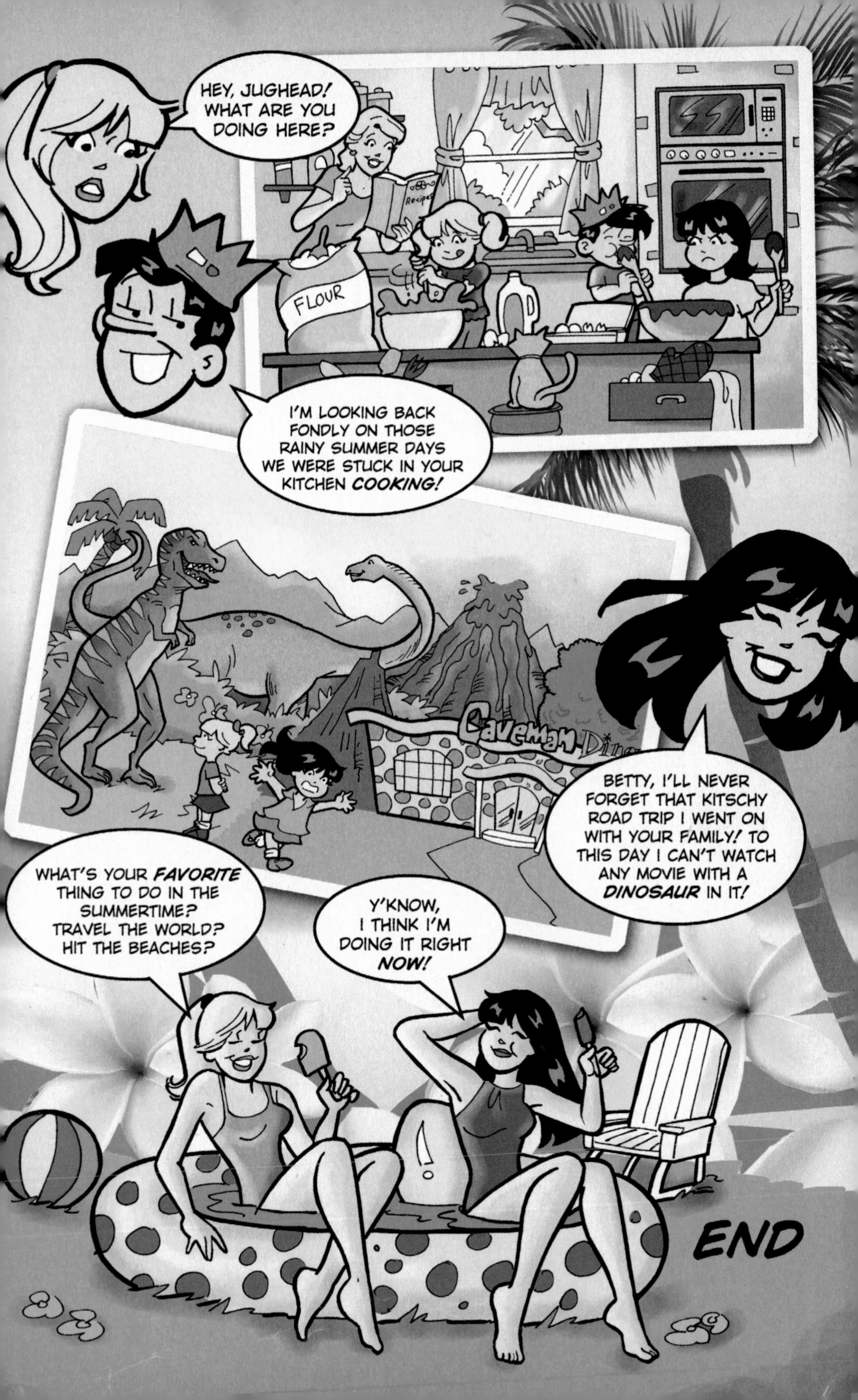
HEY, JUGHEAD! WHAT ARE YOU DOING HERE?
Recipes
FLOUR
I'M LOOKING BACK FONDLY ON THOSE RAINY SUMMER DAYS WE WERE STUCK IN YOUR KITCHEN COOKING!
Caveman Dine
BETTY, I'LL NEVER FORGET THAT KITSCHY ROAD TRIP I WENT ON WITH YOUR FAMILY! TO THIS DAY I CAN'T WATCH ANY MOVIE WITH A DINOSAUR IN IT!
WHAT'S YOUR FAVORITE THING TO DO IN THE SUMMERTIME? TRAVEL THE WORLD? HIT THE BEACHES?
Y'KNOW, I THINK I'M DOING IT RIGHT NOW!
END

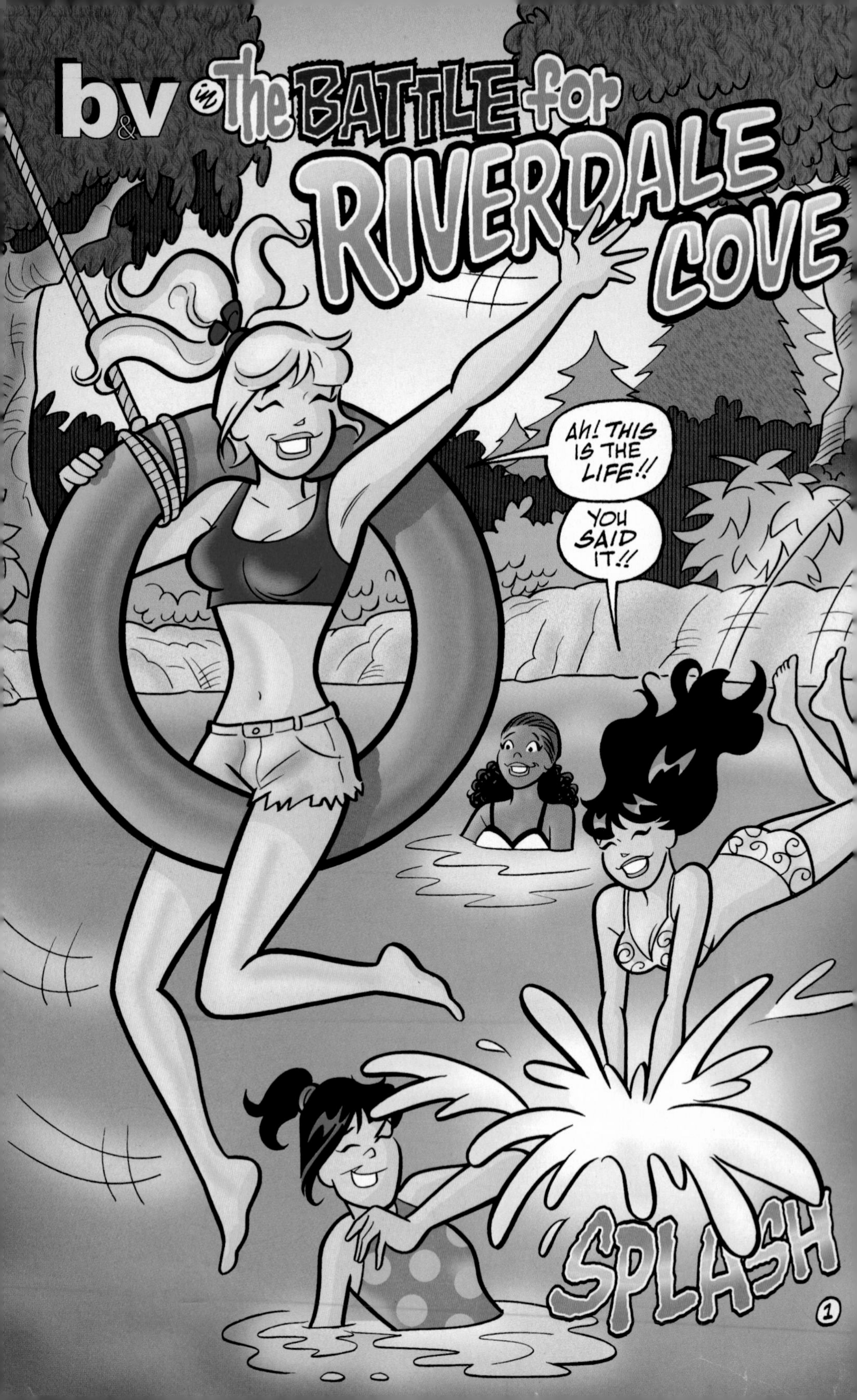
b&v in
The BATTLE for RIVERDALE COVE
Ah! THIS IS THE LIFE!!
YOU SAID IT!!
SPLASH
1

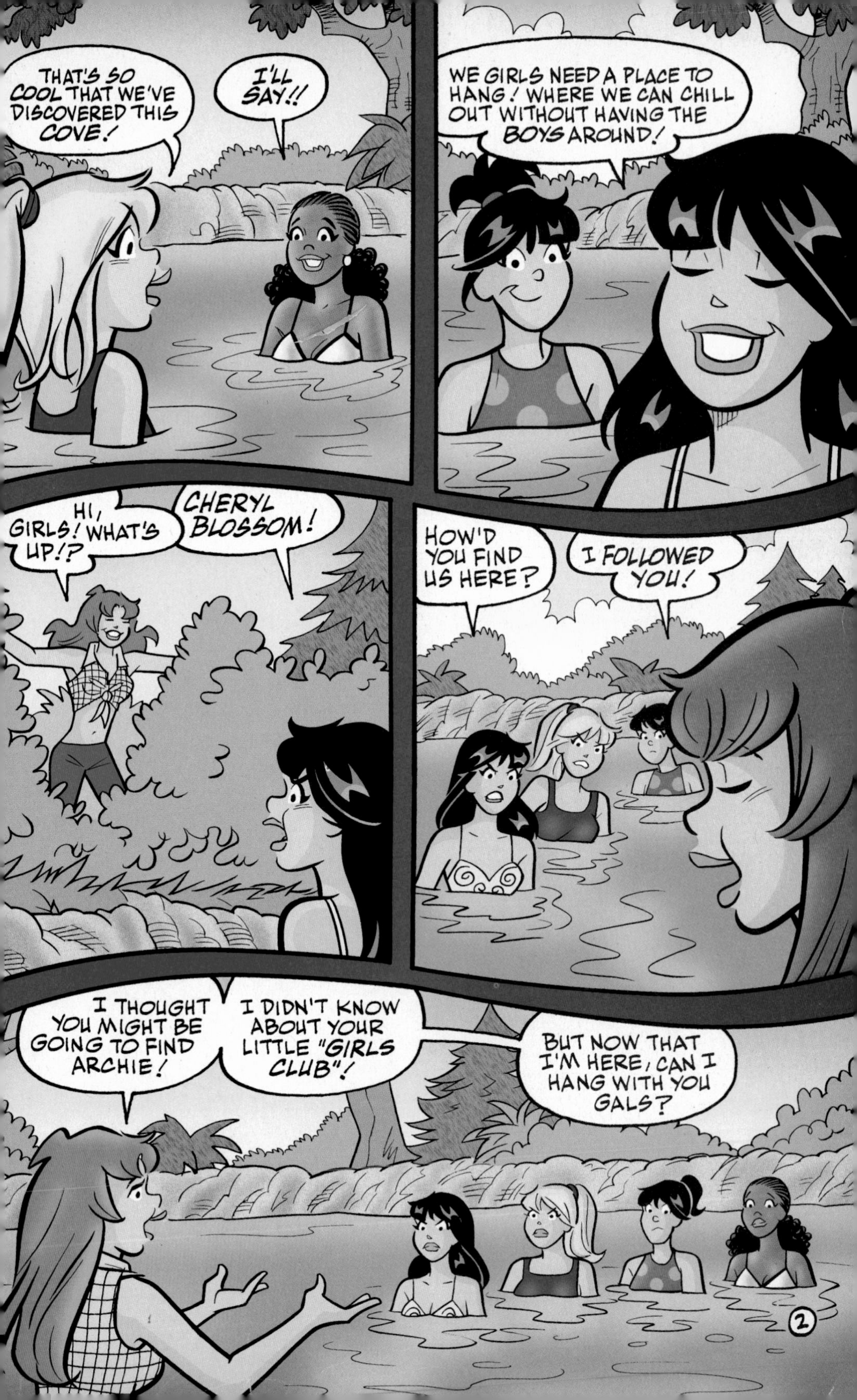
THAT'S SO COOL THAT WE'VE DISCOVERED THIS COVE!
I'LL SAY!!
WE GIRLS NEED A PLACE TO HANG! WHERE WE CAN CHILL OUT WITHOUT HAVING THE BOYS AROUND!
HI, GIRLS! WHAT'S UP!?
CHERYL BLOSSOM!
HOW'D YOU FIND US HERE?
I FOLLOWED YOU!
I THOUGHT YOU MIGHT BE GOING TO FIND ARCHIE!
I DIDN'T KNOW ABOUT YOUR LITTLE "GIRLS CLUB"!
BUT NOW THAT I'M HERE, CAN I HANG WITH YOU GALS?
2

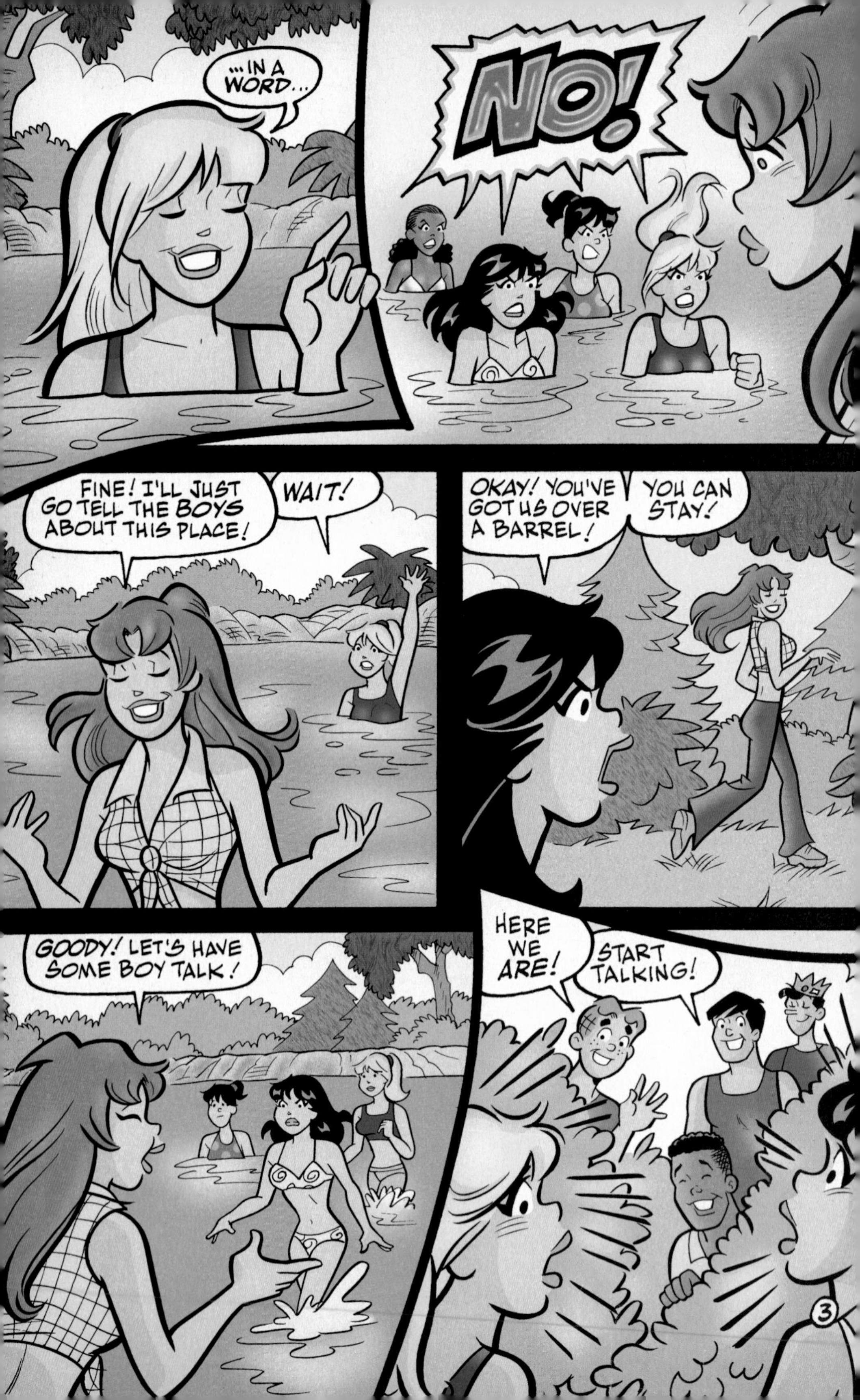
...IN A WORD...
NO!
FINE! I'LL JUST GO TELL THE BOYS ABOUT THIS PLACE!
WAIT!
OKAY! YOU'VE GOT US OVER A BARREL!
YOU CAN STAY!
GOODY! LET'S HAVE SOME BOY TALK!
HERE WE ARE!
START TALKING!
3

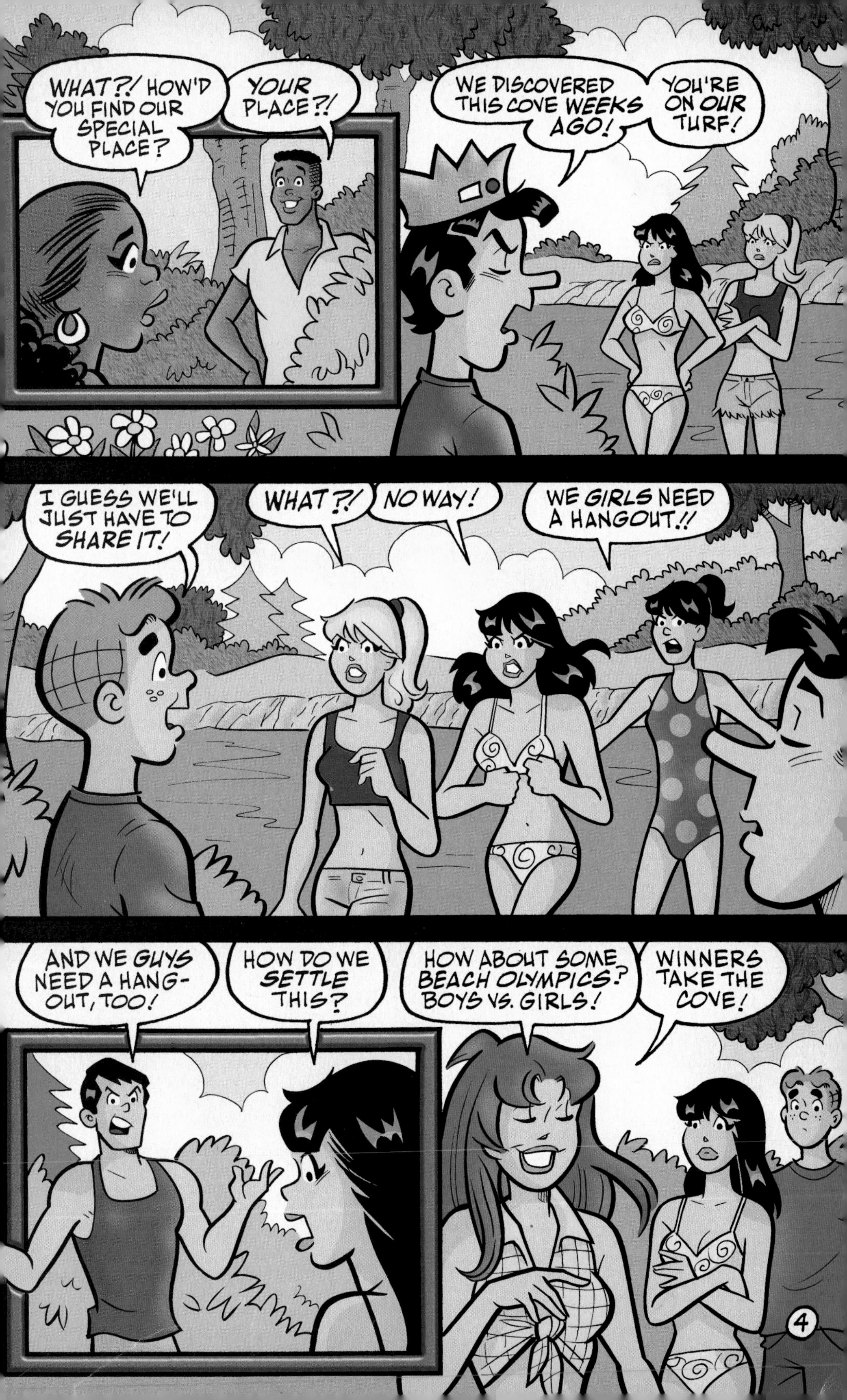
WHAT?! HOW'D YOU FIND OUR SPECIAL PLACE?
YOUR PLACE?!
WE DISCOVERED THIS COVE WEEKS AGO!
YOU'RE ON OUR TURF!
I GUESS WE'LL JUST HAVE TO SHARE IT!
WHAT?!
NO WAY!
WE GIRLS NEED A HANGOUT!!
AND WE GUYS NEED A HANG-OUT, TOO!
HOW DO WE SETTLE THIS?
HOW ABOUT SOME BEACH OLYMPICS? BOYS VS. GIRLS!
WINNERS TAKE THE COVE!
4

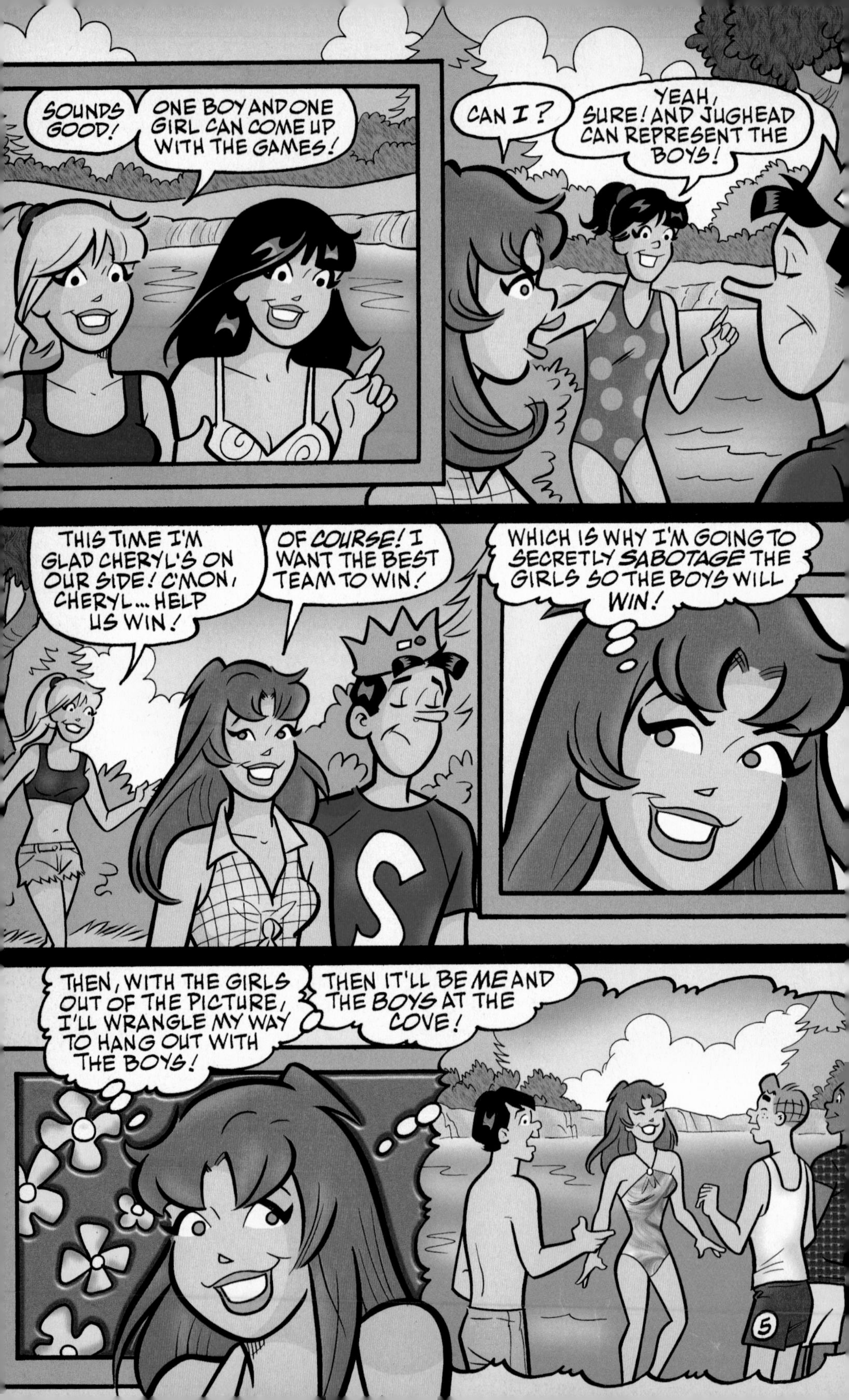
SOUNDS GOOD!
ONE BOY AND ONE GIRL CAN COME UP WITH THE GAMES!
CAN I?
YEAH, SURE! AND JUGHEAD CAN REPRESENT THE BOYS!
THIS TIME I'M GLAD CHERYL'S ON OUR SIDE! C'MON, CHERYL... HELP US WIN!
OF COURSE! I WANT THE BEST TEAM TO WIN!
WHICH IS WHY I'M GOING TO SECRETLY SABOTAGE THE GIRLS SO THE BOYS WILL WIN!
THEN, WITH THE GIRLS OUT OF THE PICTURE, I'LL WRANGLE MY WAY TO HANG OUT WITH THE BOYS!
THEN IT'LL BE ME AND THE BOYS AT THE COVE!

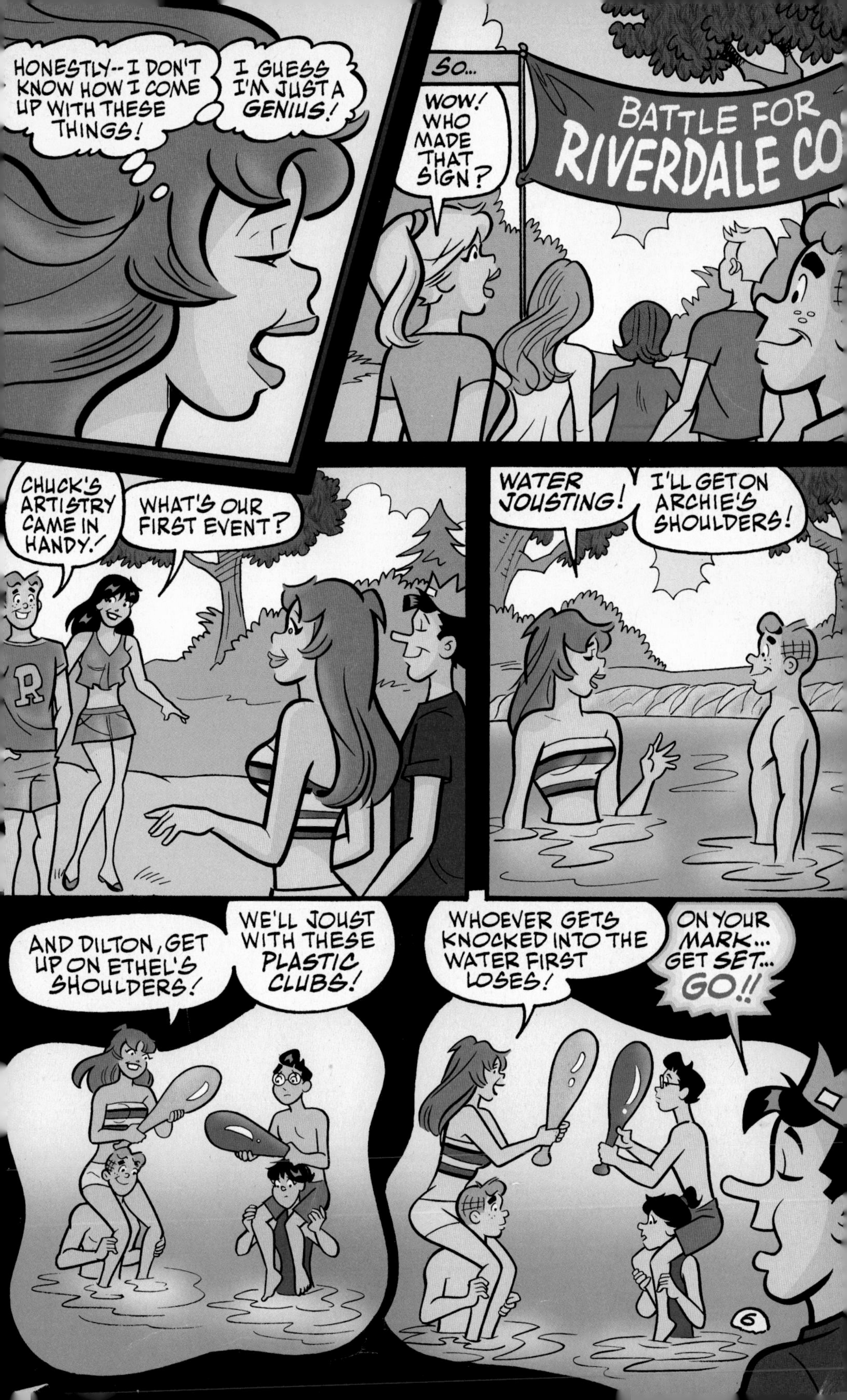

HONESTLY--I DON'T KNOW HOW I COME UP WITH THESE THINGS!
I GUESS I'M JUST A GENIUS!
SO...
WOW! WHO MADE THAT SIGN?
BATTLE FOR RIVERDALE CO
CHUCK'S ARTISTRY CAME IN HANDY!
WHAT'S OUR FIRST EVENT?
WATER JOUSTING!
I'LL GET ON ARCHIE'S SHOULDERS!
AND DILTON, GET UP ON ETHEL'S SHOULDERS!
WE'LL JOUST WITH THESE PLASTIC CLUBS!
WHOEVER GETS KNOCKED INTO THE WATER FIRST LOSES!
ON YOUR MARK... GET SET... GO!!
6

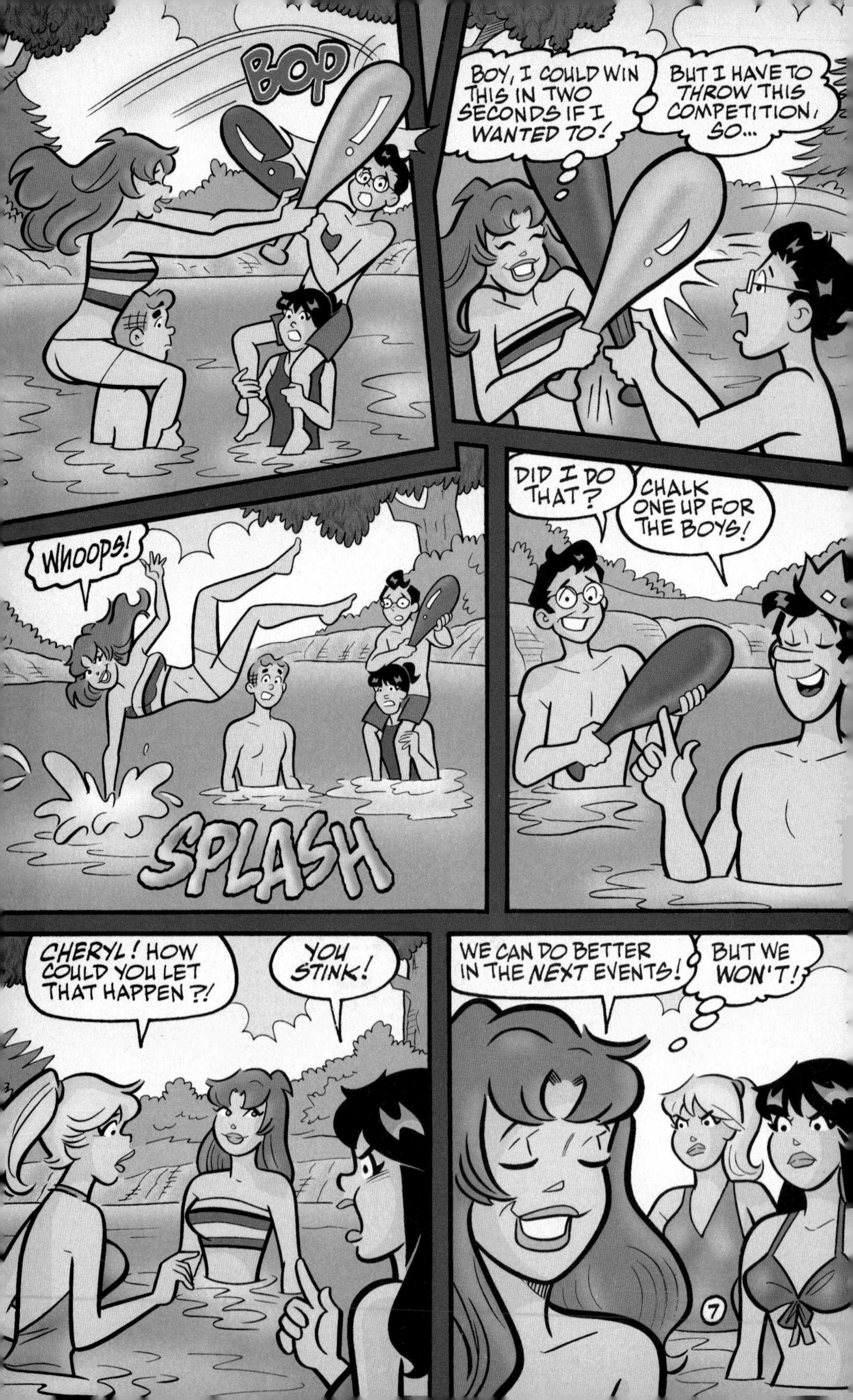
BOP
BOY, I COULD WIN THIS IN TWO SECONDS IF I WANTED TO!
BUT I HAVE TO THROW THIS COMPETITION, SO...
WHOOPS!
SPLASH
DID I DO THAT?
CHALK ONE UP FOR THE BOYS!
CHERYL! HOW COULD YOU LET THAT HAPPEN?!
YOU STINK!
WE CAN DO BETTER IN THE NEXT EVENTS!
BUT WE WON'T!
7

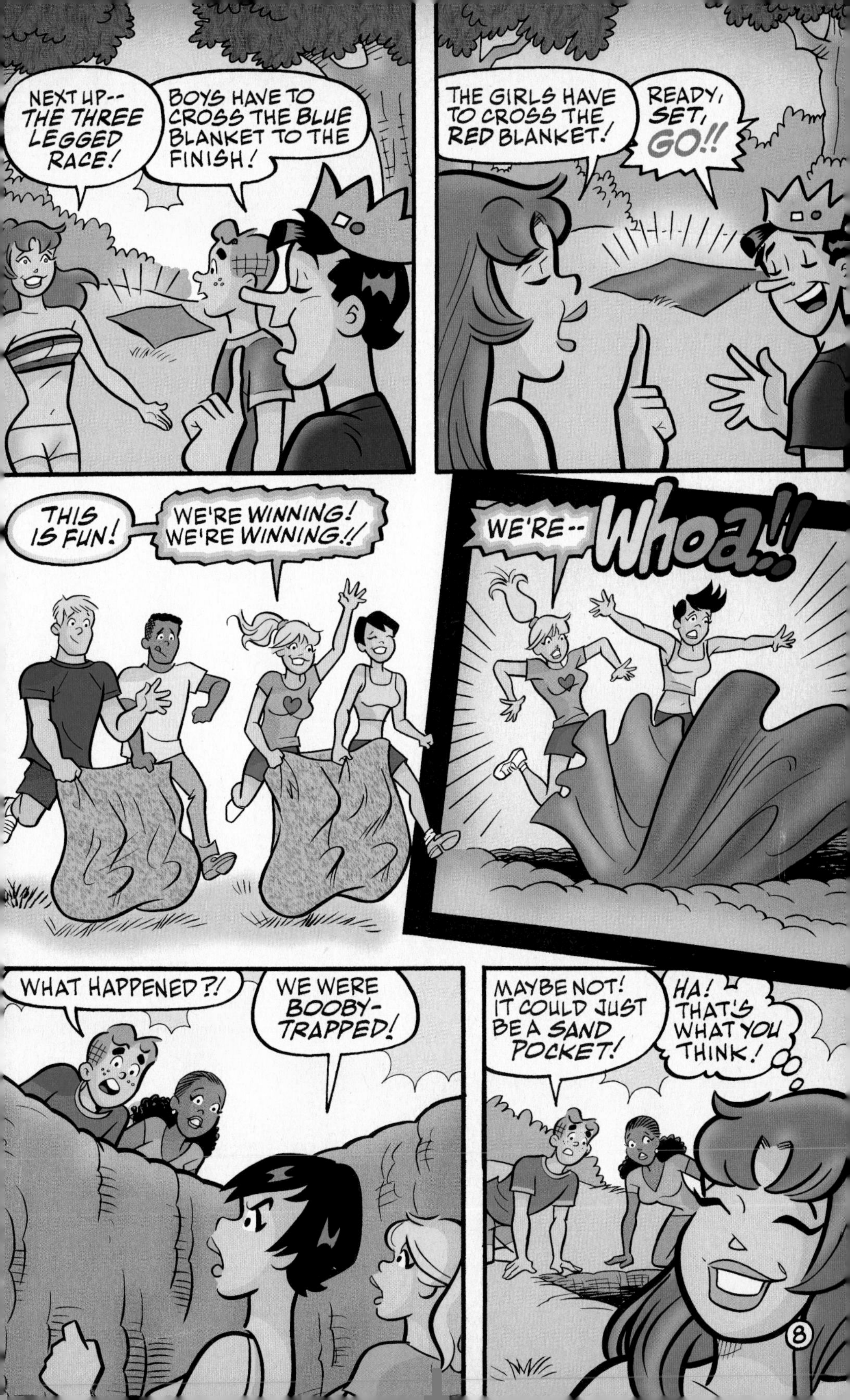

NEXT UP-- THE THREE LEGGED RACE!
BOYS HAVE TO CROSS THE BLUE BLANKET TO THE FINISH!
THE GIRLS HAVE TO CROSS THE RED BLANKET!
READY, SET, GO!!
THIS IS FUN!
WE'RE WINNING! WE'RE WINNING!!
WE'RE-- Whoa!!
WHAT HAPPENED?!
WE WERE BOOBY-TRAPPED!
MAYBE NOT! IT COULD JUST BE A SAND POCKET!
HA! THAT'S WHAT YOU THINK!

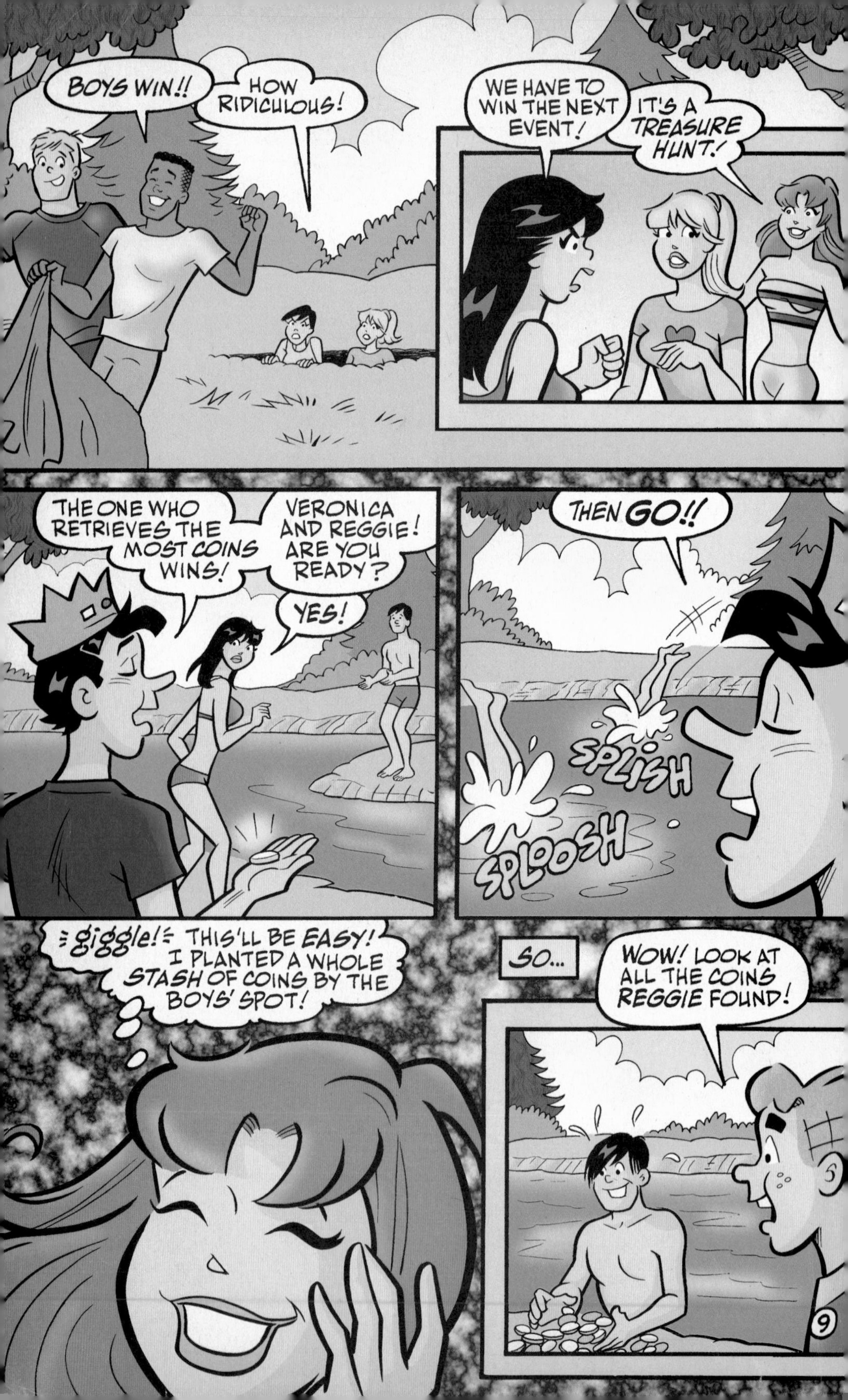
BOYS WIN!!
HOW RIDICULOUS!
WE HAVE TO WIN THE NEXT EVENT!
IT'S A TREASURE HUNT!
THE ONE WHO RETRIEVES THE MOST COINS WINS!
VERONICA AND REGGIE! ARE YOU READY?
YES!
THEN GO!!
SPLISH
SPLOOSH
giggle! THIS'LL BE EASY! I PLANTED A WHOLE STASH OF COINS BY THE BOYS' SPOT!
SO...
WOW! LOOK AT ALL THE COINS REGGIE FOUND!
9

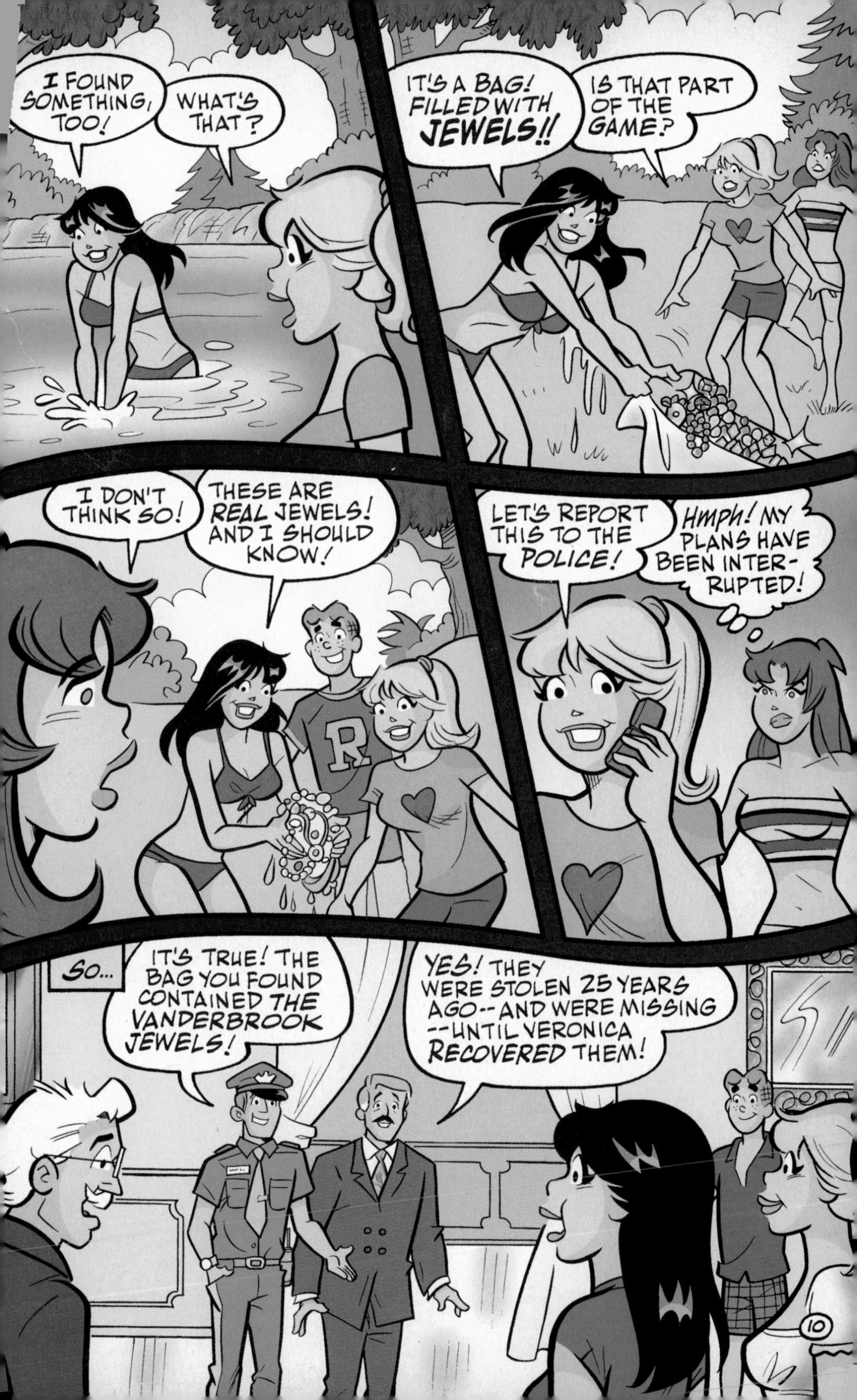

I FOUND SOMETHING, TOO!
WHAT'S THAT?
IT'S A BAG! FILLED WITH JEWELS!!
IS THAT PART OF THE GAME?
I DON'T THINK SO!
THESE ARE REAL JEWELS! AND I SHOULD KNOW!
LET'S REPORT THIS TO THE POLICE!
Hmph! MY PLANS HAVE BEEN INTER-RUPTED!
SO...
IT'S TRUE! THE BAG YOU FOUND CONTAINED THE VANDERBROOK JEWELS!
YES! THEY WERE STOLEN 25 YEARS AGO--AND WERE MISSING --UNTIL VERONICA RECOVERED THEM!
10

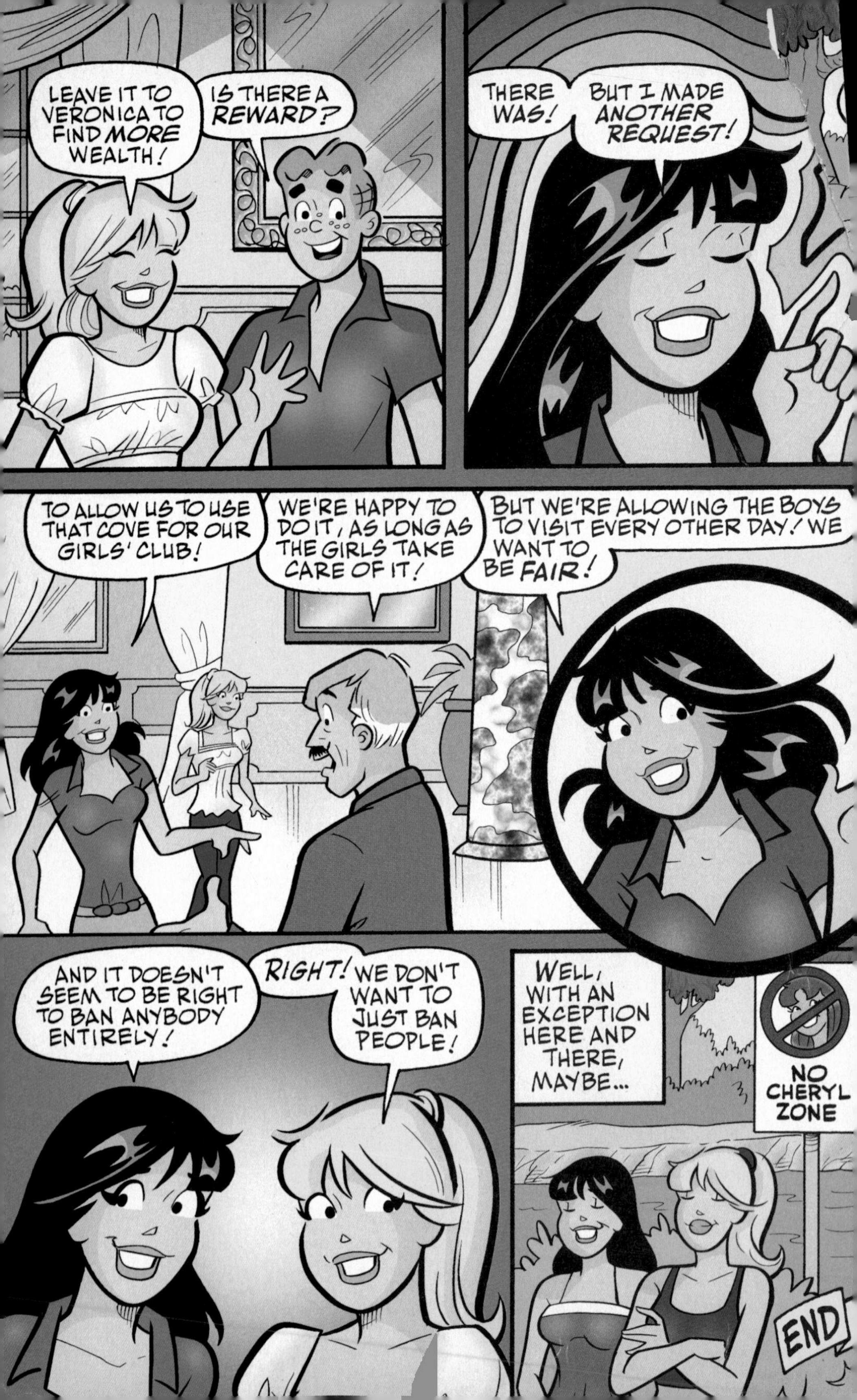
LEAVE IT TO VERONICA TO FIND MORE WEALTH!
IS THERE A REWARD?
THERE WAS!
BUT I MADE ANOTHER REQUEST!
TO ALLOW US TO USE THAT COVE FOR OUR GIRLS' CLUB!
WE'RE HAPPY TO DO IT, AS LONG AS THE GIRLS TAKE CARE OF IT!
BUT WE'RE ALLOWING THE BOYS TO VISIT EVERY OTHER DAY! WE WANT TO BE FAIR!
AND IT DOESN'T SEEM TO BE RIGHT TO BAN ANYBODY ENTIRELY!
RIGHT! WE DON'T WANT TO JUST BAN PEOPLE!
WELL, WITH AN EXCEPTION HERE AND THERE, MAYBE...
NO CHERYL ZONE
END

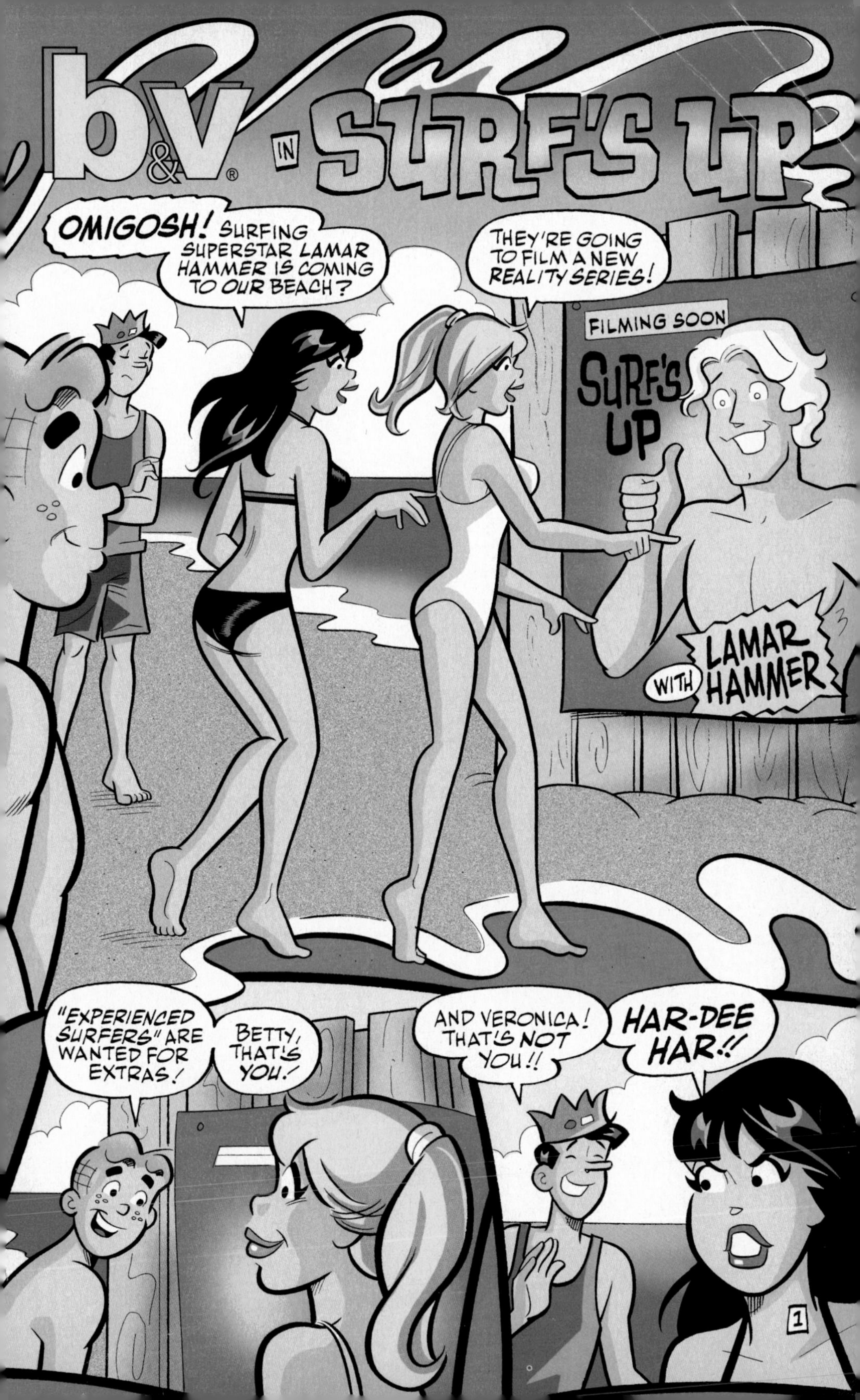
B&V IN SURF'S UP
OMIGOSH! SURFING SUPERSTAR LAMAR HAMMER IS COMING TO OUR BEACH?
THEY'RE GOING TO FILM A NEW REALITY SERIES!
FILMING SOON
SURF'S UP
WITH LAMAR HAMMER
"EXPERIENCED SURFERS" ARE WANTED FOR EXTRAS!
BETTY, THAT'S YOU!
AND VERONICA! THAT'S NOT YOU!!
HAR-DEE HAR!!
1

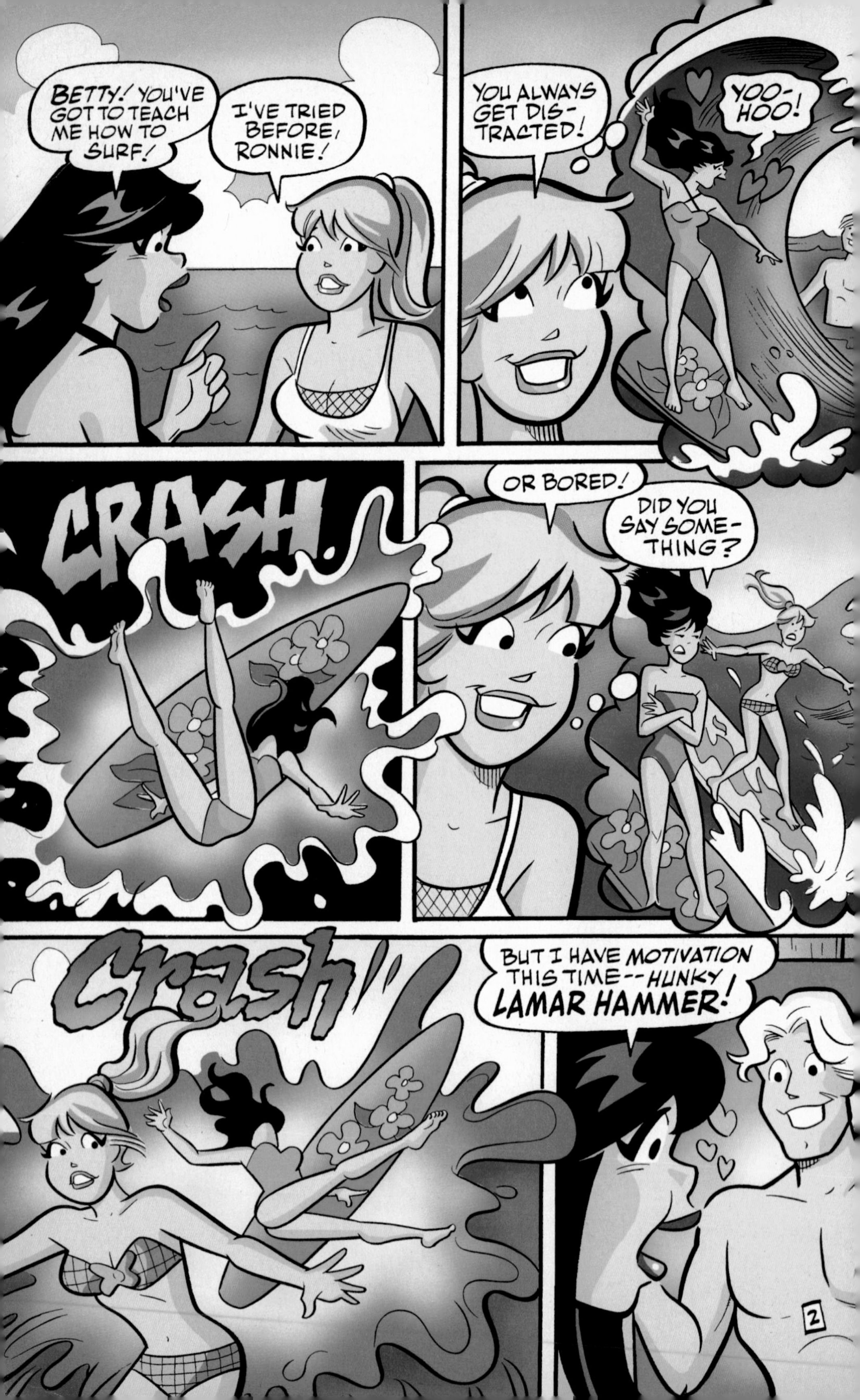
BETTY! YOU'VE GOT TO TEACH ME HOW TO SURF!
I'VE TRIED BEFORE, RONNIE!
YOU ALWAYS GET DIS-TRACTED!
YOO-HOO!
CRASH
OR BORED!
DID YOU SAY SOME-THING?
Crash
BUT I HAVE MOTIVATION THIS TIME--HUNKY LAMAR HAMMER!
2

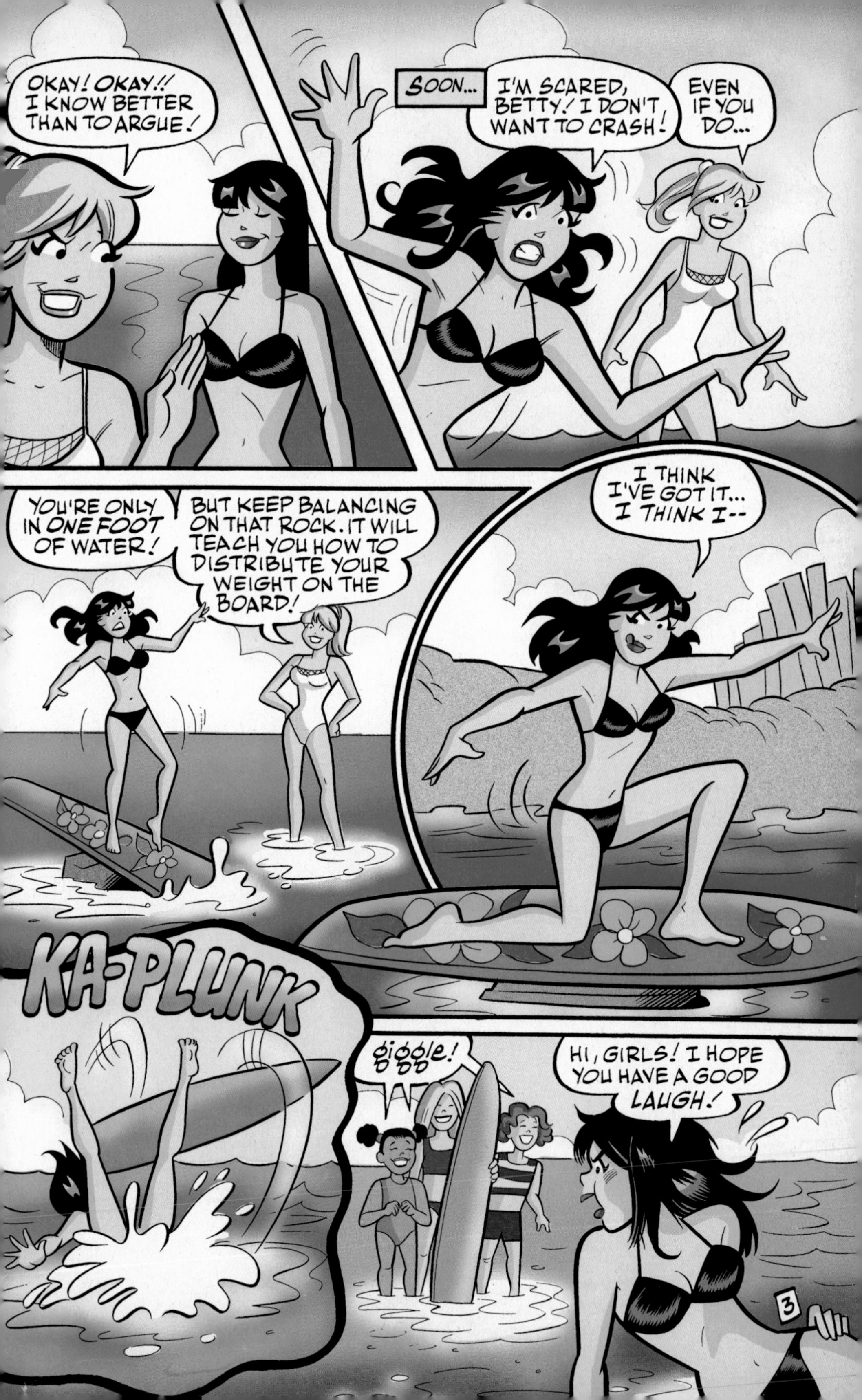
OKAY! OKAY!! I KNOW BETTER THAN TO ARGUE!
SOON...
I'M SCARED, BETTY! I DON'T WANT TO CRASH!
EVEN IF YOU DO...
YOU'RE ONLY IN ONE FOOT OF WATER!
BUT KEEP BALANCING ON THAT ROCK. IT WILL TEACH YOU HOW TO DISTRIBUTE YOUR WEIGHT ON THE BOARD!
I THINK I'VE GOT IT... I THINK I--
KA-PLUNK
giggle!
HI, GIRLS! I HOPE YOU HAVE A GOOD LAUGH!
3

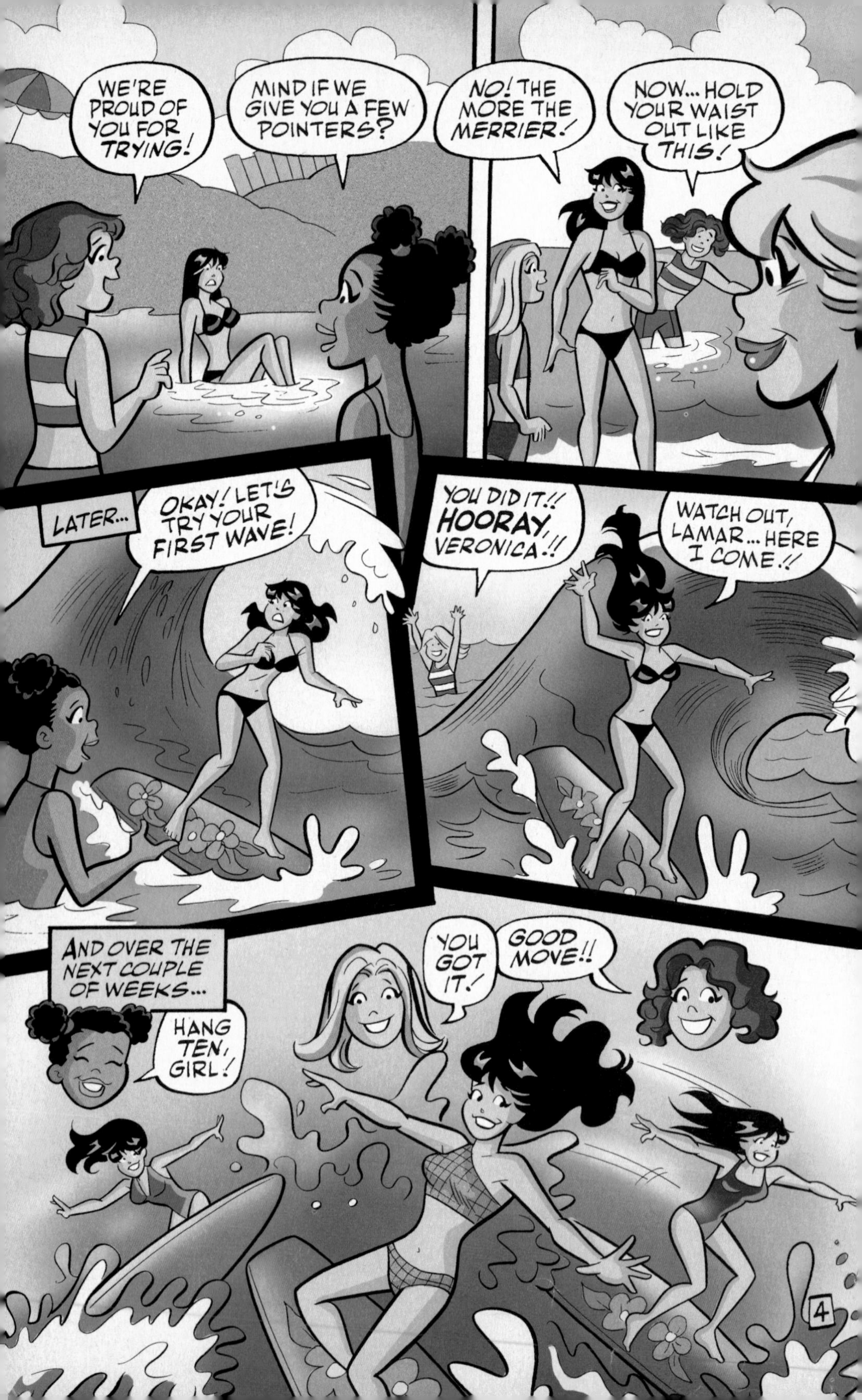
WE'RE PROUD OF YOU FOR TRYING!
MIND IF WE GIVE YOU A FEW POINTERS?
NO! THE MORE THE MERRIER!
NOW... HOLD YOUR WAIST OUT LIKE THIS!
LATER...
OKAY! LET'S TRY YOUR FIRST WAVE!
YOU DID IT!! HOORAY, VERONICA!!
WATCH OUT, LAMAR... HERE I COME!!
AND OVER THE NEXT COUPLE OF WEEKS...
HANG TEN, GIRL!
YOU GOT IT!
GOOD MOVE!!
4

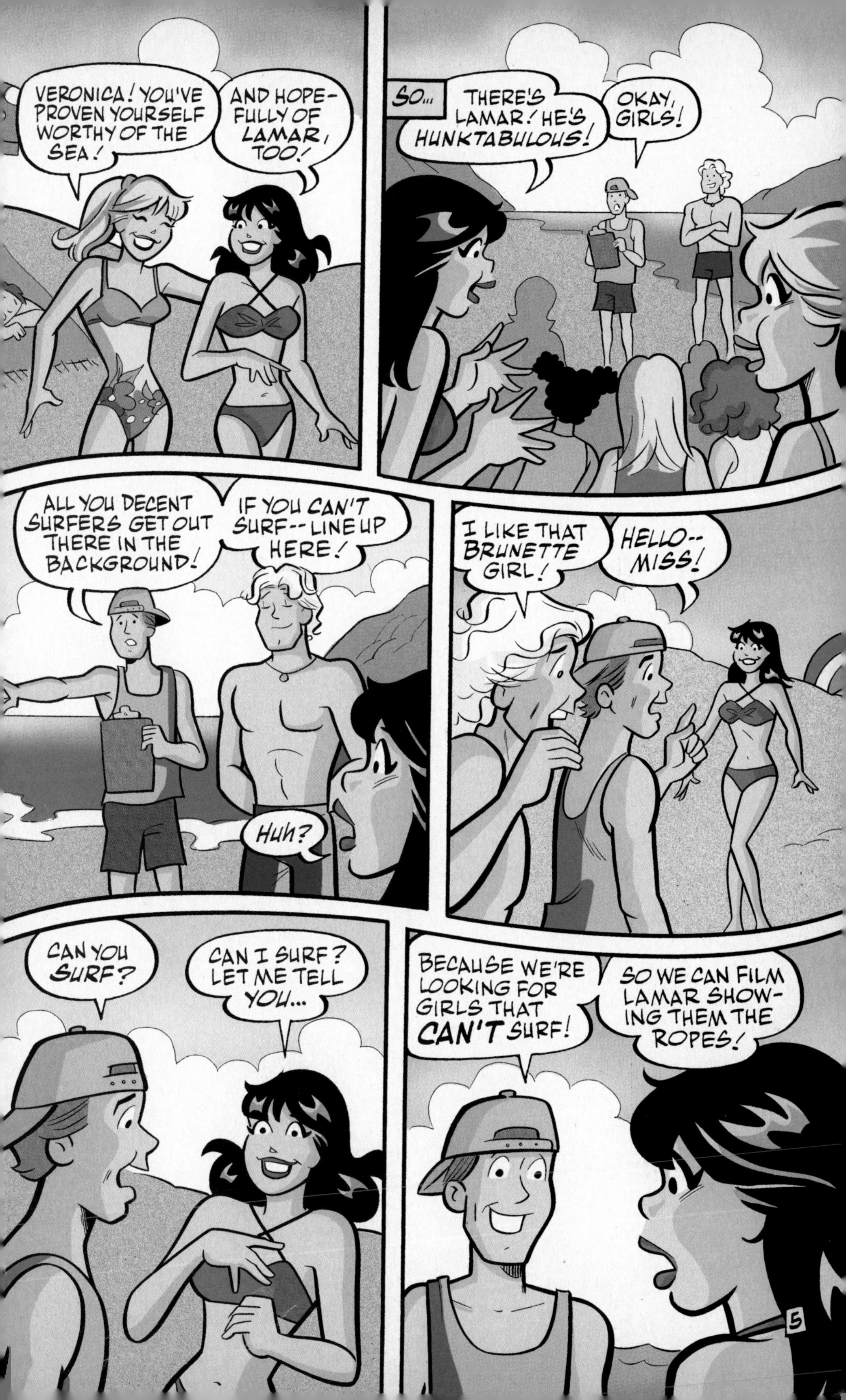
VERONICA! YOU'VE PROVEN YOURSELF WORTHY OF THE SEA!
AND HOPE-FULLY OF LAMAR, TOO!
SO...
THERE'S LAMAR! HE'S HUNKTABULOUS!
OKAY, GIRLS!
ALL YOU DECENT SURFERS GET OUT THERE IN THE BACKGROUND!
IF YOU CAN'T SURF-- LINE UP HERE!
HUH?
I LIKE THAT BRUNETTE GIRL!
HELLO-- MISS!
CAN YOU SURF?
CAN I SURF? LET ME TELL YOU...
BECAUSE WE'RE LOOKING FOR GIRLS THAT CAN'T SURF!
SO WE CAN FILM LAMAR SHOWING THEM THE ROPES!
5

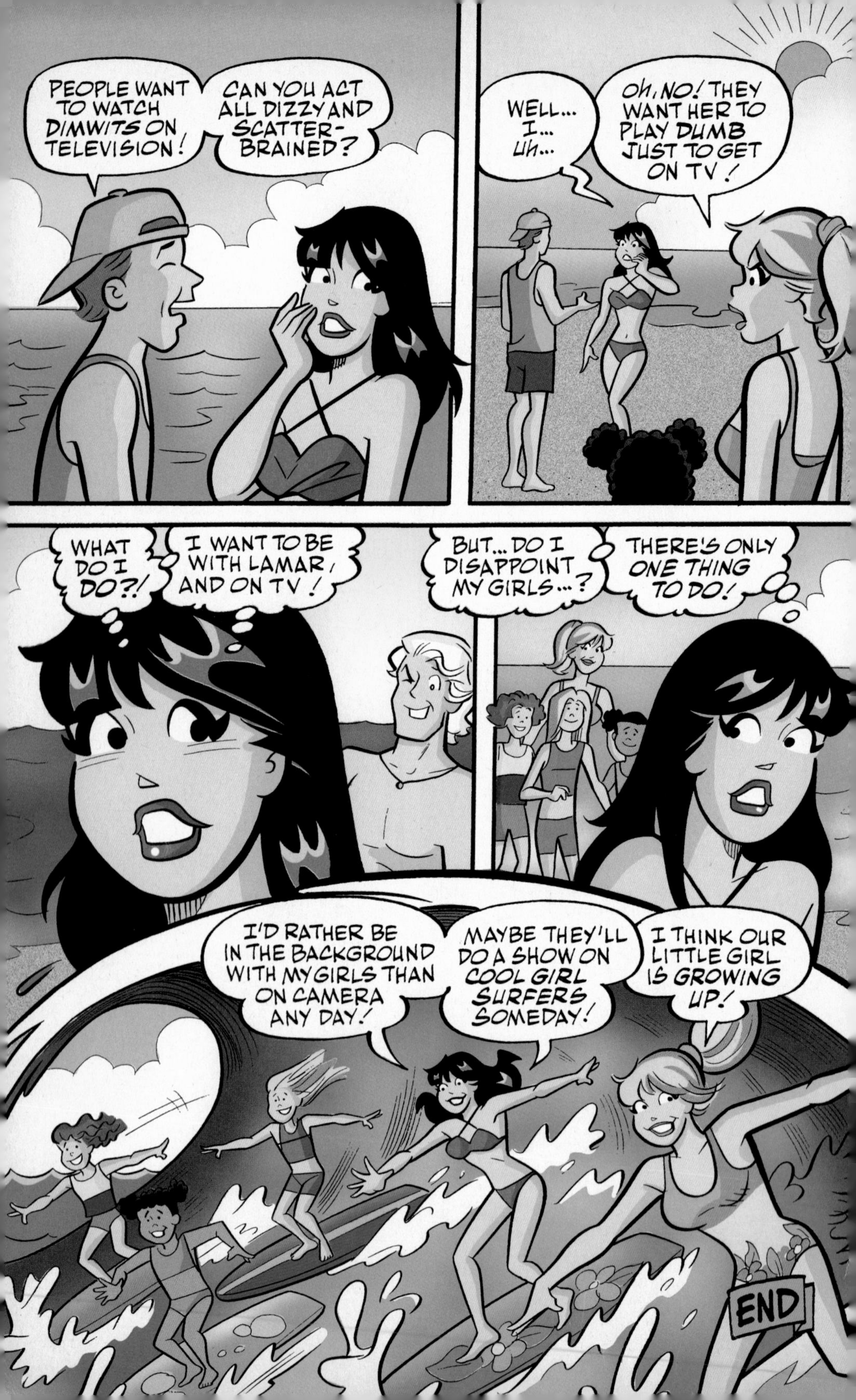
PEOPLE WANT TO WATCH DIMWITS ON TELEVISION!
CAN YOU ACT ALL DIZZY AND SCATTER-BRAINED?
WELL... I... uh...
Oh, NO! THEY WANT HER TO PLAY DUMB JUST TO GET ON TV!
WHAT DO I DO?!
I WANT TO BE WITH LAMAR, AND ON TV!
BUT... DO I DISAPPOINT MY GIRLS...?
THERE'S ONLY ONE THING TO DO!
I'D RATHER BE IN THE BACKGROUND WITH MY GIRLS THAN ON CAMERA ANY DAY!
MAYBE THEY'LL DO A SHOW ON COOL GIRL SURFERS SOMEDAY!
I THINK OUR LITTLE GIRL IS GROWING UP!
END

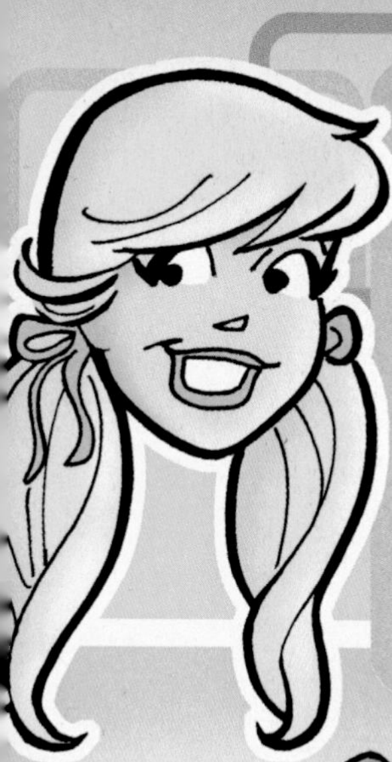

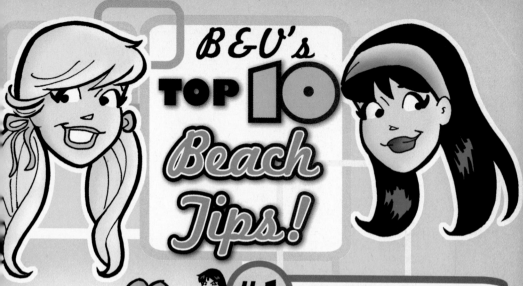

B&V's TOP 10 Beach Tips!

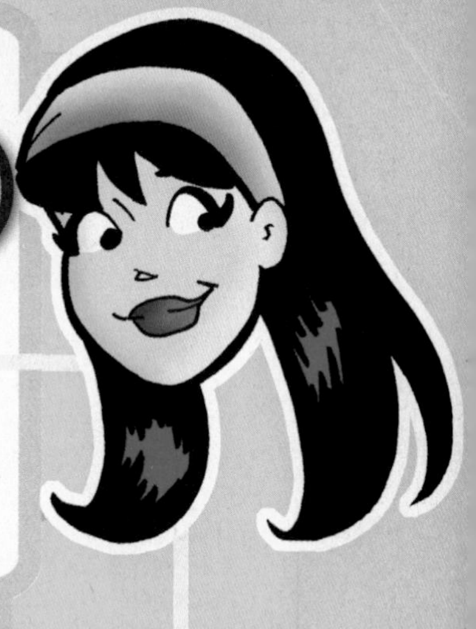

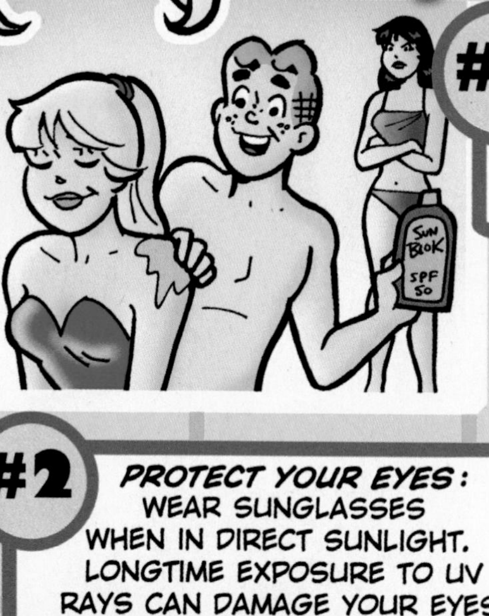
SUN BLOK
SPF 50

#1 ***PROTECT YOUR SKIN :***
USE A SUNBLOCK TO AVOID EXPOSURE TO THE SUN. USE A SUNBLOCK WITH AN SPF OF 40 OR MORE.

#2 ***PROTECT YOUR EYES :***
WEAR SUNGLASSES WHEN IN DIRECT SUNLIGHT. LONGTIME EXPOSURE TO UV RAYS CAN DAMAGE YOUR EYES.

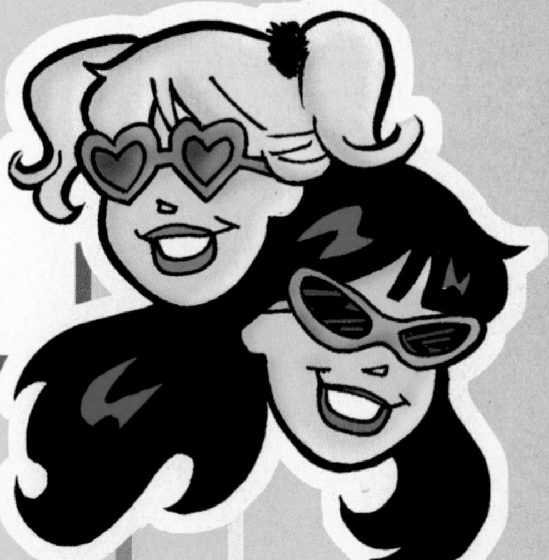

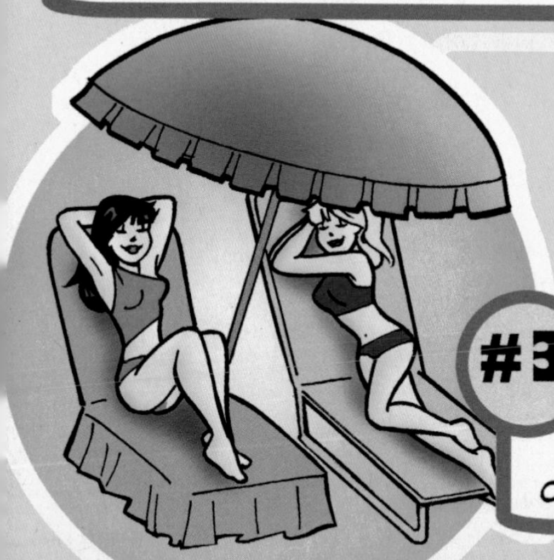

#3 ***STAY COOL :***
PREVENT OVERHEATING AND DEHYDRATION BY KEEPING YOUR BODY COOL AND NOT OVERDOING IT IN DIRECT SUNLIGHT.

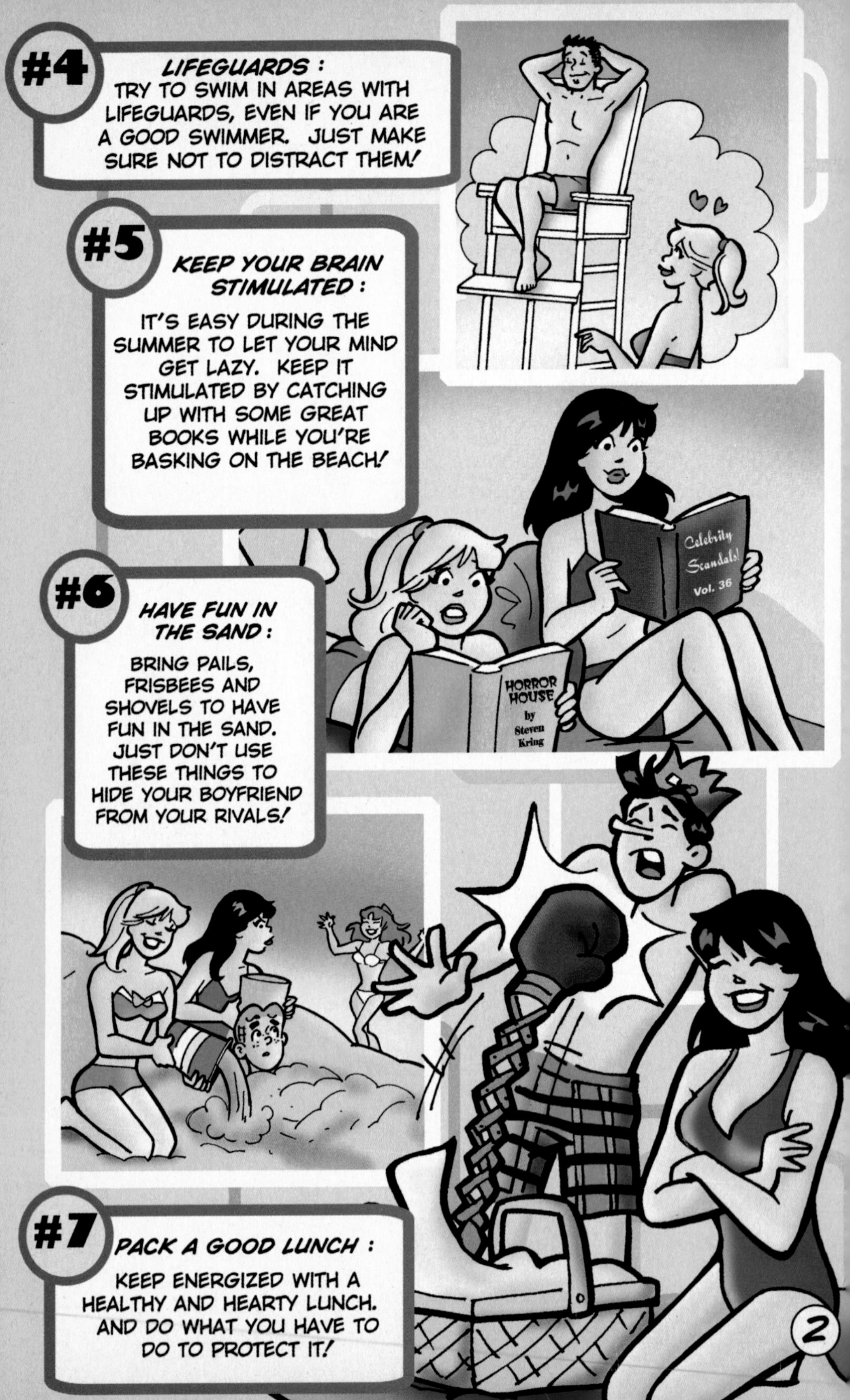
#4
LIFEGUARDS :
TRY TO SWIM IN AREAS WITH LIFEGUARDS, EVEN IF YOU ARE A GOOD SWIMMER. JUST MAKE SURE NOT TO DISTRACT THEM!
#5
KEEP YOUR BRAIN STIMULATED :
IT'S EASY DURING THE SUMMER TO LET YOUR MIND GET LAZY. KEEP IT STIMULATED BY CATCHING UP WITH SOME GREAT BOOKS WHILE YOU'RE BASKING ON THE BEACH!
Celebrity Scandals! Vol. 36
HORROR HOUSE by Steven Kring
#6
HAVE FUN IN THE SAND :
BRING PAILS, FRISBEES AND SHOVELS TO HAVE FUN IN THE SAND. JUST DON'T USE THESE THINGS TO HIDE YOUR BOYFRIEND FROM YOUR RIVALS!
#7
PACK A GOOD LUNCH :
KEEP ENERGIZED WITH A HEALTHY AND HEARTY LUNCH. AND DO WHAT YOU HAVE TO DO TO PROTECT IT!

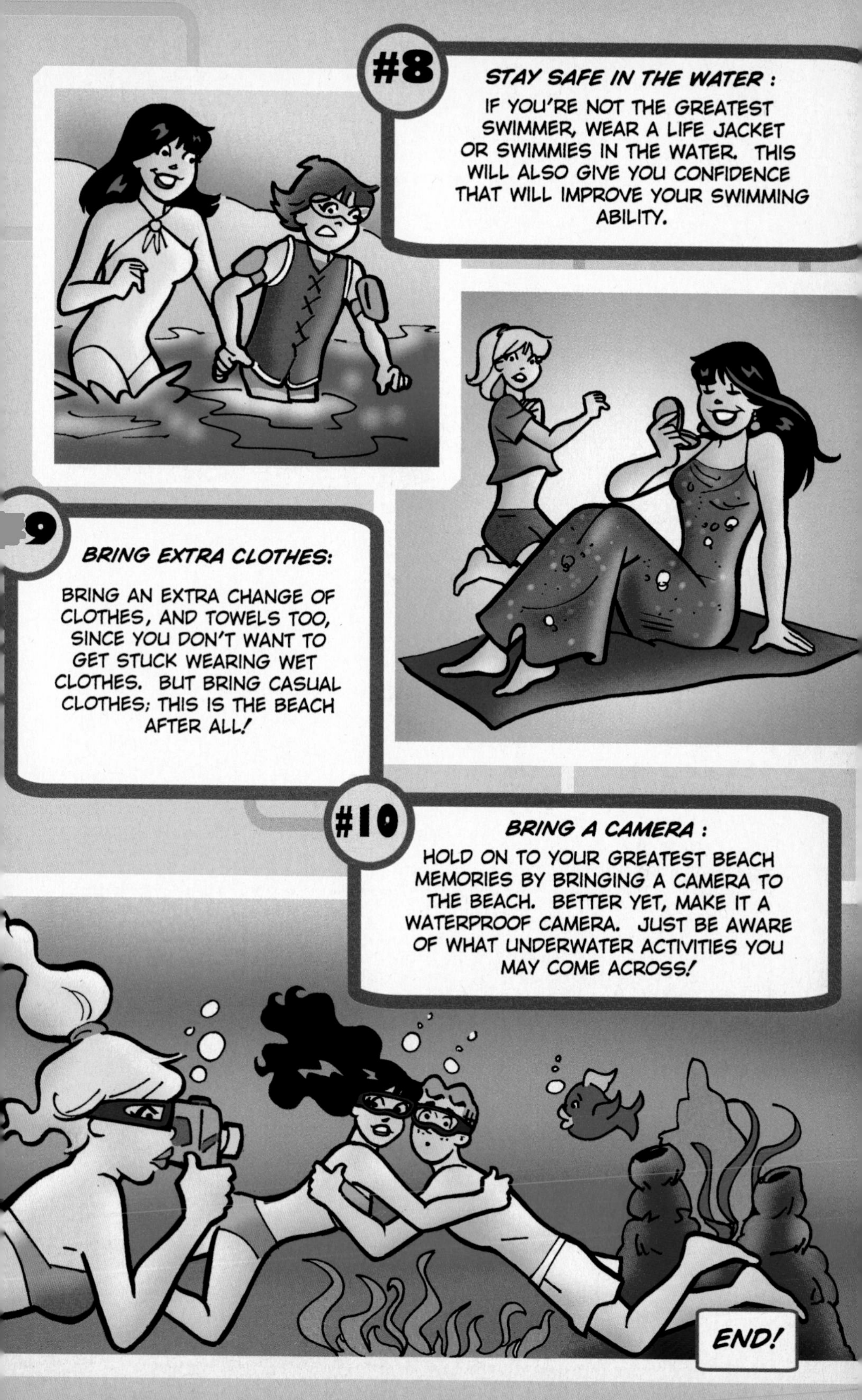
#8
STAY SAFE IN THE WATER :
IF YOU'RE NOT THE GREATEST SWIMMER, WEAR A LIFE JACKET OR SWIMMIES IN THE WATER. THIS WILL ALSO GIVE YOU CONFIDENCE THAT WILL IMPROVE YOUR SWIMMING ABILITY.
9
BRING EXTRA CLOTHES:
BRING AN EXTRA CHANGE OF CLOTHES, AND TOWELS TOO, SINCE YOU DON'T WANT TO GET STUCK WEARING WET CLOTHES. BUT BRING CASUAL CLOTHES; THIS IS THE BEACH AFTER ALL!
#10
BRING A CAMERA :
HOLD ON TO YOUR GREATEST BEACH MEMORIES BY BRINGING A CAMERA TO THE BEACH. BETTER YET, MAKE IT A WATERPROOF CAMERA. JUST BE AWARE OF WHAT UNDERWATER ACTIVITIES YOU MAY COME ACROSS!
END!

Betty and Veronica in LOSERS CAN BE CHOOSERS

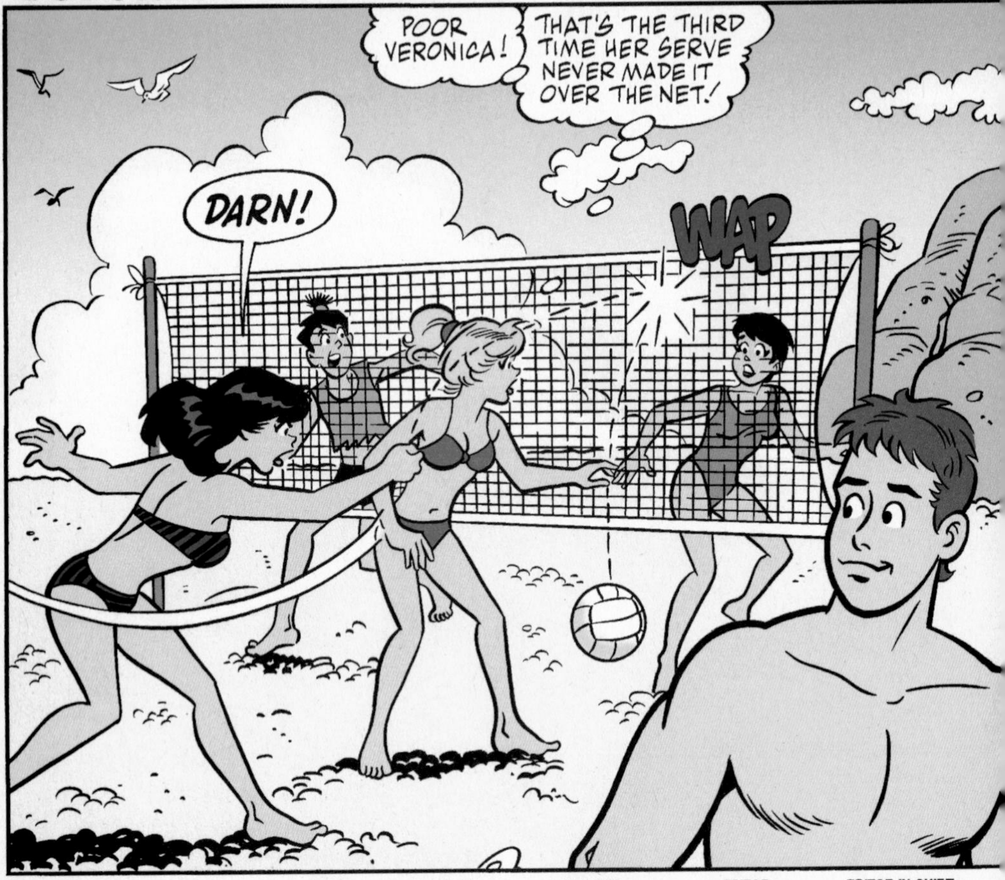
POOR VERONICA!
THAT'S THE THIRD TIME HER SERVE NEVER MADE IT OVER THE NET!
DARN!
WAP

SCRIPT: GEORGE GLADIR · PENCILS: JEFF SHULTZ · INKING: AL MILGROM · LETTERING: JACK MORELLI · COLORING: BARRY GROSSMAN · EDITOR: VICTOR GORELICK · EDITOR-IN-CHIEF: RICHARD GOLDWATER

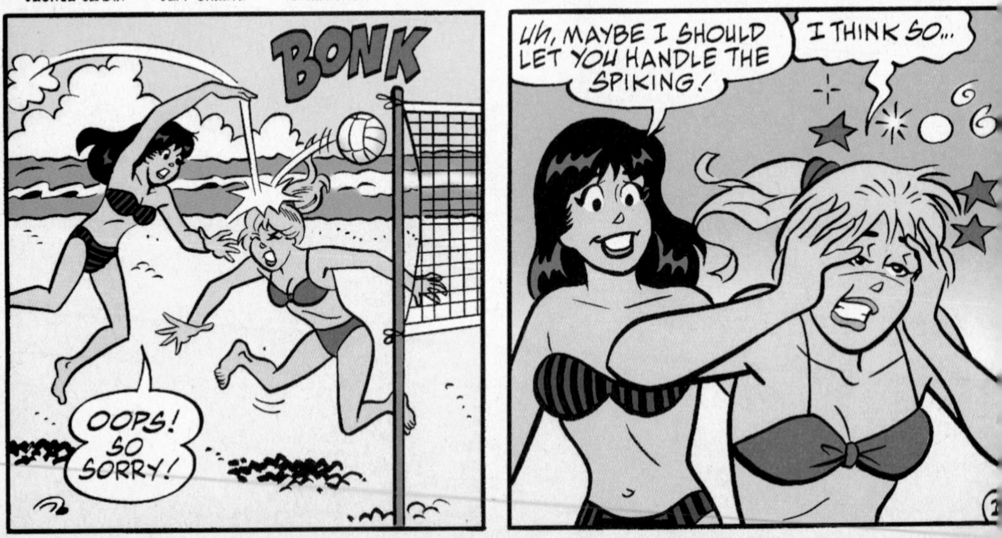
BONK
OOPS! SO SORRY!
UH, MAYBE I SHOULD LET YOU HANDLE THE SPIKING!
I THINK SO...

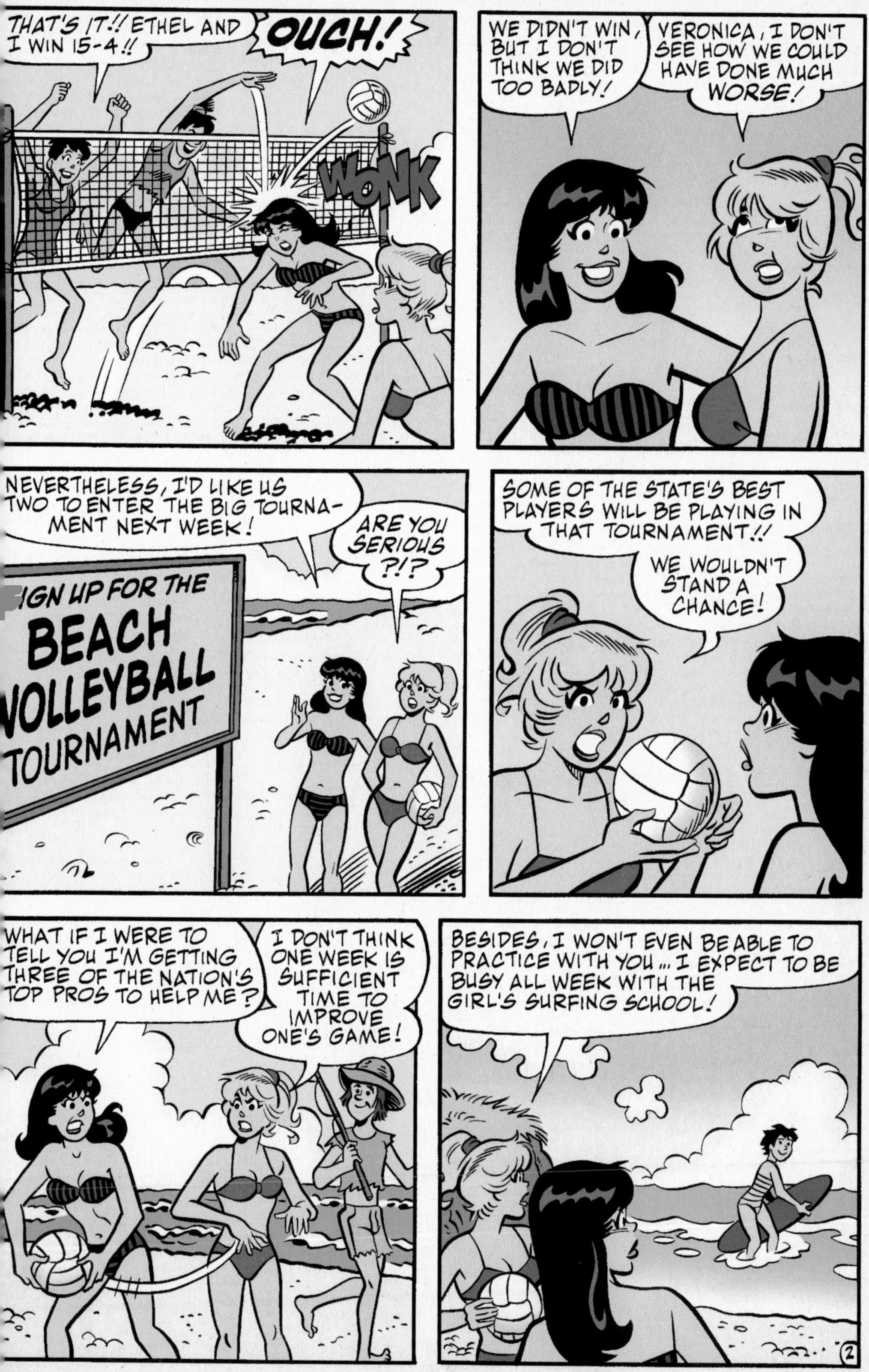
THAT'S IT!! ETHEL AND I WIN 15-4!!
OUCH!
WONK
WE DIDN'T WIN, BUT I DON'T THINK WE DID TOO BADLY!
VERONICA, I DON'T SEE HOW WE COULD HAVE DONE MUCH WORSE!
NEVERTHELESS, I'D LIKE US TWO TO ENTER THE BIG TOURNAMENT NEXT WEEK!
ARE YOU SERIOUS ?!?
BEACH VOLLEYBALL TOURNAMENT
SOME OF THE STATE'S BEST PLAYERS WILL BE PLAYING IN THAT TOURNAMENT!!
WE WOULDN'T STAND A CHANCE!
WHAT IF I WERE TO TELL YOU I'M GETTING THREE OF THE NATION'S TOP PROS TO HELP ME?
I DON'T THINK ONE WEEK IS SUFFICIENT TIME TO IMPROVE ONE'S GAME!
BESIDES, I WON'T EVEN BE ABLE TO PRACTICE WITH YOU ... I EXPECT TO BE BUSY ALL WEEK WITH THE GIRL'S SURFING SCHOOL!
2

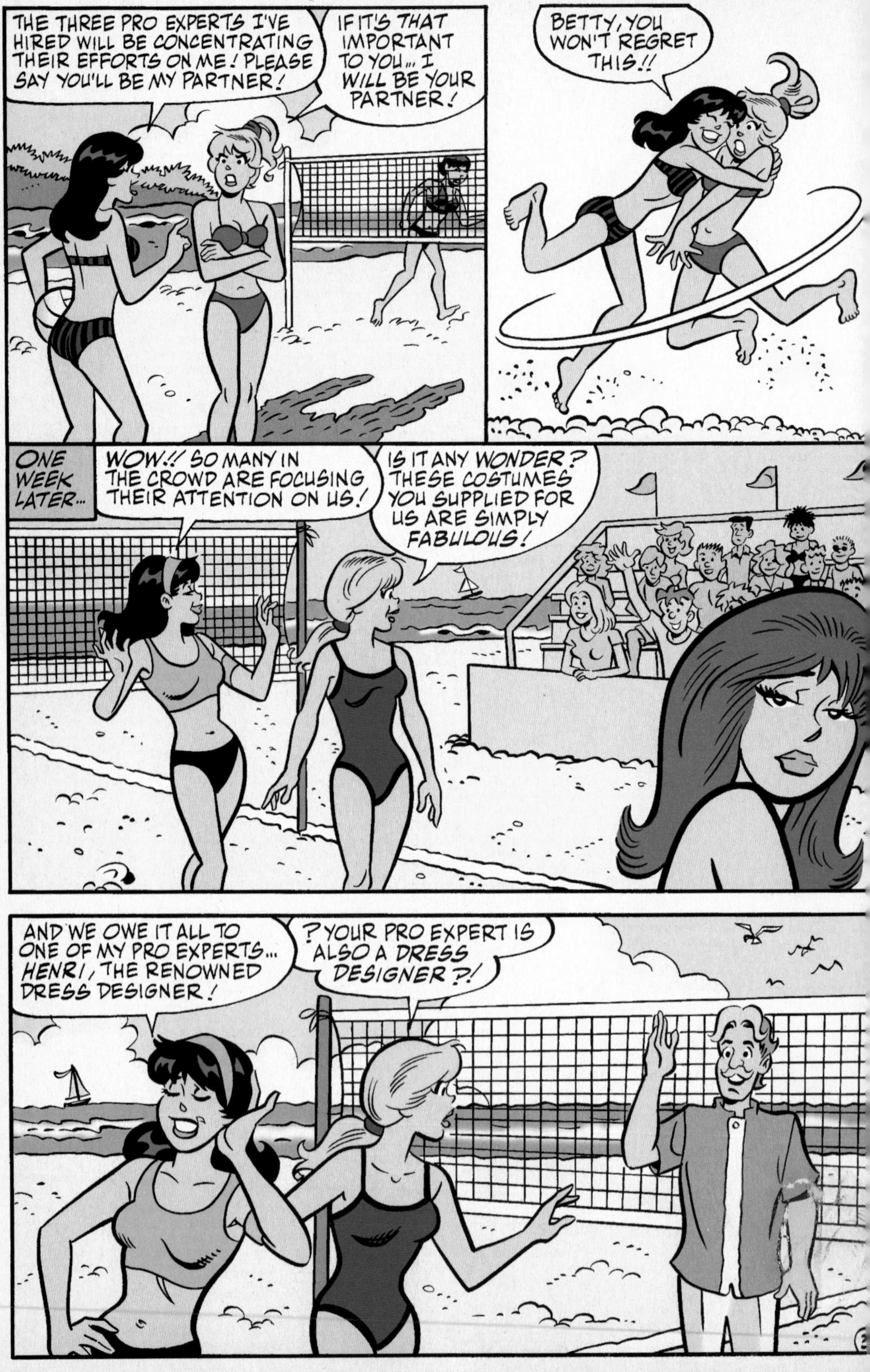
THE THREE PRO EXPERTS I'VE HIRED WILL BE CONCENTRATING THEIR EFFORTS ON ME! PLEASE SAY YOU'LL BE MY PARTNER!
IF IT'S THAT IMPORTANT TO YOU... I WILL BE YOUR PARTNER!
BETTY, YOU WON'T REGRET THIS!!
ONE WEEK LATER...
WOW!! SO MANY IN THE CROWD ARE FOCUSING THEIR ATTENTION ON US!
IS IT ANY WONDER? THESE COSTUMES YOU SUPPLIED FOR US ARE SIMPLY FABULOUS!
AND WE OWE IT ALL TO ONE OF MY PRO EXPERTS... HENRI, THE RENOWNED DRESS DESIGNER!
? YOUR PRO EXPERT IS ALSO A DRESS DESIGNER?!

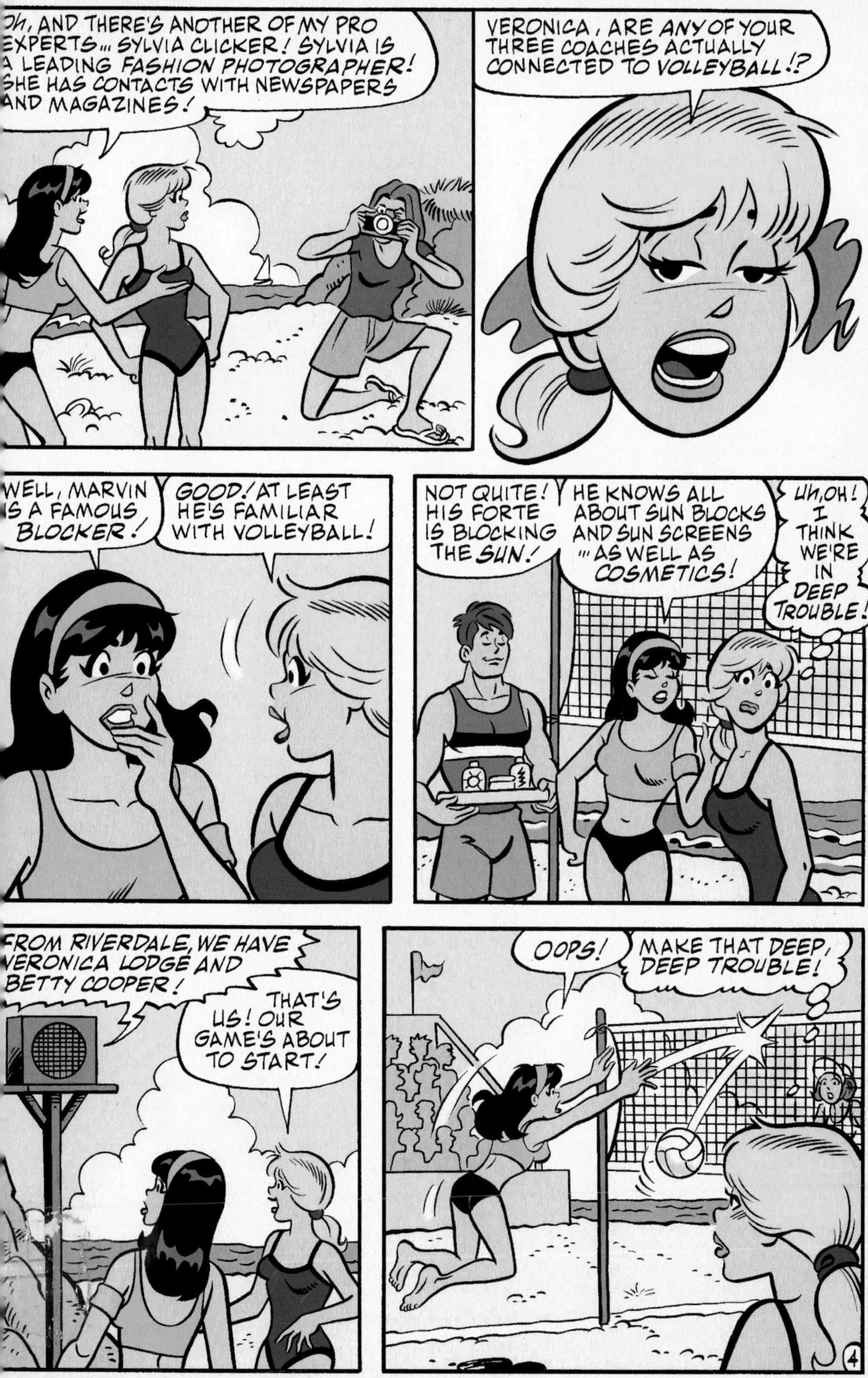
OH, AND THERE'S ANOTHER OF MY PRO EXPERTS... SYLVIA CLICKER! SYLVIA IS A LEADING FASHION PHOTOGRAPHER! SHE HAS CONTACTS WITH NEWSPAPERS AND MAGAZINES!
VERONICA, ARE ANY OF YOUR THREE COACHES ACTUALLY CONNECTED TO VOLLEYBALL!?
WELL, MARVIN IS A FAMOUS BLOCKER!
GOOD! AT LEAST HE'S FAMILIAR WITH VOLLEYBALL!
NOT QUITE! HIS FORTE IS BLOCKING THE SUN!
HE KNOWS ALL ABOUT SUN BLOCKS AND SUN SCREENS ... AS WELL AS COSMETICS!
UH,OH! I THINK WE'RE IN DEEP TROUBLE!
FROM RIVERDALE, WE HAVE VERONICA LODGE AND BETTY COOPER!
THAT'S US! OUR GAME'S ABOUT TO START!
OOPS!
MAKE THAT DEEP, DEEP TROUBLE!
4

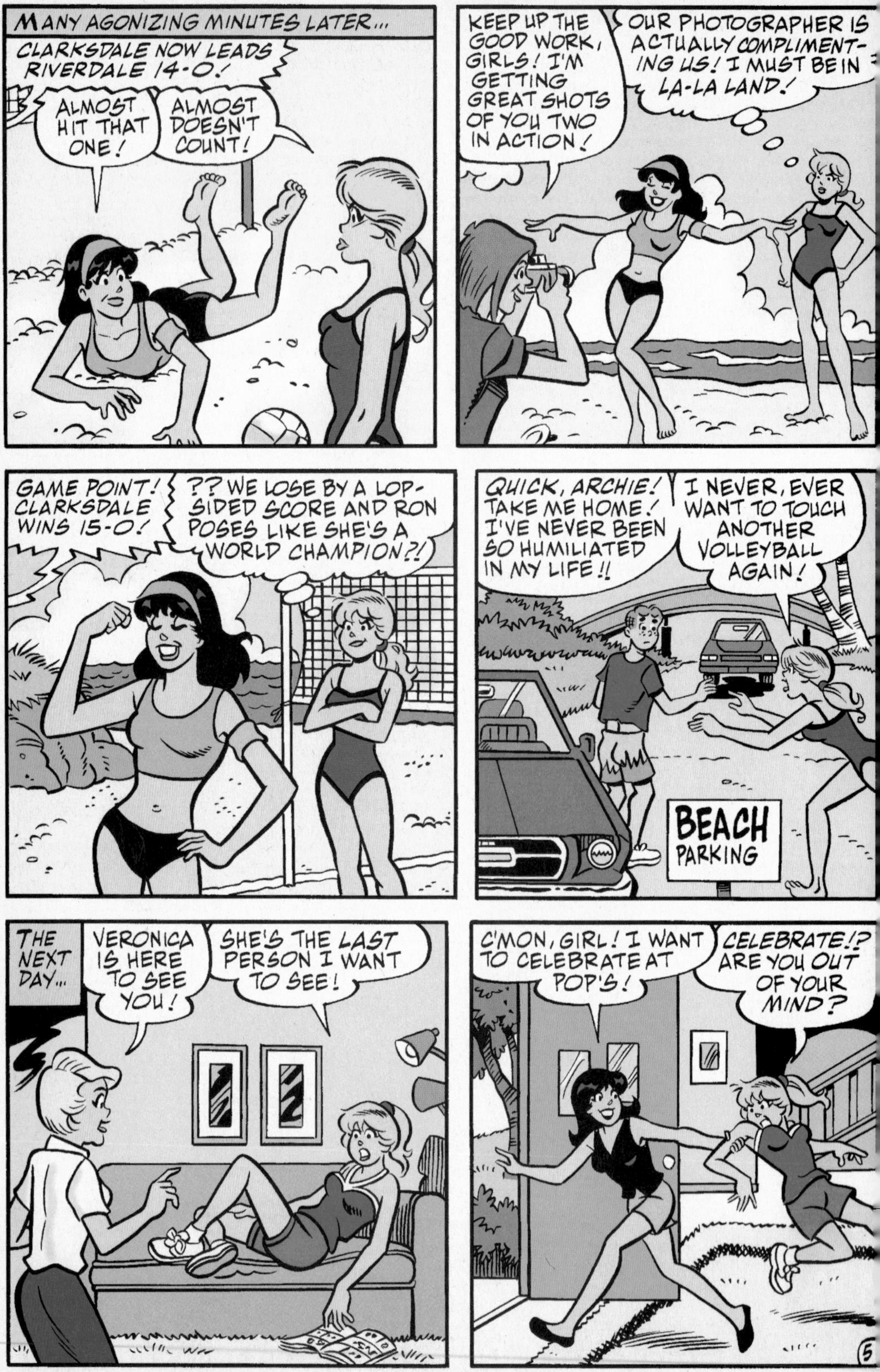
MANY AGONIZING MINUTES LATER...
CLARKSDALE NOW LEADS RIVERDALE 14-0!
ALMOST HIT THAT ONE!
ALMOST DOESN'T COUNT!
KEEP UP THE GOOD WORK, GIRLS! I'M GETTING GREAT SHOTS OF YOU TWO IN ACTION!
OUR PHOTOGRAPHER IS ACTUALLY COMPLIMENTING US! I MUST BE IN LA-LA LAND!
GAME POINT! CLARKSDALE WINS 15-0!
?? WE LOSE BY A LOP-SIDED SCORE AND RON POSES LIKE SHE'S A WORLD CHAMPION?!
QUICK, ARCHIE! TAKE ME HOME! I'VE NEVER BEEN SO HUMILIATED IN MY LIFE!!
I NEVER, EVER WANT TO TOUCH ANOTHER VOLLEYBALL AGAIN!
BEACH PARKING
THE NEXT DAY...
VERONICA IS HERE TO SEE YOU!
SHE'S THE LAST PERSON I WANT TO SEE!
C'MON, GIRL! I WANT TO CELEBRATE AT POP'S!
CELEBRATE!? ARE YOU OUT OF YOUR MIND?
5

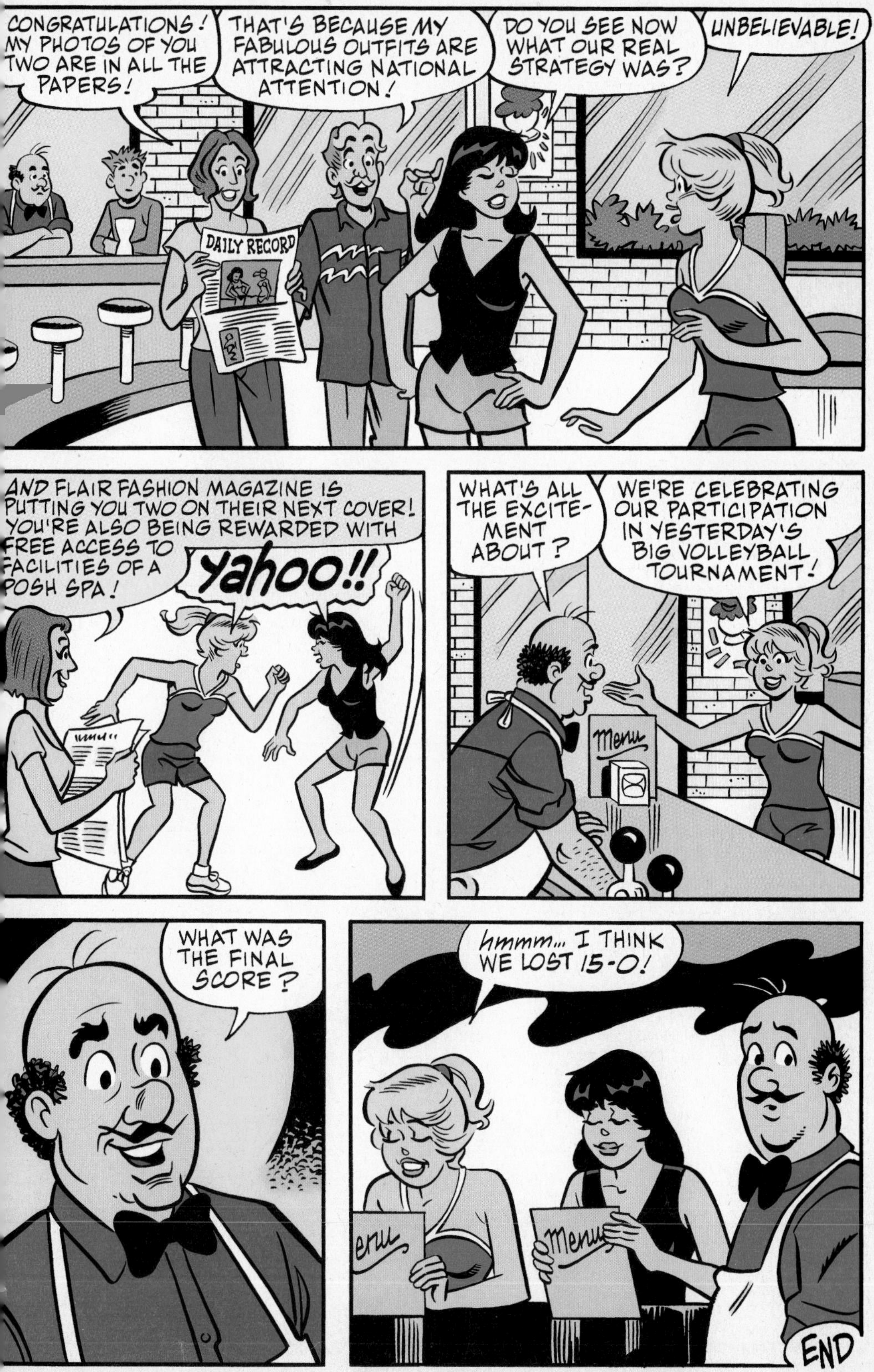
CONGRATULATIONS! MY PHOTOS OF YOU TWO ARE IN ALL THE PAPERS!
THAT'S BECAUSE MY FABULOUS OUTFITS ARE ATTRACTING NATIONAL ATTENTION!
DAILY RECORD
DO YOU SEE NOW WHAT OUR REAL STRATEGY WAS?
UNBELIEVABLE!
AND FLAIR FASHION MAGAZINE IS PUTTING YOU TWO ON THEIR NEXT COVER! YOU'RE ALSO BEING REWARDED WITH FREE ACCESS TO FACILITIES OF A POSH SPA!
yahoo!!
WHAT'S ALL THE EXCITE-MENT ABOUT?
WE'RE CELEBRATING OUR PARTICIPATION IN YESTERDAY'S BIG VOLLEYBALL TOURNAMENT!
Menu
WHAT WAS THE FINAL SCORE?
hmmm... I THINK WE LOST 15-0!
Menu
END

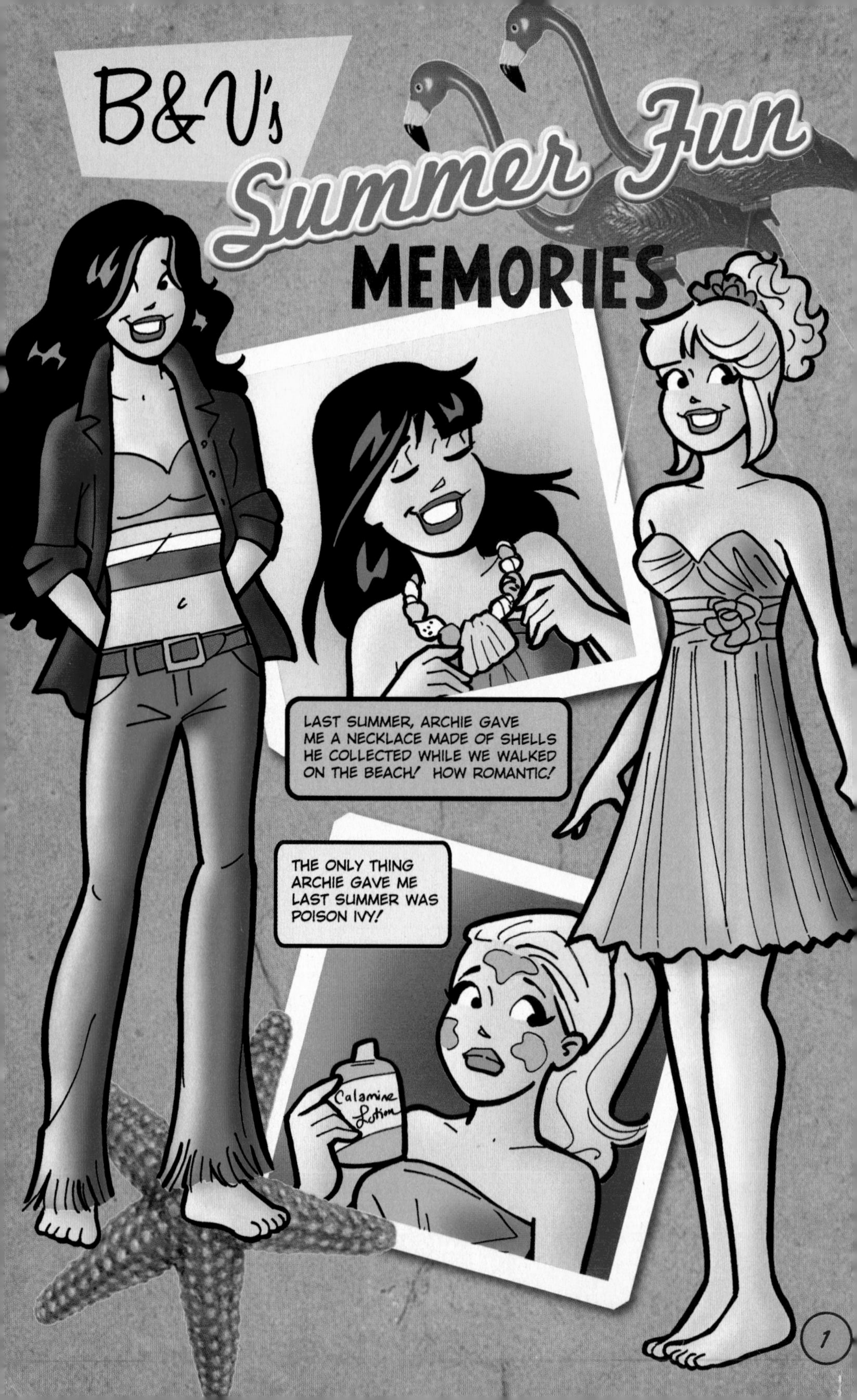
B&V's Summer Fun MEMORIES
LAST SUMMER, ARCHIE GAVE ME A NECKLACE MADE OF SHELLS HE COLLECTED WHILE WE WALKED ON THE BEACH! HOW ROMANTIC!
THE ONLY THING ARCHIE GAVE ME LAST SUMMER WAS POISON IVY!
Calamine Lotion

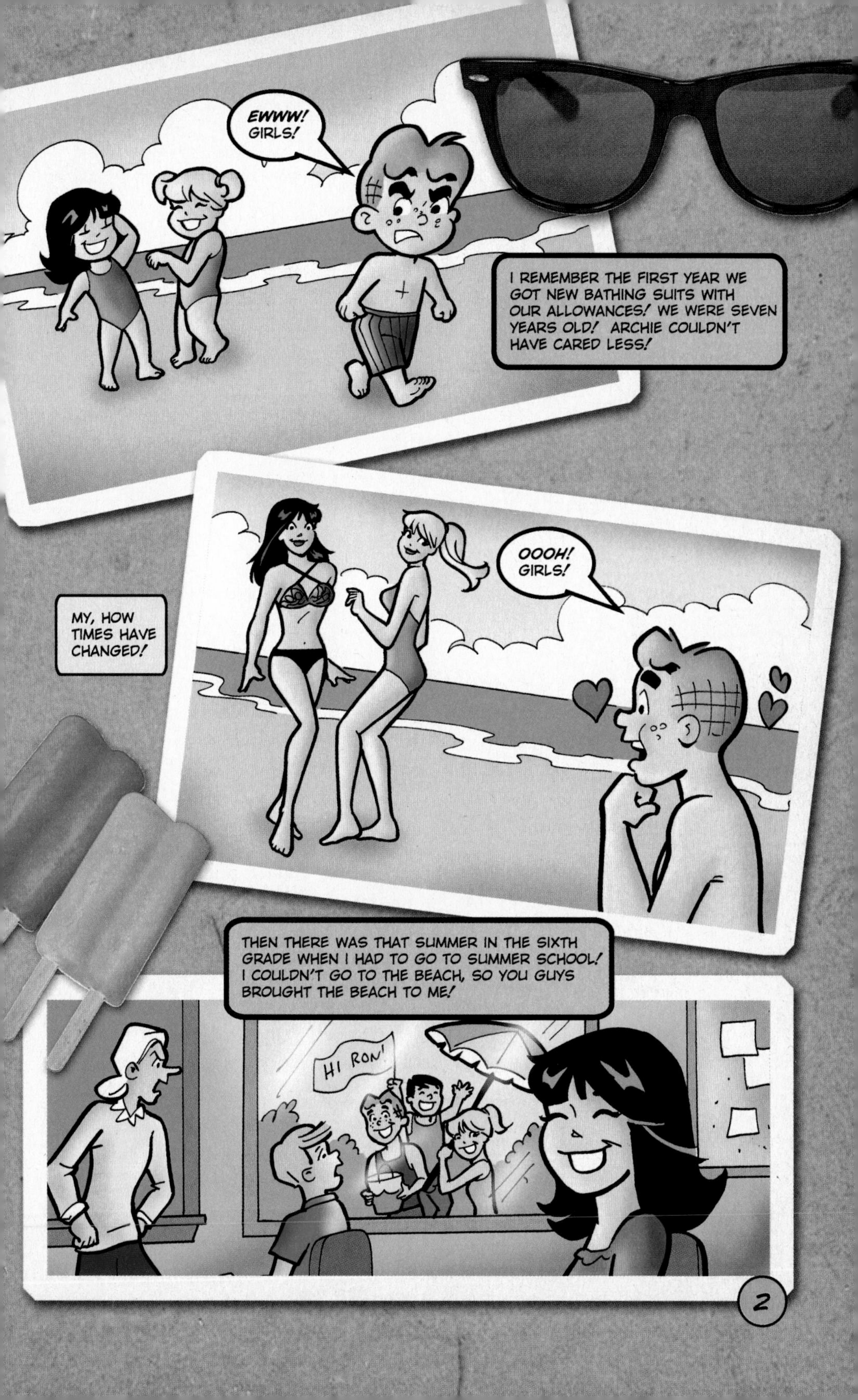
EWWW! GIRLS!
I REMEMBER THE FIRST YEAR WE GOT NEW BATHING SUITS WITH OUR ALLOWANCES! WE WERE SEVEN YEARS OLD! ARCHIE COULDN'T HAVE CARED LESS!
MY, HOW TIMES HAVE CHANGED!
OOOH! GIRLS!
THEN THERE WAS THAT SUMMER IN THE SIXTH GRADE WHEN I HAD TO GO TO SUMMER SCHOOL! I COULDN'T GO TO THE BEACH, SO YOU GUYS BROUGHT THE BEACH TO ME!
HI RON!

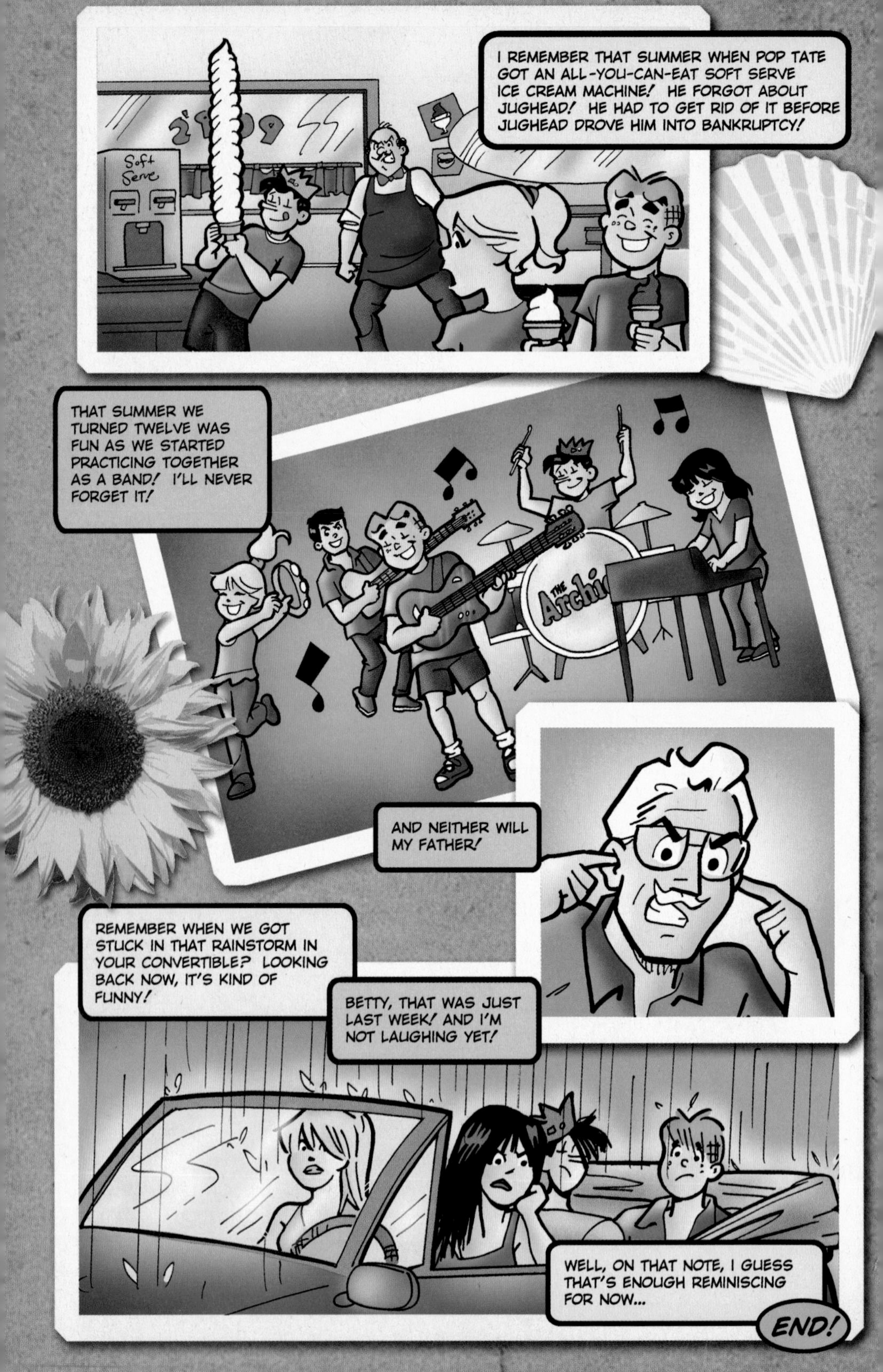
I REMEMBER THAT SUMMER WHEN POP TATE GOT AN ALL-YOU-CAN-EAT SOFT SERVE ICE CREAM MACHINE! HE FORGOT ABOUT JUGHEAD! HE HAD TO GET RID OF IT BEFORE JUGHEAD DROVE HIM INTO BANKRUPTCY!
Soft Serve
THAT SUMMER WE TURNED TWELVE WAS FUN AS WE STARTED PRACTICING TOGETHER AS A BAND! I'LL NEVER FORGET IT!
AND NEITHER WILL MY FATHER!
REMEMBER WHEN WE GOT STUCK IN THAT RAINSTORM IN YOUR CONVERTIBLE? LOOKING BACK NOW, IT'S KIND OF FUNNY!
BETTY, THAT WAS JUST LAST WEEK! AND I'M NOT LAUGHING YET!
WELL, ON THAT NOTE, I GUESS THAT'S ENOUGH REMINISCING FOR NOW...
END!

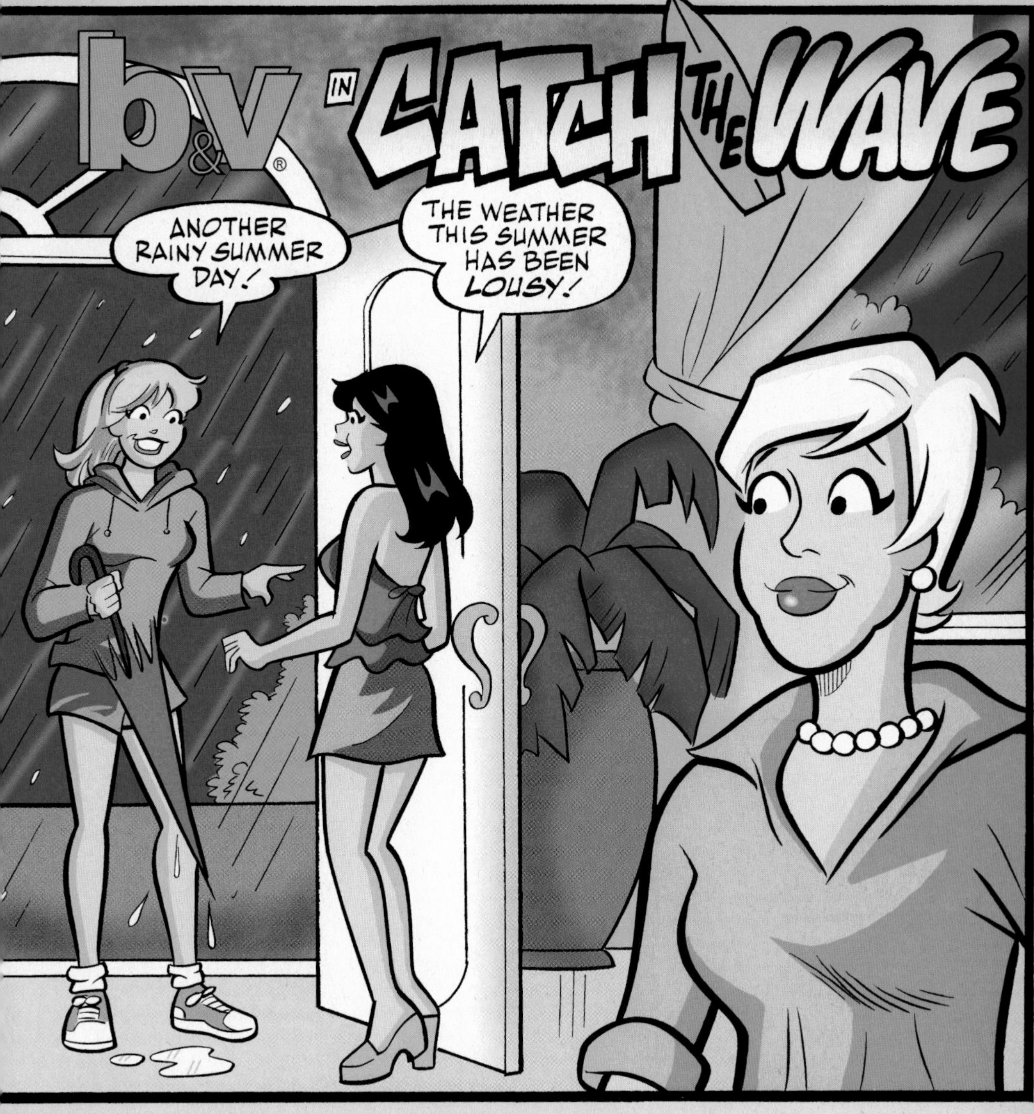
b&v® IN CATCH THE WAVE
ANOTHER RAINY SUMMER DAY!
THE WEATHER THIS SUMMER HAS BEEN LOUSY!

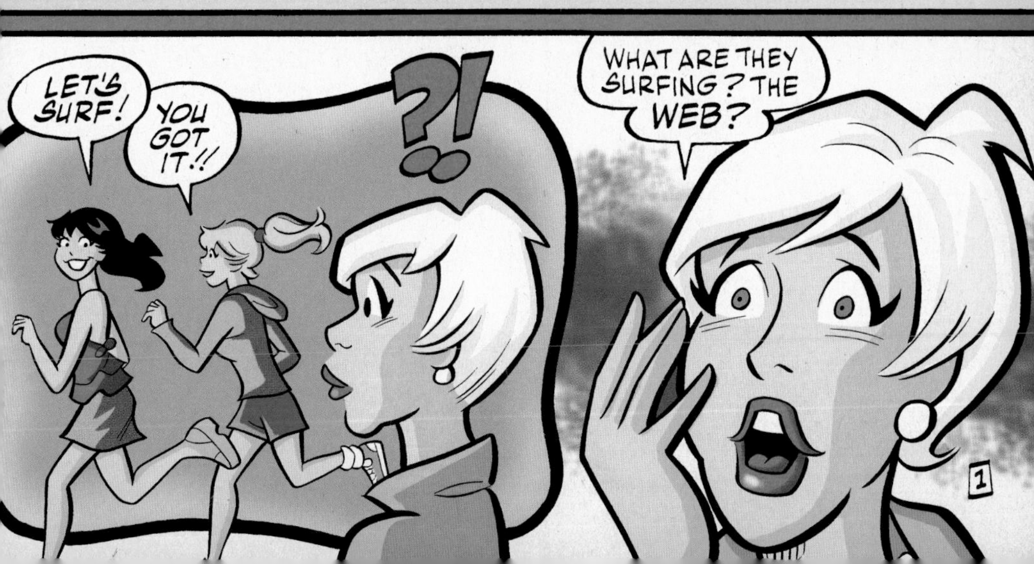
LET'S SURF!
YOU GOT IT!!
?!
WHAT ARE THEY SURFING? THE WEB?
1

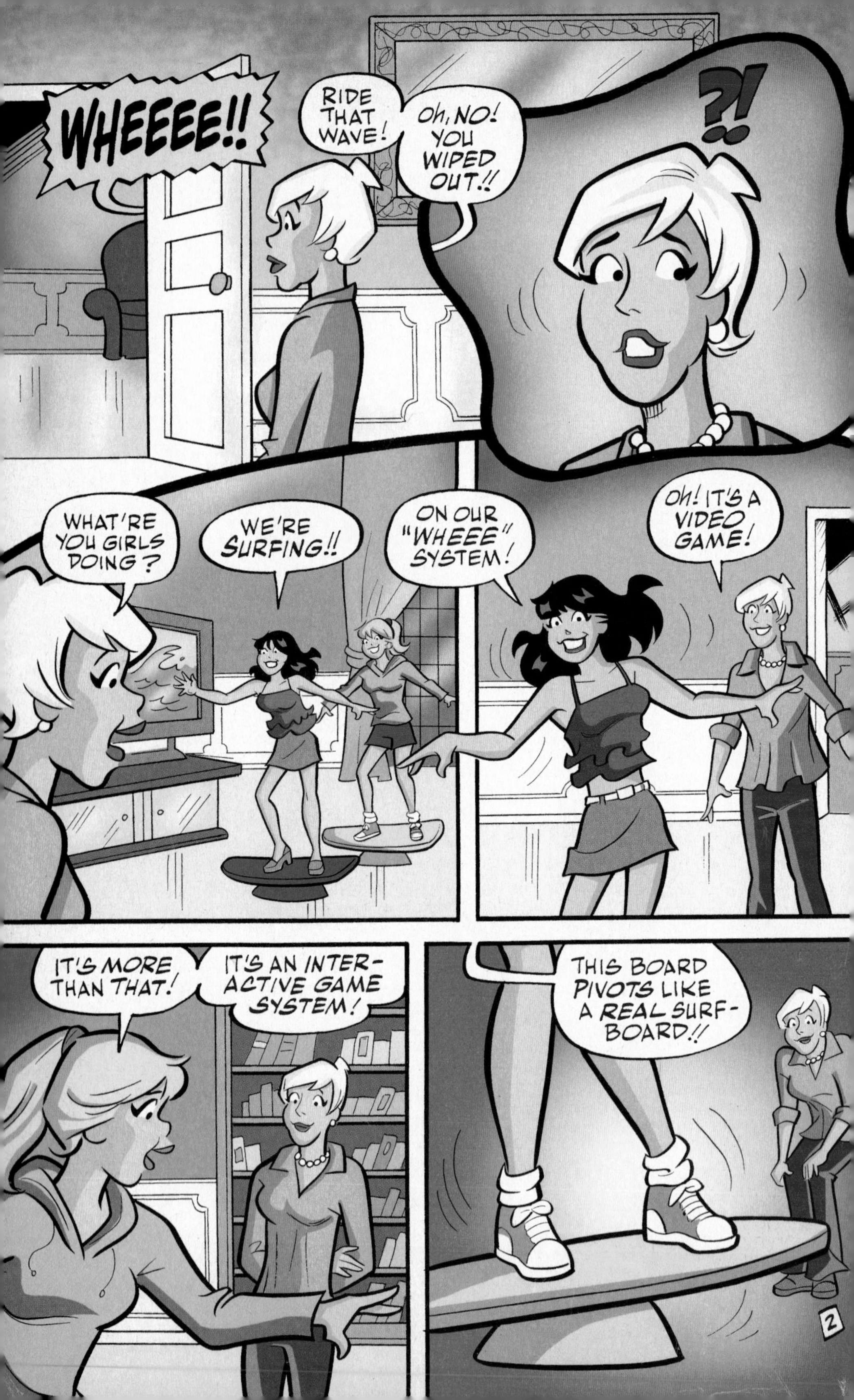
WHEEEEE!!
RIDE THAT WAVE!
Oh, NO! YOU WIPED OUT!!
?!
WHAT'RE YOU GIRLS DOING?
WE'RE SURFING!!
ON OUR "WHEEE" SYSTEM!
Oh! IT'S A VIDEO GAME!
IT'S MORE THAN THAT!
IT'S AN INTER-ACTIVE GAME SYSTEM!
THIS BOARD PIVOTS LIKE A REAL SURF-BOARD!!
2

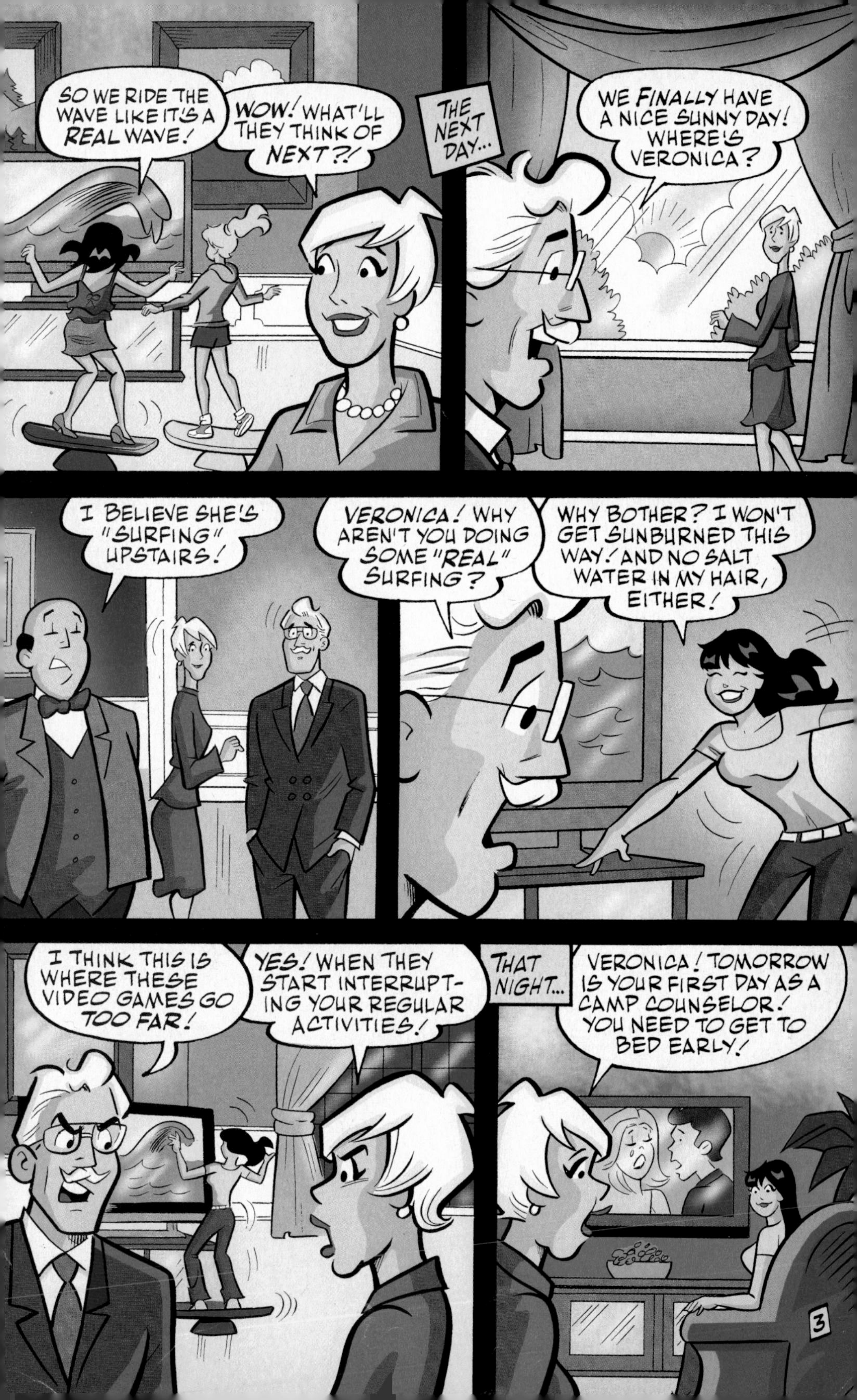
SO WE RIDE THE WAVE LIKE IT'S A REAL WAVE!
WOW! WHAT'LL THEY THINK OF NEXT?!
THE NEXT DAY...
WE FINALLY HAVE A NICE SUNNY DAY! WHERE'S VERONICA?
I BELIEVE SHE'S "SURFING" UPSTAIRS!
VERONICA! WHY AREN'T YOU DOING SOME "REAL" SURFING?
WHY BOTHER? I WON'T GET SUNBURNED THIS WAY! AND NO SALT WATER IN MY HAIR, EITHER!
I THINK THIS IS WHERE THESE VIDEO GAMES GO TOO FAR!
YES! WHEN THEY START INTERRUPTING YOUR REGULAR ACTIVITIES!
THAT NIGHT...
VERONICA! TOMORROW IS YOUR FIRST DAY AS A CAMP COUNSELOR! YOU NEED TO GET TO BED EARLY!
3

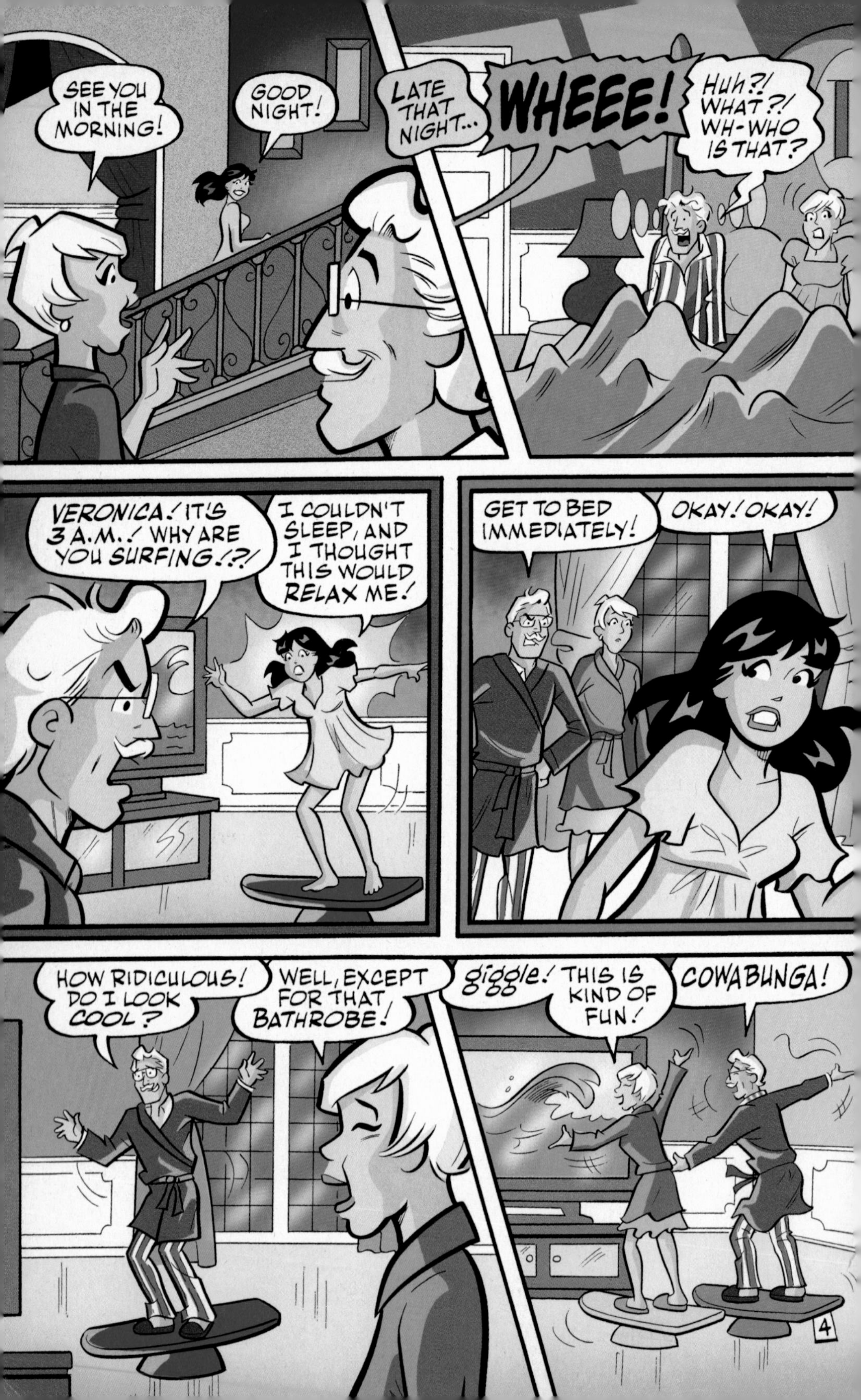

SEE YOU IN THE MORNING!
GOOD NIGHT!
LATE THAT NIGHT...
WHEEEE!
Huh?! WHAT?! WH-WHO IS THAT?
VERONICA! IT'S 3 A.M.! WHY ARE YOU SURFING!?!
I COULDN'T SLEEP, AND I THOUGHT THIS WOULD RELAX ME!
GET TO BED IMMEDIATELY!
OKAY! OKAY!
HOW RIDICULOUS! DO I LOOK COOL?
WELL, EXCEPT FOR THAT BATHROBE!
giggle! THIS IS KIND OF FUN!
COWABUNGA!
4

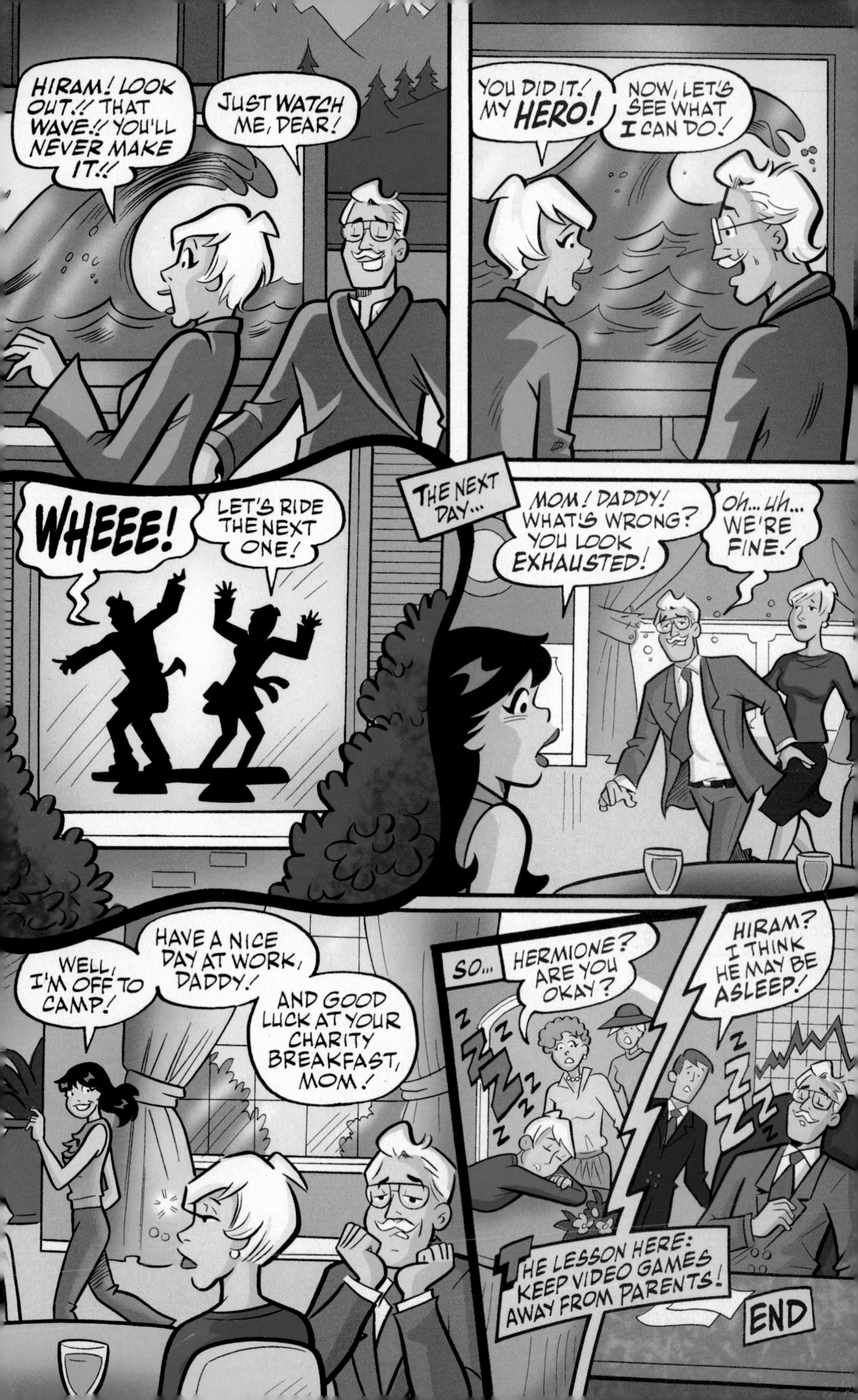
HIRAM! LOOK OUT!! THAT WAVE!! YOU'LL NEVER MAKE IT!!
JUST WATCH ME, DEAR!
YOU DID IT! MY HERO!
NOW, LET'S SEE WHAT I CAN DO!
WHEEEE!
LET'S RIDE THE NEXT ONE!
THE NEXT DAY...
MOM! DADDY! WHAT'S WRONG? YOU LOOK EXHAUSTED!
Oh... uh... WE'RE FINE!
WELL, I'M OFF TO CAMP!
HAVE A NICE DAY AT WORK, DADDY!
AND GOOD LUCK AT YOUR CHARITY BREAKFAST, MOM!
SO...
HERMIONE? ARE YOU OKAY?
HIRAM? I THINK HE MAY BE ASLEEP!
THE LESSON HERE: KEEP VIDEO GAMES AWAY FROM PARENTS!
END

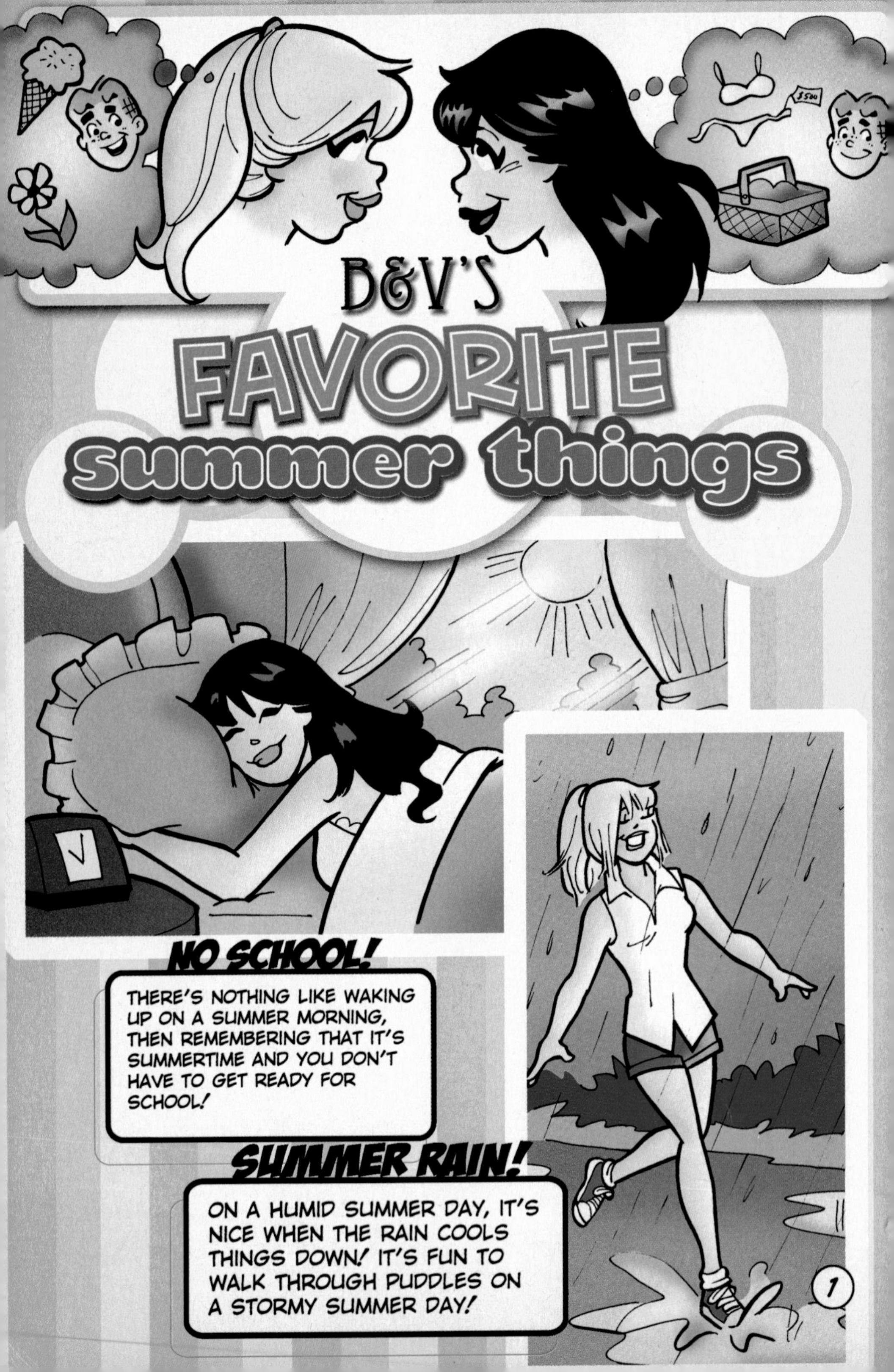
B&V'S
FAVORITE summer things
NO SCHOOL!
THERE'S NOTHING LIKE WAKING UP ON A SUMMER MORNING, THEN REMEMBERING THAT IT'S SUMMERTIME AND YOU DON'T HAVE TO GET READY FOR SCHOOL!
SUMMER RAIN!
ON A HUMID SUMMER DAY, IT'S NICE WHEN THE RAIN COOLS THINGS DOWN! IT'S FUN TO WALK THROUGH PUDDLES ON A STORMY SUMMER DAY!
1

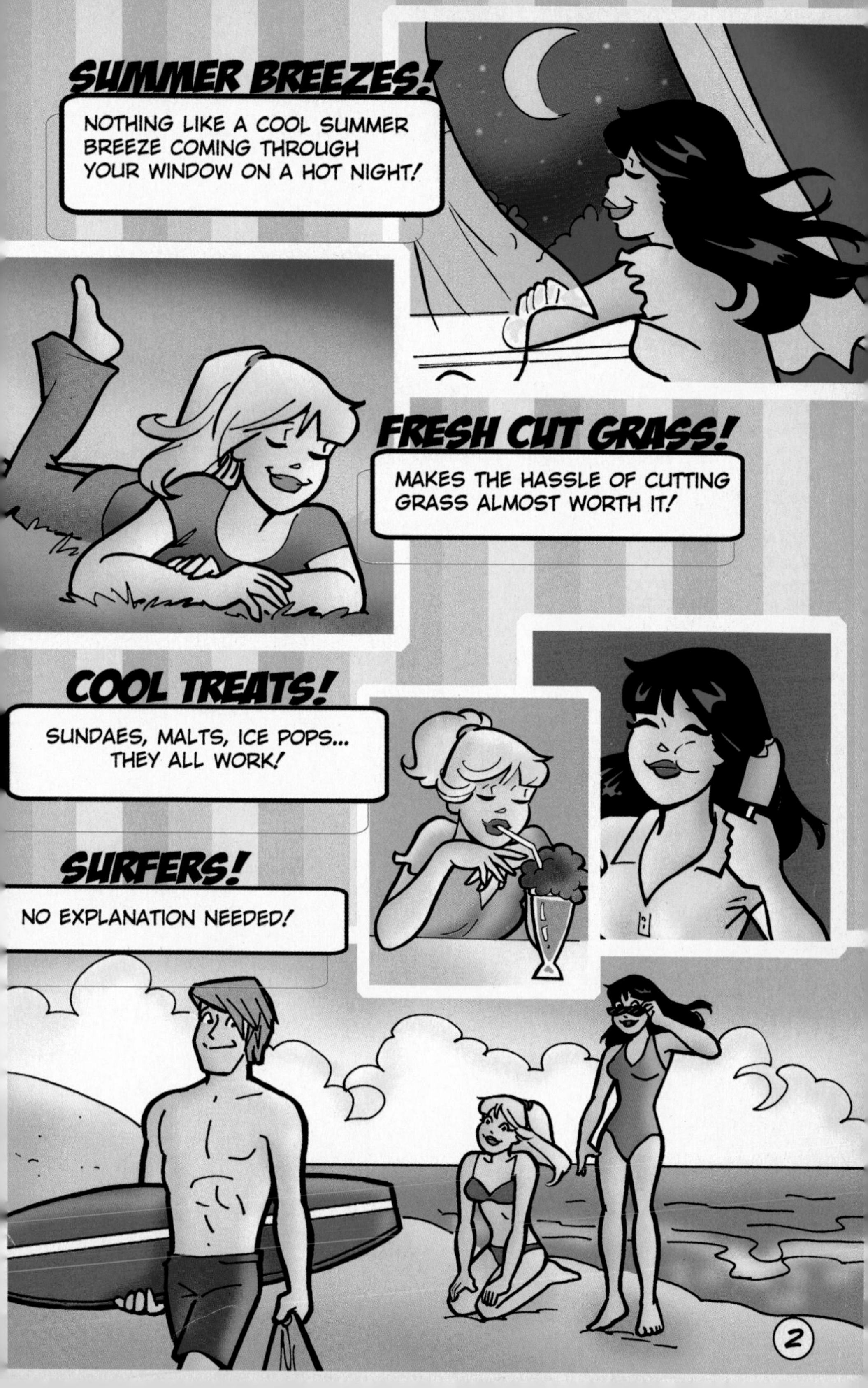
SUMMER BREEZES!
NOTHING LIKE A COOL SUMMER BREEZE COMING THROUGH YOUR WINDOW ON A HOT NIGHT!
FRESH CUT GRASS!
MAKES THE HASSLE OF CUTTING GRASS ALMOST WORTH IT!
COOL TREATS!
SUNDAES, MALTS, ICE POPS... THEY ALL WORK!
SURFERS!
NO EXPLANATION NEEDED!

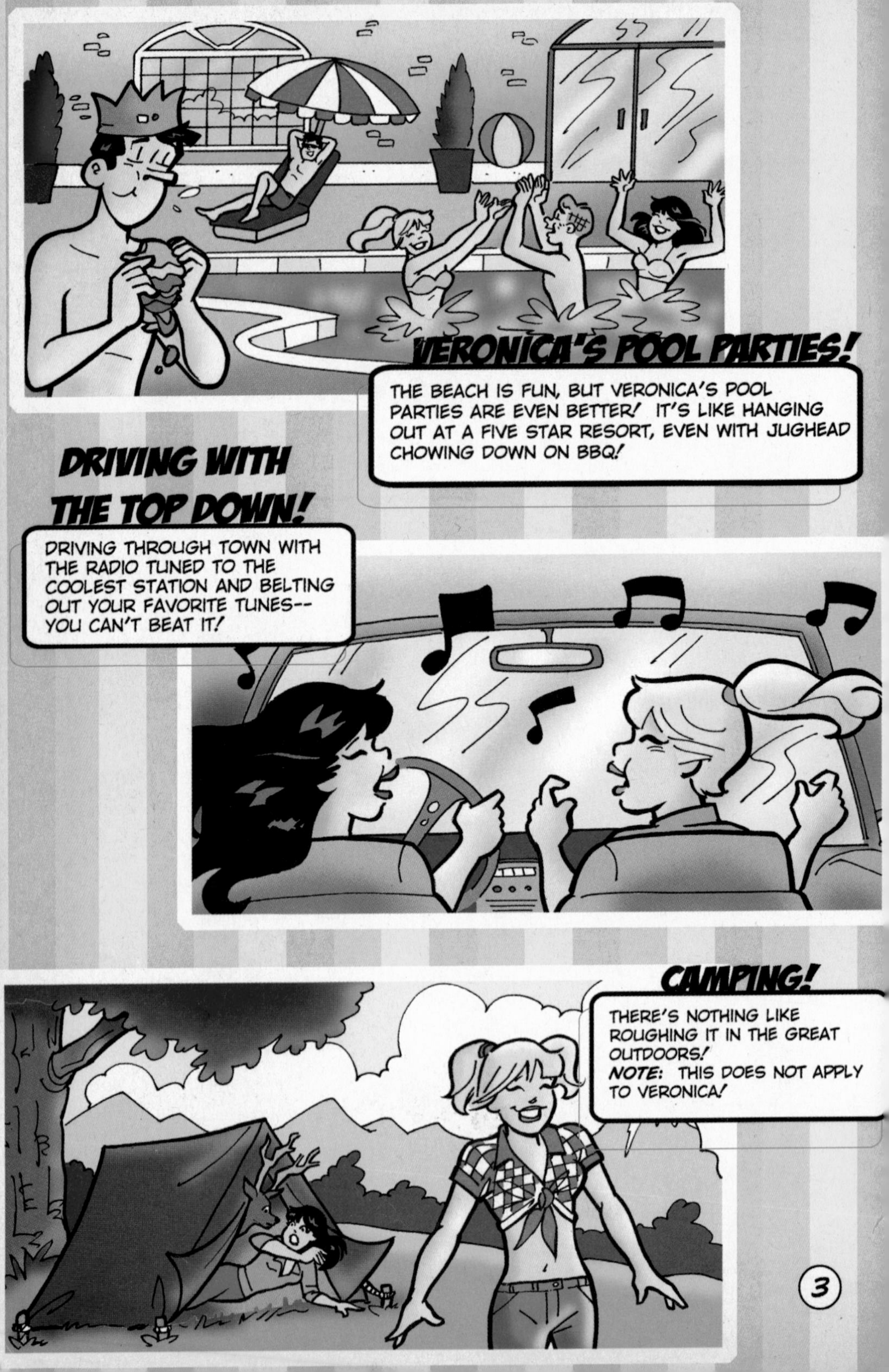
VERONICA'S POOL PARTIES!
THE BEACH IS FUN, BUT VERONICA'S POOL PARTIES ARE EVEN BETTER! IT'S LIKE HANGING OUT AT A FIVE STAR RESORT, EVEN WITH JUGHEAD CHOWING DOWN ON BBQ!
DRIVING WITH THE TOP DOWN!
DRIVING THROUGH TOWN WITH THE RADIO TUNED TO THE COOLEST STATION AND BELTING OUT YOUR FAVORITE TUNES-- YOU CAN'T BEAT IT!
CAMPING!
THERE'S NOTHING LIKE ROUGHING IT IN THE GREAT OUTDOORS!
NOTE: THIS DOES NOT APPLY TO VERONICA!

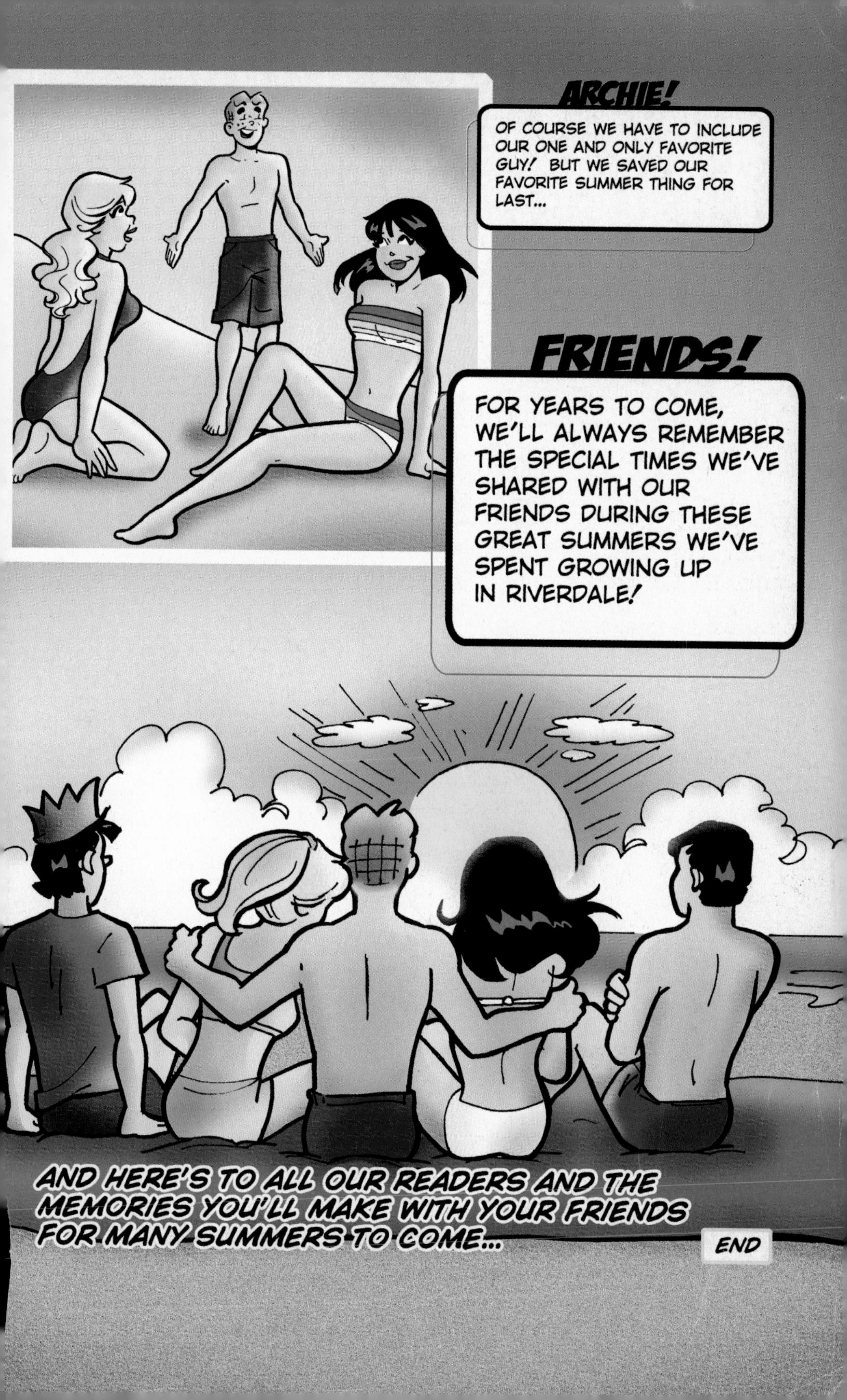
ARCHIE!
OF COURSE WE HAVE TO INCLUDE OUR ONE AND ONLY FAVORITE GUY! BUT WE SAVED OUR FAVORITE SUMMER THING FOR LAST...
FRIENDS!
FOR YEARS TO COME, WE'LL ALWAYS REMEMBER THE SPECIAL TIMES WE'VE SHARED WITH OUR FRIENDS DURING THESE GREAT SUMMERS WE'VE SPENT GROWING UP IN RIVERDALE!
AND HERE'S TO ALL OUR READERS AND THE MEMORIES YOU'LL MAKE WITH YOUR FRIENDS FOR MANY SUMMERS TO COME...
END

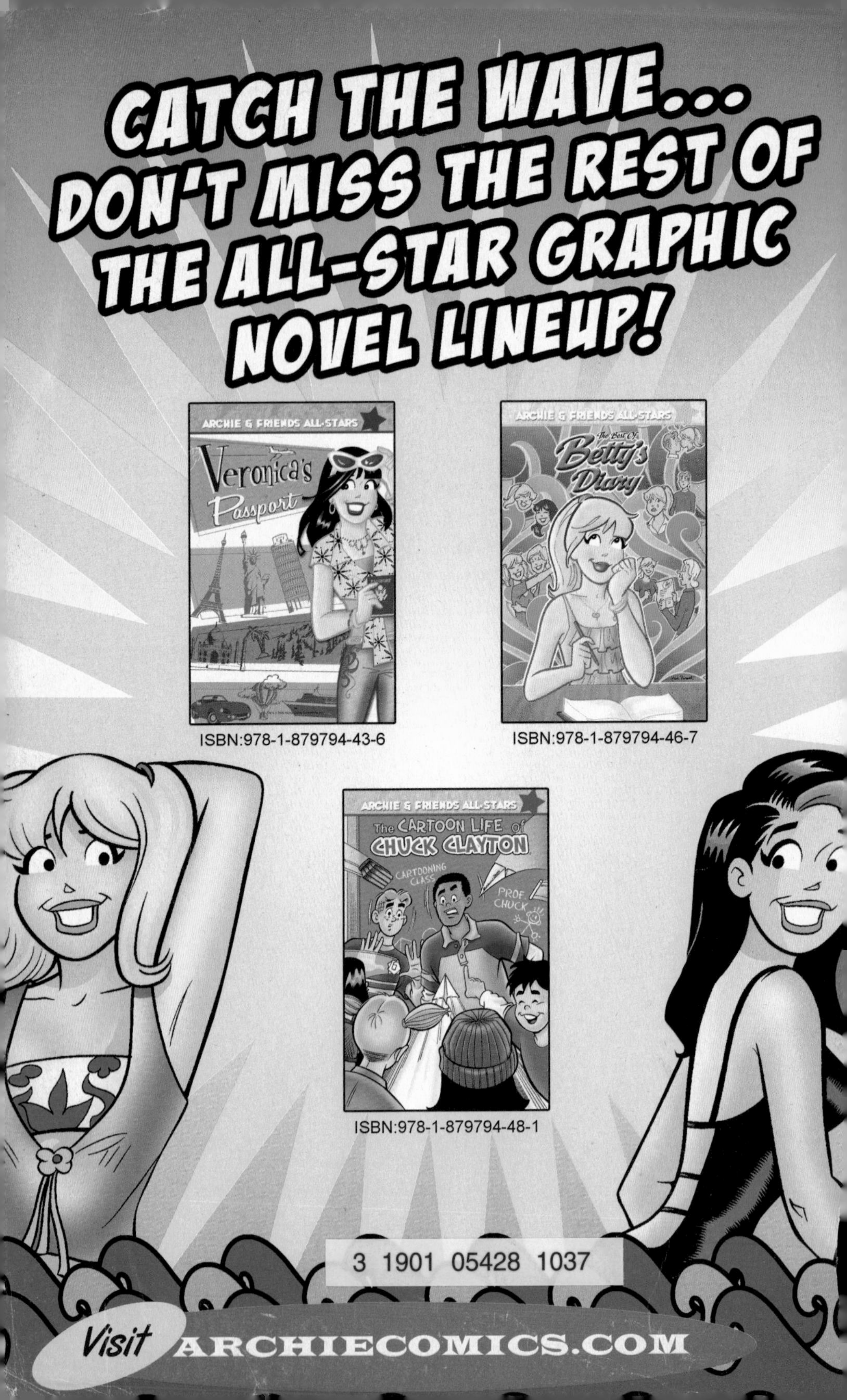
CATCH THE WAVE...
DON'T MISS THE REST OF THE ALL-STAR GRAPHIC NOVEL LINEUP!
ARCHIE & FRIENDS ALL-STARS
Veronica's Passport
ISBN:978-1-879794-43-6
ARCHIE & FRIENDS ALL-STARS
The Best Of Betty's Diary
ISBN:978-1-879794-46-7
ARCHIE & FRIENDS ALL-STARS
The CARTOON LIFE of CHUCK CLAYTON
CARTOONING CLASS
PROF CHUCK
ISBN:978-1-879794-48-1
Visit ARCHIECOMICS.COM